QUEEN
IN

CW00794373

QUEENIE AND CO
IN
JAPAN

Francesca Jones

First published in Great Britain in 1993
by Nexus
332 Ladbroke Grove
London W10 5AH

Copyright © James Hallums 1993
Letter from Esme copyright © Esme Ombreux 1993
Phototypeset by Intype Ltd, London
Printed and bound in Great Britain by
Cox & Wyman Ltd, Reading, Berkshire

ISBN 0 352 32852 5

This book is a work of fiction.
In real life, make sure you practise safe sex.

For Lies, Lovingly

Chapter One

Danger! Girls at Work . . .

Coco Qua Min Baker, Co to her friends, dropped to one designer-jean-clad knee, balanced her Nikon on it with both green-nailed hands and carefully aimed its lens. Her gleaming black hair was bunched into a pony-tail reaching the small of her back. Half Philippino, on her mother's side, half American, Coco, the twenty-two year-old award-winning photographer whose startlingly life-like work had appeared in practically every major world publication in recent years, was indulging her favourite photographic passion. When she was not hot on the trail of a photo-journalistic reportage with her ravishing partner and girlfriend, Queenie Granville, she loved to shoot erotic pictures for which the magazines concerned payed her handsomely – knowing they were getting the best results in the business.

London's mid-September streets were drizzle-dreary, but here in the splendidly-appointed studios of Britain's most daringly explicit sex magazine, *Sophisticats*, arc-light manufactured sunshine filtered through lush jungle greenery on to the back of a magnificent, restlessly pacing Bengal tiger. Coco, however, was in no danger of being devoured by the beast. Between it and her and two nubile young lovelies, who were going through lesbian contortions on astroturf in the jungle foreground, was a massive sheet of plate glass.

The model girls, one corn-blonde, the other brunette, were skimpily dressed in pieces of animal hide: zebra for the blonde, bear for the brunette. Their pointy, quivering breasts were loose, the hides crudely knotted at their waists and just reaching the tops of shapely thighs. Neither one was wearing panties.

As Coco fired her carefully paced and focused shots, a middle-aged man with two cameras hanging around his neck – the one not in use resting on a T-shirted beer gut – barked a string of instructions at the girls in a gratingly nasal, effeminate voice.

'*Wide* open beaver, please, Clare, *dar*ling,' he directed at the blonde. 'Spread it and . . . *hold* it. Now, Lucy, you're about to go down on it but first I want you to make love to it with your eyes. Lick your lips as you do, desire it, *worship* it.'

Coco was engrossed in her task but, unlike the average, sexually-detached professional in erotic photography, she began as usual to get turned on by the scene before her. She smiled as she listened to her associate's expressive choice of words. The man, Joe, was not impressed with Lucy's 'acting'.

'For Christ's *sake*, sweetheart,' he complained. 'You're staring at Clare's twat as if it was something the fucking *cat* brought in. It *is* the cat. Soft, gentle, *sweet* pussycat. You *love* it. You just *know* it's going to taste more *heav*enly than Beluga caviar. That's *it. Much* better. Now – *eat*. Eat, eat, *eat*. Close your *eyes*, Clare, roll your head around. And moan, darling, *moan*. You're wild, that tongue's driving you *wild*. You're in a *frenzy*.'

Coco deftly reloaded her camera and continued to shoot steadily, personally caught up in the action. Dropping to both knees, her thighs unconsciously rubbed gently on the crotch-seam of her jeans as the girls straddled one another in the classic sixty-nine position. Their tongues went busily to work, tasting, licking, probing while the tiger prowled with ceaseless feline grace back and forth through the plastic jungle behind them.

A lustful need for seventeen-year-old Clare's body began to grow within Coco. The blonde's ultra-desirable flesh shone white as a fresh fall of snow beneath the lights. Her svelte curves sinuously accommodated the plumper ones of Lucy, her nipples taut and thrusting and her delightfully downy pubic thatch in harmony with her hair.

'*Rip* that animal skin *off* Clare now, Lucy,' insisted Joe, his words almost a snarl. 'This *is* the *jungle*, remember. You're fucking *savage* in your lust. Roll, Clare, *roll* as the studs pop, all the way across the grass. Then sit up and stretch your arms towards Lucy. Im*plore*, you're *des*perate for more of her. *Do* it, dar*lings*.'

As this sequence was enacted and came to an end, Coco once more ran out of film. Her sexual patience was close to exhaustion, too. She positively craved the delectable Clare. 'Let's take a break, huh, Joe?' she suggested, her slightly American accent visited by the trace of a tremor.

'Anything you say, Co dear,' Joe responded, long lashes flickering in unconcealed, amused curiosity as he watched Coco stand and hold a hand out towards Clare. The man had worked with Coco before; he was aware of what would probably happen next.

'Like some coffee, Clare?' Coco suggested, and the girl nodded, saying nothing, and studded herself into her scrap of zebra skin. Clare's large, watery blue eyes lingered with faint wariness on their two locked hands as Coco, nervously excited, led her into an empty, adjoining office, sat her on a soft, white leather sofa and then let go of her hand to lock the door.

'Shit. Coffee's cold,' said Coco, feeling a small machine which stood near the door. 'Sorry.'

'What's the business of locking us in?' asked Clare, but calmly with a hint of East London in her speech.

Coco shrugged, cracking a dimple with her smile. 'I did, didn't I?' she murmured. 'Thought perhaps we wouldn't want to be disturbed.'

Clare blinked at her several times. 'I heard you sometimes take a bit of a fancy to one of the models.'

'Did you? And they sometimes fancy me,' Coco

3

responded. Going to Clare, she once again took her hand. 'You really like girls, don't you?'

'I suppose. Shows then, does it? But I'm not so keen in front of cameras, though. And with a bleeding tiger behind me!'

Coco chuckled. 'I think I can understand that. Glass or not, he looks like he's going to spring right through it at any second.' She folded herself into the sofa and covered the back of Clare's clasped hand with her other one. Ebony eyes searing into Clare's, her words falling thickly one on the other, she murmured, 'I like girls. And I'm good.'

'*All* . . . All right.' There is a catch in Clare's voice, she runs the tip of her tongue over her pink-tinged lips, making them glisten. Seconds later the clicks of press studs popping sound unnaturally loud in the room. Taking Clare's naked body in her arms, Coco eagerly mingles mouths with hers, but with breathtaking tenderness. Her tongue explores just enough to discover the fleshy underside of the girl's lips as her hands, soft as the skin of a baby, roam caressingly over unshrinking, smooth flesh.

This brief sampling of the delights to come serves to inflame Coco almost unbearably. She unhands her prize to stand and, impatient, fumbling, she gets out of her jeans, unbuttons her canary blouse and drops it, peels delicate lace panties down her shapely, olive-skinned legs and steps out of them; her eyes never leave Clare's once during this hasty striptease. She sinks to her knees on an Afghan rug as Clare's legs welcomingly part in front of her.

'You have a brilliant body,' Clare murmurs as her hands reach for the back of Coco's dipping head.

Throatily, Coco mutters, 'I have a brilliant tongue, too.'

With her fingers indenting the inside of Clare's thighs, she carefully parts Clare's vaginal lips with her long nails, breathing the scent of her. Eagerly she begins

4

to nibble, lick, kiss, tongue, suck the girl, who draws in her breath in an ecstatic moan, clutching Coco's hair in rising need, yanking at it.

Her body wriggles, her thighs shudder, her head rolls.

It had been nothing like this in the studio, thought Clare. And reading her mind, Coco said, 'This is for real, baby!'

Eyes closed, Clare allows herself to be laid on her back on the sofa; her entire body from the soles of her feet to the top of her cornfield head is kissed and caressed with a touch as cool and light and exhilarating as that of a soft summer's breeze.

Fires rage within Coco. She centres all of her loving attention on the coveted pussy, spoiling it with her wealth of expertise as Clare squeaks and grunts in animal delight. Then Coco rolls between Clare's wide-parted thighs, like a man about to penetrate her, crotch against crotch, clitoris teasing clitoris, her tense buttocks rising and falling, fucking the girl, imagining in the final, mutually explosive moments that she is the man with his cock rammed right up her. Then she softly groans in orgasm as Clare comes with a drawn-out, contented sigh.

They lie embraced in one another's arms for several long, relaxing minutes. Then Coco, wonderfully replete, untangles herself from Clare, rises to her feet and climbs languidly, happily, back into her clothes. 'That was divine, honey,' she murmurs. 'But I guess they're waiting for us in there. Let's get back to the phony stuff that makes our bread!'

At that moment, less than a mile away as the crow flies, or forty-five minutes in a taxi through the appalling traffic, Queenie Granville was, unknowingly, about to walk into a somewhat different though equally libidinous situation. Parking her slightly worse-for-wear, much-loved red Mercedes 280SL on the ancient cobbles of Eaton Mews West, Belgravia, she slid her long, sleekly-stockinged legs out into the rain, ducked from the car and hurried to the shelter of the porch of number 23B. Behind the antique front door with its old, black iron knocker, resided world-famous, Irish suspense novelist Sean Magee whom Queenie had lined up for an interview.

She had of course seen pictures of the writer, but she had never met him in the flesh and was unprepared for the sheer charisma of the man who opened the door. He stood well over six feet in his socks – he *was* in his socks, black ones with thinning heels – and he was broad too. His ruggedly handsome, vaguely tanned face – with its forty-eight-year-old shock of grey hair – was split almost from ear to ear with a welcoming smile as he extended his hand to the beautiful young woman who graced his doorstep.

'Well I'm . . .' he said appreciatively in a soft brogue. 'I was rather expecting a . . . Do come in.'

Queenie stepped into the open-planned, lower level of the house which, like its owner, exuded warmth. There was a wealth of knotty wood, a number of tasteful antiques and a twisted, beamed ceiling. An old, oak staircase cut the opposite wall diagonally in two. The armchairs and the sofa were modern, clean-lined, comfortable-looking and strewn with colourful silk cushions.

'Expecting a what?' asked Queenie as Magee took her raincoat.

Holding the coat in one hand, he frankly appraised her; she was wearing a smartly-cut Hubert Givenchy blazer over a frilly white blouse with a shoestring tie and a tight little skirt cut halfway up her thighs. 'Beautifully dressed, willowy, sensuous and hair the colour of a sunset over Galway Bay. And gloriously young!' He stowed the raincoat in a cupboard and showed her to a chair.

Queenie, pleased with this reception, sat with a smile, unconsciously showing a great deal of leg. 'Not so young. I'm twenty-three.'

'Twenty-three is it now? And already famous in your field, as well-known as myself in your way. What I expected was someone fortyish, intense, academic-looking and frowzily dressed.' His mild, grey eyes rested a moment on her knees then held her palest of green ones. 'I propose to celebrate this most propitious meeting with a drop of the finest Scotch malt whisky,' he said, his accent falling pleasantly on her ears. 'You'll be joining me?'

'Why not?' responded Queenie, already intrigued by the man.

He grinned. 'What is more she's not averse to a drop of the hard stuff at four in the afternoon. Perfection indeed. I'll bet you drive a fast car, too.'

Queenie jutted her chin. 'You're suggesting I'm a fast woman?' She had not meant to be bold; the words somehow slipped out. Sean Magee had put her entirely at ease within two minutes.

'Am I now?' He went to a mahogany sideboard whose shining top was covered with liquor bottles. 'Ice?'

'Please.'

'But we shan't insult the beverage with soda or water. This is a Glenmorangie, which also means no more than one lump of ice.'

She watched muscles rippling in his broad back as he poured two generous measures of the malt into two heavy, cut crystal glasses, ice cracking as he did so. He was wearing jeans with a casual, white cotton shirt and as he turned she noticed that no middle-aged gut spilled over the silver buckle of his wide leather belt. Suddenly she realised that she was admiring the physical appearance of the man. She found him distinctly attractive in a most masculine way – twice her age or not.

'The demon drink,' he said, handing her her glass and clinking it with his own.

'Your very good health.'

'Cheers.' Queenie's eyes smiled at him over the rim of her glass as she carefully sipped the raw spirit which slid easily down her throat, filling her belly with a warm glow.

Magee sat himself in a chair close to her, savouring his malt with healthy appreciation. 'Do you use a tape recorder?'

'Yes.' She dipped into her handbag and brought out a small Sony. 'Just this simple little device.'

'Okay. This would seem as good a time as any to begin my third degree. Fire away.'

'Right.' She switched the recorder on. 'We'll just chat generally if you don't mind – it's sort of my technique.'

'No pre-prepared lists of rather boring questions?'

'Good grief, no. What I try to do is, I try to get some life breathed into my interviews, Mr Magee.'

'Do you now? You sure as hell breathed life into me the moment I opened the door.' He assessed her still further with dancing eyes which may have been laughing. 'The name is Sean, Miss Granville.'

She stared unblinkingly back at him. 'The name is Queenie, Sean.'

Thus began a conversation into which Magee breathed more life – all the colours of the rainbow – than Queenie could have dared to hope for. It was a lengthy discussion of the lively world of Sean Magee: of his early life in his beloved Killarny; of rough and tough days as a mercenary; of his complicated, tempestuous loves and three marriages; of adventures all over the globe which brought inspiration for his thrillers. Queenie found herself enthralled, more so than she could remember with any previous interviewee. By the time they were halfway through their second whiskys she realised with a slight jolt that she was not merely captivated, she was becoming seriously sexually aroused by this man. It was an incredible, unexpected development and it began to play havoc with her composure. About three-quarters of an hour had elapsed and Queenie was losing concentration on the interview as thoughts of what it would be like to be made love to by the Irishman began to crowd out objectivity.

8

He was saying, as many successful writers have before, '. . . you know, what happens to me when things start to flow is a form of self-hypnosis. The inner recesses of my brain open up. I . . .' He paused, staring at her intently, searchingly, in silence.

'Yes?' Queenie stammered, a symptom of what was happening to her insides.

'Only the tape recorder's listening, Queenie.'

'I . . . No, I . . .' Confusion.

'I was speaking of hypnosis. It's sometimes used in mind-reading, and, to be sure, I can see clean into yours at this moment.'

'You can?' Almost a whisper.

'I can.' He reached for her hand. 'There is a pressing need in you. There is a similar need in myself. What is more, there is a simple remedy.' Standing, he took her firmly by the elbow and drew her to her feet, his hand burning through the sleeve of her blazer as her heart pounded and her head whirled. 'The presumptious, bold, brash Irish within me insists I take you upstairs to my bed.'

'To bed? Yes, to bed.' These were the last words of any intelligence which Queenie was to utter in a while.

He hooked an arm under the backs of her legs, swung her off her feet and, in classic Clark Gable *Gone With the Wind* fashion, rushed her up the old, oak staircase to his old oak-framed, canopied bed, where a spring twanged as he dumped her on it. She bounced once, wobbled, and lay still on her back, gazing at him in a sort of rapturous wonder, her stomach churning as she looked up at him. He stood above her, enjoying the moment of triumph, breathing only slightly more heavily than normal.

Then, wordlessly, he perched on the edge of the bed and, his neatly manicured fingers – both eager and practised – found the buttons of her blouse beneath her blazer. Undoing them slowly, carefully, as if each were a cherished prize, he eased the blouse out of her waist-band and opened it wide. Queenie's full breasts jutted

9

provocatively at him through a lacy white bra which hooked at the front; he undid it and they tumbled quiveringly free whilst their owner remained motionless, barely breathing within her sexual spell. Vague, needful thoughts crowded her brain – touch them, go on, touch my tits, suck my nipples – but for the moment he left her flesh alone, finding instead the zip at the side of her skirt and whispering it down. Her first movement on that massive bed was to help him by raising her hips as he dragged the skirt down and over her feet, taking her shoes off as well. Briefly, she regretted wearing tights. Had she known this was going to happen, she would most certainly have selected stockings and one of her many skimpy suspender belts. He very quickly had them off her, her knickers joining them on the ride down her legs. She suddenly felt gloriously, shamelessly, raunchily exposed, her nakedness accentuated by the dishabille of blazer, blouse and bra.

His Irish eyes managed a crooked smile through their passion before latching onto her pubic mound. 'It seems I found myself a natural redhead, then,' he breathed, and ducked to her.

Queenie gasps and shudders as the first carnal contact this extraordinary man makes with her is with his tongue wetly touching the inside of her thigh. She watches the thick grey hair on the back of his head move slowly towards her belly as he traces a delicate saliva trail up her leg, then she softly squeals as his tongue tip reaches and ferrets amongst her pubic thatch. Gently, he prises her thighs further apart, moves his head between them and his tongue finds its way inside her damp and welcoming pussy, which at that moment is the centre of her existence.

He eats Queenie Granville, Mr Thriller-Writer Sean Magee, with the same hungry intensity with which he has been known to describe such an act in his novels. He thrusts his tongue in and out of her like a practised little cock, pausing to flicker it over her clitoris, stabbing inside her again. Rushing already to orgasm, Queenie draws her knees up high and crosses her feet on his back. Rocking her hips in time to her moans, with his tongue plunging she comes with a loud grunt followed by a long sigh, her thighs tightly clenching his head, twitching, then finally relaxing.

Magee sits up and gazes at her, wiping the back of his hand across his glistening lips.

The grey eyes no longer have room for a smile, they are crowded out by lust which ravages her body as he quickly undoes his shirt, strips it off, stands and gets out of his jeans and white underpants. A fine, thick erection swaying before him, he straddles her face, his buttocks resting lightly on her breasts as he slides his hands through her luscious red hair to the back of her neck and pulls her head into his groin.

Queenie takes this new lover's, old friend's, stranger's cock deep into her mouth whilst with one hand she cradles his heavy balls and with the other clutches his buttock and this simple combination of acts triggers her libido once more. With fresh juices flowing between her legs, she sucks, she squeezes, she licks, she plunders. She runs her tongue down the back of his throbbing cock and over his balls then draws both his balls into her mouth, rubbing his cock, which is pressed against her nose and forehead, with her flat palm. Her fingertip finds his anus and as it does so he tenses so violently she thinks he is going to come right then, to shoot his seed into her hair. But he holds back – just – walks his knees down on either side of her body and mounts her, his hands crawling up her back and around her shoulders beneath the blouse and jacket, fingers digging into her, not quite clawing.

This is to be no controlled fuck, and neither does Queenie – riding on a mammoth sexual high, devoured by her libido – want it to be. Sean pounds his cock into her, going at her like a piston, slamming into her pussy, his buttocks taut, toes curling, teeth clenched. Queenie matches his pelvic thrusts with her own wild bucking until together, with a final, climatic heave they reach a gasping, sweaty, shouted orgasm and Sean slowly collapses sideways with Queenie fully impaled, taking her over with him.

It was a full five minutes before their genitals parted company. With a sigh of satisfaction the Irishman rolled away from Queenie onto his back, his flaccid penis flopping out of her and leaving a short, wet trail on the inside of her thigh. 'Holy Mary,' he muttered irreverently.

'Too right,' was Queenie's mumbled response. She glanced down at herself. 'Shit, what a mess.' Sitting up, she stripped off her jacket and blouse, holding the jacket in critical examination. 'Creased to hell.'

He grinned. 'Somehow there didn't seem to be the time to take it off.'

'Right.' She looked at him archly and ran a hand through her hair. 'Wow!' Swinging her legs to the carpet she bent forward and draped blouse and jacket over a chair, then shrugged out of her bra.

'Then you weren't considering the possibility of getting dressed? Not that the notion would fill me with delight.'

She treated him to a wicked little smirk. 'It's raining outside. Besides, I've an interview to finish.' Her eyes fell on the tape recorder which she had not let go of until the moment of being dropped on the bed. It lay by the edge of a pillow and, suddenly realising something, she picked it up. 'It's still running.'

'It is?' He raised an amused eyebrow. 'Then it will have recorded . . . ah, would it not?'

'I guess.'

'It would be perhaps a rather di*dactic* exercise to listen to that, no?'

'I'm also good with words, Sean, and you're being wonderfully facetious. Morally instructive it is *un*likely to be.'

'Nevertheless, I do believe I might like to hear it.'

12

'We both would.' Queenie stopped the tape and pressed the rewind button. Seconds later they were listening to a remarkably clear rerun of their gamut of sexual noises, a titillating assortment of muttered words of sex, grunts and moans and Queenie's squeals, to the background of heavy breathing and irregular creaking from the bedsprings, all of which conspired very quickly to turn Queenie on again. As she heard herself shouting 'I'm coominnng,' she wrapped her fingers around Magee's cock, gratified to feel the instant response.

This time it was less of a frantic, lust-filled assault on one another's bodies. Instead, it was more tender as they pleasured one another for over an hour, going through slow, inventive, consuming sexual contortions, each coming to soaring climaxes twice more. Finally, contentedly replete, as they shared a cigarette, Sean stated the obvious, 'That had to be sex at its glorious best.'

'It was lousy.'

He laughed. 'And here am I, scheduled to go off on an important trip tomorrow. You've almost convinced me to cancel it, to be sure you have. This is too good to walk away from when it's only just begun.'

She frowned, but her eyes smiled. 'Nothing's just begun, Sean. We had sex. It was great, but I don't tend to commit.'

'Do you not? You know, there might even be something tough about words like that from such a pretty mouth.'

'Tough? I suppose I can be. But the real reason is that I have a girlfriend.' She dragged briefly at the cigarette and gave it back to him. 'It's fairly serious. We, ah, we make it together.'

'Oh.' This was too much of a man of the world to be surprised. 'In that case you do commit, Queenie.'

'To a point. It's an easy arrangement, no room for jealousy. She also likes men – and the occasional other girl in the sack. There are no secrets, but most of the time we live together and share our lives. It kind of

13

keeps us from other entanglements.' She shrugged. 'It's great.'

'Good for you. However, you are looking at one hot-blooded Irishman who would most definitely like to entangle some more.'

She planted a kiss amongst chest hairs almost as thick as those of his head, ran her green-painted fingernails through the mat, then rested her cheek on it. 'Me too, of course. But then, you're going away tomorrow.'

He stubbed out the cigarette and lazily stroked her hair. 'I am, I am. But I'll be back.'

'Where are you off to?'

'Japan, to research a new book.'

She shifted her head, swivelling her eyes to him in surprise. 'How very odd. So am I. I happen to have finalised a contract with *Time* magazine for an in-depth article on the lifestyle of the Japanese businessman. How long were you planning to be there?'

'As long as it takes. Three weeks. Four, maybe.'

'Tokyo?'

'As a base, yes. You?'

'As well. One of life's curious coincidences. We were planning to leave next week.' She snuggled closer to him, happy with this turn of events.

'We? You and Coco Baker, the photographer?'

'Right.'

'Is she your girlfriend as well as your partner?'

'You got it.'

'Is that going to present any difficulty about you and I getting it together out there?'

'Didn't I just tell you there's no jealousy between us.' She kissed his chest. 'Tell you what, Co will adore you.'

'Uh-huh. Does that by any chance imply what I think it does?'

'You should be so lucky.' She dipped the tip of a finger in his belly-button. 'But sure, why not? Maybe we can all three get it together.'

'*Jesus*! And me a good Catholic lad!'

'If the idea daunts you, wait until you see Coco.'

'My dear girlie, nothing in this life daunts me except perhaps taking leave of it.' He picked her head up so that she was staring straight at him and looked deep into her eyes. 'What in the name of God have I found myself here?'

'A simple hedonist?'

'I would tend to disregard the word simple. Try complicated. And not one of your nymphomaniacs by any chance, is it?'

'What, me?' She giggled. 'Well, perhaps just a teeny bit.'

'In that case I doubt if I'll even get to see you in Tokyo. It's a city which tends to walk on the sexual wild side.'

'Is it now? But then, I tend to be selective.' She ran her fingers down over his tight stomach and playfully tugged his pubic hair. 'You'll see me all right.' Her hand moved lower. 'Fancy one for the road?'

Chapter Two

Steam-mates

The 747 had been descending slowly for ten minutes. As it began to bank to port, turning in a slow, graceful arc like some giant, gliding seabird, Coco leant across Queenie to look out of the window. The plane nosed through a hazy layer of cloud. Gradually a patchwork of pale green fields, symmetrically criss-crossed with perfectly straight furrows, was unveiled some twelve thousand feet below – a pleasingly elegant, welcoming carpet for Honshu, Japan's principal island. In the distance the snow-crowned cone of Honshu's majestic king, the extinct volcano Mount Fuji, was buried in cloud.

Japan was hardly the Philippines but the half of Coco which belonged to the Orient was excited to be paying it a visit. Her hand found the inside of Queenie's denim-covered thigh and lovingly squeezed. Queenie responded with a kiss on the back of her head.

Queenie, too, was experiencing stirrings of excitement. A previously unseen country and a strange and alien place by Western standards, lay minutes below them. A new challenge was down there in the steaming metropolis of Tokyo – a major article to tackle with high rewards. There would probably be some interesting sex as a bonus – certainly a carnal romp with Sean Magee who was very much on her mind.

The note of the engines dropped; there was a dull thunk as the wheels came down. The plane began to sink faster, banking into the flight-path for Narita Airport. But the only evidence that Tokyo itself was somewhere ahead was a thick pall of smog drifting out from its heavily industrialised areas. Seconds latter the 747 was surrounded by the smog; the only view from the window was the winking lights at the tip of a ghostly wing.

'Charming,' remarked Coco, sitting up and fastening her safety belt.

'We're going to get a lot of that filthy stuff,' said Queenie. 'It tends to hang around here. Air inversion apparently.'

'Which is?'

'A freaky metrological situation. There's often a layer of air next to the ground which is cooler than that higher up. It traps all the pollution – result, smog. I thought about bringing us masks.'

'Good for you,' said Coco, hooking her arm through Queenie's. 'Always prepared for anything.' She produced a delightfully crooked smile. 'I wonder what adventures await us this trip?'

'How about I write my story, you take your photographs, we stick to wrapping the article up and go home?'

'Fat chance,' said Coco.

The presence of the man was remarkable compared to the average Japanese. He was wearing an Yves Saint Laurent suit in pale blue silk, subtly cut to compliment his enormous bulk, a dull-coloured, hand-painted silk tie and a fussy pocket handkerchief. Makita Noguchi, multi-millionaire industrialist and president of Nippon Petrochemicals, sat behind his enormous, maroon lacquered desk in a huge, European-styled office. He was concluding a telephone conversation. As he hung up he briefly bowed his head to the telephone, one of four, and turned his attention to the two, young, western female reporters whose visit he had been anticipating as only an irritating disturbance to his busy day's routine.

17

Queenie and Coco sat across the room from him in black leather armchairs near a low antique coffee table. His eyes had rarely left them during his conversation. Their business-like clothing did little to conceal their obvious sensuality; the low chairs meant they were unavoidably showing a great deal of stockinged leg. Noguchi was possessed of a responsibility to match his sumo wrestler proportions, but he also had an eager eye for female flesh and what those eyes, coal black and piercing, had been dwelling on was flesh indeed.

He left his desk to join them at the coffee table, his step curiously elegant and light. The shiny black brogue shoes seemed a little too small for his frame as they indented a thick-piled carpet of faintest strawberry.

'Would you like tea?' he offered as he parked his frame, with which he was clearly perfectly at home, on a sofa and pressed a button in the table. A tiny, young woman in a crisp, white shirt instantly appeared and then melted away after he asked her, in English and without having had any reply from Queenie or Coco, for tea.

Queenie launched into her series of unprepared questions just the tiniest bit disconcerted by Noguchi's eyes which were subtly practised in the art of penetrating female clothes. As he answered Queenie's questions, Noguchi's fantasies were in full swing. Girls not as sexually tuned in as Queenie and Coco would perhaps not have been aware of this since the Japanese man, as custom demanded, was being polite to the point of deference to his visitors. His occasional dropping of his gaze to below face level was a mere, discreet dart, but by the time the tea arrived, both girls were aware that they had been mentally stripped naked.

The tea was green. The young woman knelt and poured it from a steaming porcelain pot into three delicate, prettily designed cups, firstly preparing it with a reed whisk. It was also strangely frothy. When the young woman left, Noguchi sipped his contentedly whilst Queenie, taken by surprise by its intensely bitter

18

taste, managed to disguise her dislike and suffered in silence.

'Tell me about the hotels for executives who stay overnight during the week, Mr Noguchi,' said Queenie, having bravely finished her tea and equally bravely declined more which the industrialist offered to pour. 'Is it true that the rooms are little more than cubby holes and that they cannot stand in them?'

'I am sorry if you have not enjoyed my tea,' replied Noguchi, eyes straying for a fraction of a second to her knees. 'Would you like something else?'

'Thank you, it was fine. A taste to be acquired, I imagine.' She paused. 'The, er, cubby holes?'

'They are small, yes.' He glanced around his massive office with its walls of fine prints as if to belie his next words. 'Space, regrettably, is at a premium in Tokyo. But the executive niches are equipped with every luxury. They are really most comfortable.'

Coco, who had been silent up to that point, asked if she might take some photographs.

'By all means, Miss Baker,' he agreed. His eyes sped over Coco as she got to her feet and undid her camera case. 'Forgive my forwardness, but do you have oriental blood?' he asked.

'On mum's side,' said Coco cheerfully, taking a light reading. 'Dad was a GI during the Vietnam war. Mum's Philippino.'

'Ah. Well you certainly appeared to enjoy the tea. Perhaps you have inborn sensitivity for eastern ways?'

Coco fiddled with her flash attachment. 'Just a little. But I was brought up in the States.'

She seemed to have touched a raw nerve, because Noguchi suddenly abandoned his stilted politeness. His large, fleshy mouth stern, he said, 'Regrettably Americans have no sensitivity, no culture. No . . .' He paused, as if weighing his words carefully, replenishing his cup and Coco's, then he said, 'It will be eternally impossible for the Americans to understand us.' Shifting his bulk on the sofa, he picked up a letter opener whose ivory handle was ornately worked into writhing tigers. He pointed it at Coco. 'You must forgive me for saying it, but my considered opinion is that the average American is little more than a barbarian.'

'Dad would be pleased to hear that,' chirped Coco, her cheerfulness unruffled as she peered through the viewfinder which had last framed the lesbian couple at the *Sophisticats* studio.

Noguchi was immediately contrite. 'I doubt one as bright as yourself has an average man for a father. Sorry, I occasionally get carried away on the subject of America. No doubt your father is a man of refined tastes.'

'Not especially. He's a movie actor.' She fired off a picture, making Noguchi squint.

'Yes, well,' said Queenie slowly. 'One of the background reasons for this in-depth article, apart from the purely informative, is to try to bring some understanding of the Japanese life to the West, Mr Noguchi. East and West are working hand in glove in the business world. You Japanese are buying into every free country, and heavily. We want to understand you.'

'And need to, Miss Granville.' He bowed his head. 'I will therefore be as helpful as I am able.' There seemed to be a trace of irony in his words.

An hour later, as Queenie and Coco were about to leave, Noguchi said, while his eyes travelled over both of them, lingering a little longer than previously, 'I will help your understanding of us further along if you would accept an invitation tomorrow evening to my penthouse on the top floor of this building. I shall invite a few close friends. Your company will be most welcome.' He paused, the hint of a smile appearing at the corners of his lips. 'You may learn something of the ways of the Japanese male.'

That evening, Queenie, with a case of the galloping hots for Sean Magee, rang the number he had given her three times. He was staying at a flat of his Japanese publisher which was at his disposal, but there was no reply. Disappointed, she took solace that night in Coco's arms.

The close friends of Noguchi's the following evening were few indeed; five, all men, were ceremoniously waited upon and entertained by gloriously dressed geisha girls, in traditional clothes; their hair was ornate and high and their faces pancake white in which their lips were vivid slashes. Dressed in slinky, ankle-length evening wear, Queenie and Coco at first felt slightly out of place, but men and geishas alike swiftly relaxed them with their delightful civility.

Noguchi's penthouse was forty-eight stories up in the air. Outside, as evening commenced, the smog had cleared and a dying sun, hidden behind a confusion of ultra-modern skyscrapers, was turning the sky through yellow to magenta. The flat was evidently a luxury, home-away-from-home for the industrialist and, unlike his office, was decorated in Japanese fashion. It was fairly plain, pleasantly airy, with sliding, decorated paper partitions in wooden frames.

Proceedings began with the men and Queenie and Coco sitting on cushions on the floor around a long, low – no higher than eighteen inches – white lacquered table. The five geishas kneeled strategically at their backs and served hot sake in tiny, delicate porcelain cups, which they constantly replenished as was the custom as soon as a sip was taken, so that the cups were always full with the fermented rice wine.

The wooden floor was strewn with reed mats, which Noguchi explained were known as *tatamis* and that the size of a room in Japan was defined by the number of *tatamis* it contained. This was a large room – a ten-*tatami* room – the smallest rooms were one *tatamis*, just two metres by one.

The men were chatty, evidently most happy to have such lovely western girls in their company, and between passing compliments they made jokes in Japanese which sent them into peals of laughter. They

21

seemed, except for their sober dress, extraordinarily different in temperament from the businessmen of the daytime. The sixth man, a little more inscrutable than the rest, was flamboyantly dressed in a heavy chalk-striped suit, a dark blue shirt with a white silk tie, with heavy gold bracelets on one wrist and a Rolex Oyster on the other. He was missing the top joint of a little finger. This man was introduced to the girls by Noguchi as one Ankoku Nangi; he omitted to explain that Nangi was a gangster leader whose top joint of his right little finger had been amputated in his youth as a token of loyalty to his then gangster boss.

The sake flowed, as far as flowing could be a description of drinking from such tiny cups. The geishas enacted a little mime play for them and sang and danced with great skill and prettiness. The level of conversation and number of jokes rose. There began to creep into the atmosphere hints of sexuality. The jokes, now in English, turned smutty and eyes which had earlier only smiled and laughed now burned, not just with desire for the geishas but for Queenie and Coco too. As the girls, unaccustomed to being constantly plied with liquor, grew pleasantly woozy, Noguchi's black eyes in particular, lingered on Coco, then Queenie, then Coco again, penetrating, stripping, growing smoky with rising lust.

A marked difference appeared in the relationship between men and geishas. Suddenly the geishas were no longer mere humble servants with their only function to fawn upon the men, to serve them sake, to dance, act and sing. Encouraged by the men, they closed in on them and, in allowing themselves to be touched in intimate ways, they lost their humbleness and responded suggestively, bawdily even.

No hand was laid, however, on the honoured female guests who sat on their cushions with their knees tucked under them, rather relishing the atmosphere but beginning, as at the start of the evening, to feel just slightly out of place with Japanese eyes constantly

22

washing over them while the owner's hands sought geisha flesh through heavy dresses.

Ankoku Nangi was the first to leave the room. Staggering slightly, he got to his feet, took the elbow of the tallest geisha and urged her before him through a half-open paper door. This seemed to be a general signal for revelries to continue elsewhere. One by one, the not quite sober men took a geisha from the room until Queenie and Coco were alone with Noguchi.

'Most admirable young ladies, are they not?' observed Noguchi. 'What is not known about them in the West is that only a very select few are trained to take pleasuring men to the ultimate conclusion. With most it stops with serving and general entertainment. Mine are from that elite band of perfectionists and will even now be starting to indulge my guests in pleasures exquisite.'

Coco glanced towards the paper door, now closed. 'And they will be doing this communally?'

'Not in this instance, no. Each couple are at this moment in their own one *tatumi* room where they will enjoy together many and diverse acts of love on a *futon*, that is to say a most comfortable and accommodating padded floor quilt.'

Queenie smiled lazily as Noguchi momentarily blurred before her eyes. 'And this, this entertainment . . . is all part of the everyday life of the Japanese executive?' She managed to only slightly trip over her words.

Noguchi's eyes dwelt hotly on her breasts, searing through the Ballenciago satin. But his voice remained steady. He, unlike the rest of the party, appeared to be the only one unaffected by the liquor. 'Everyday, no – though no doubt he would like it to be. Occasionally, certainly. He needs to conserve his energy for his principal duty in life – his company. However, these particular friends of mine are all rich and powerful. For them, a rather different set of rules applies.'

At that moment, from somewhere very close on the other side of the paper walls, came the sound of a loud grunt. Coco and Queenie glanced in the general direction of the noise, which was repeated, and Nogu-chi, his eyes pigging on Queenie above a face which now positively leered, muttered, 'The pleasure noises will of course multiply. My guests cannot see each other's activities with their geishas but the construction of this apartment makes it inevitable that they will hear each other. The excitement of this naturally adds to the overall pleasure.'

Coco giggled. 'How come you are without a geisha, Mr Noguchi?'

His eyes did to her what they had been doing to Queenie. 'I would hardly be so crassly rude as to go off and leave my guest of honour alone.' He paused, allowing himself his first overt sexual move as his hand lightly rested on Queenie's knee. 'Besides, I have amusing plans for the three of us.'

Queenie looked warily at the pudgy-fingered hand with its gold rings, one weighted with an enormous diamond. The thought of sex with its owner was daunting and unattractive; nevertheless, the atmosphere was getting to her and the sake had thrown off all inhibition.

A long-drawn-out male groan of pleasure intruded on their ears, a girl laughed, another squealed. 'What I decided that we three should indulge together,' said Noguchi, 'is my sauna and massage room. From there we shall also be isolated from the intrusive sounds of lovemaking.' With surprising grace and agility he raised his bulk from the floor, gesturing that the girls should do the same, his attitude precluding any refusal.

In their stockinged feet, Queenie and Coco followed Noguchi through the same door through which the rest had exited and along a narrow corridor past several paper doors behind which the sounds of sexual enjoyment were on the increase.

At the end of the passageway was a heavy teak door, beyond it a small room with a cedar-slatted floor and low lighting. There were some empty wire hangers on hooks on the wall and several thin, white, towelling robes. Noguchi shut them in and nodded at another door. 'Come through there when you're quite ready.'

'Ready being exactly . . . ?' asked Coco.

'It's a sauna, dear girl. Doubtless it will not be your first time. I shall be sending for my massage girls. Ready is without clothes beneath a bathrobe. As I myself shall be.' His eyes travelled probingly over both their bodies, he bowed his head at each of them briefly in a way which may have been mocking, and left.

'Randy son-of-a-bitch,' observed Coco.

Grinning, tottering a little, Queenie began to slide down a zipper. 'So let's get on with it,' she said. 'If only he weren't so damned fat.'

'You don't suppose he has in mind . . . ?' asked Coco rhetorically as she struggled with a button.

'Bet your sweet life he does.'

Queenie stepped out of her dress and draped it over a hanger. On the other side of the opposite wall, a coal-black eye was glued lustfully to a carefully concealed spy-hole. Makita Noguchi, nationally respected head of one of Japan's largest companies, was naked, playing with his rapidly erecting penis as he leched at the sight of his honoured female guests climbing out of their clothes.

'Sort of nice in here,' commented Coco, as she slipped into a bathrobe, lurching somewhat as the effect of the sake combined with the strange events. The air was warmly moist, agreeable; the predominant background noise was no longer just sex, but a muffled sound of dripping water. The sleeves of Coco's robe fell over her hands and she rolled them up.

'Steam and a massage beckon with welcoming arms,' said Queenie, climbing out of her knickers and into a robe, scrunching up her knickers and slipping them into a pocket.

'Not to mention fatso,' said Coco.

'Right.' Queenie loosely tied the sash and sighed. 'Right.' Noguchi's leching eye vanished from the spy-hole.

The steam room was somewhat larger than the dressing room. It was also noisy; the gurgling water running through pipes in the walls echoed through the room and the water's regular conversion into steam sounded exactly like the noise from the boiler of an old fashioned locomotive. It was fuggy with vision almost as limited as Tokyo streets in smog and close to being stifling. Yet in its way it was strangely agreeable. Noguchi was already there, close to appearing gross now that his silk suit was substituted by a loose robe. He was seated on a cedar bench, steam swirling around him, sweating profusely, his robe gaping open over an impressively large and hairy belly. Expressionless, he patted the bench on either side of him and the girls sat down.

It was too noisy for conversation, it was necessary almost to shout to communicate, an exercise too tiring in such an environment. The three sat and silently perspired, their robes very quickly becoming heavy with moisture both inside and out. After fifteen minutes or so of this Noguchi got to his feet and beckoned. They followed him through a smallish door which tightly framed his great bulk and found themselves in a smaller, square room featuring a large, octagonal Jacuzzi, which bubbled and seethed, steam clinging to the restless surface.

Queenie and Coco exchanged questioning glances; one hardly partook of a Jacuzzi in one's bathrobe. Noguchi, watching them, produced a flat grin. Then, his restless eyes flickering from one girl to the other, he calmly stripped off his robe and let it fall at his feet. Resting his hands on the elevated edge of the bath he clambered over it and in. His large penis, earlier aroused from his Peeping Tom activity, swayed over a commendable set of testicles. He was watching for a reaction from the girls as he did so and was rewarded by Queenie's perceptibly widening eyes.

Noguchi settled down with a comfortable sigh. As the jets pounded his flesh he raised an eyebrow at the uncertainty hovering over Queenie and Coco. 'Why the hesitation?' he asked. 'We Japanese do not find nudity shocking. Come on in – it's wonderful.'

For some reason Queenie, her prurient interest inevitably tickled by the glimpse of male genitalia, was visited by a brief attack of giggles. Suddenly playful, she took Coco by surprise by yanking undone the sash of her girlfriend's robe and sliding it off over her shoulders. Laughingly protesting, Coco quickly climbed into the Jacuzzi on the opposite side from Noguchi. Then Queenie, throwing a defiant, mocking look at him, joined her in her nudity and lowered herself into the tub next to Coco.

The tub was too large, otherwise Noguchi might have begun sexual moves with toe-mingling. Instead, sitting with the pounding water just below the level of his massive shoulders, as skilful at mentally peering through agitated water as he was through female clothing, he set about graphically discussing the sexual preferences and oddities of the Oriental male as calmly as if he were talking about an average day in the office.

Queenie and Coco both found his words, in this soothing yet stimulating atmosphere, amusing, even arousing, and could Noguchi's eyes see as clearly through the water as his imagination could, they would have been rewarded by a view of Queenie's hand stealing up Coco's thigh and finding her sexual heart.

Noguchi prattles away about communally administered enemas in S&M clubs, assuming that Coco's closed eyes are demonstrating an appreciation of the combination of his words and the Jacuzzi whilst what is happening to her is that beneath the miniature waves Queenie's index and second fingers are sliding smoothly, steadily, in exactly the way she knows Coco likes – in and out of Coco's tight, wet pussy, whilst her thumb gentles her tiny nub of erect clitoris. In a remarkably short time Coco comes with a suppressed whimper, her thighs tightening in a reflex action on Queenie's hand, her nostrils flaring. Moments later her own hand is creeping up the quivering inside of Queenie's thigh with the intention of returning the compliment when Noguchi unknowingly cuts short this activity by pressing two buttons on the outside of the tub. The water stills and a young woman in a short, white housecoat, looking like a nurse, materialises bearing a heap of neatly folded, fluffy white towels.

Noguchi climbed out of the Jacuzzi, the girl carefully dried down his wobbly flesh then knotted the towel around his middle as, fascinated by the casualness of it, Queenie and Coco looked on. Then the girl beckoned to Queenie, holding a towel wide, and Queenie, unful-filled and in rising carnal need, stepped out of the water and into it. She was dried down by the girl's nimble hands, which only served to arouse her further, and the towel was secured around her breasts.

Perched on a small, wooden, folding stool, Noguchi made no disguise of his sexual interest as Coco followed Queenie out of the tub and was in turn carefully dried down and pamperingly wrapped up.

'Now,' uttered Noguchi, with emphasis. 'Now comes our greatest pleasure in the wonderful hands of my masseuses. We will experience something most special indeed which will induce in each of us a lightness of being so intense that after the heat of the steam and the pounding of the waters we shall begin to feel as if we are floating.' He paused, his eyes lingering meaning-fully on each of them in turn. 'And then, we shall see,' he added.

His bulky sides bulging over the snow-white towel, Noguchi led the way into yet another room. This one was suffused with a soft red glow from an invisible light source, and a light aroma of birch and metholated camphor pervaded the warm, moist air. There were four, aligned, chrome-legged massage tables with padded tops, alongside three of which stood a girl in a white housecoat.

'My wonderful young ladies, as you are about to discover,' said Noguchi. 'Pick yourself one each.' Propping the edge of his belly on a central table he hauled his legs up and rolled on to it with a grunt.

Queenie and Coco climbed up on either side of him. Queenie in particular was eager for the touch of strange, feminine fingers. Crossing her hands under her chin on the small, flat pillow, she turned her head sideways in time to see Noguchi's great buttocks being exposed as his girl opened his towel. Queenie noticed that there seemed to be something odd about the masseuse's movements; she appeared to have felt for the towel rather than reaching for it in the normal way.

Noguchi answered her thoughts. 'They are blind,' he said, as Queenie felt her own towel parting company with her flesh. 'From Taiwan. They are much prized for their delicate touch, which is said to be a result of their affliction.'

Incredibly sensitive hands started work on Queenie and she began immediately to appreciate what he meant. Small, strong and skilful, they commenced on her lumbar region, isolating little muscles she had hardly been aware existed. Fingers and palms smooth and busy seemed almost to blend in with the muscles as they contrived to turn them to butter. The treatment very quickly became exhilarating. Queenie's eyes grew lazy, hovering half focused on Noguchi's buttocks which trembled as his upper thighs were slapped and massaged. With a sigh she turned her head, her vision unblurring momentarily to look at the infinitely more desirable flesh of Coco whose girl was doing to her what she herself had many times done and which Coco loved – strongly massaging the muscles between neck and shoulders. Coco, eyes closed, was making little grunts of appreciation and wriggling.

The blind girl's hands began a rhythmical sweeping from Queenie's back to mid-thigh, teasing the buttocks sensually each time they fluttered over them, and Queenie's exhilaration turned to giddy euphoria. Noguchi's predictions became reality; she indeed felt as if she were floating and the sexual need which had remained with her since pleasuring Coco in the Jacuzzi increased. Closing her eyes, the lids feeling heavy with a need greater than sleep, she pressed her crotch into the padded table-top and began to gently rock with the rhythm of those magic hands, imagining them straying between her buttocks and their fingers finding her pussy.

Moments later there is a brief moment of being untouched then Queenie's salacious longing is catered for. Her buttocks are kneeded and parted, fingers slide onto the silky skin of her inner thighs, spreading them wider, then the tips of two fingers slip to the second knuckle into her damp pussy. Yet the touch, Queenie realises as she savours this so-welcome thrill, has changed. Opening her eyes she glances over her shoulder. The girl has vanished. In her place stands Noguchi. His pudgy lips are open, his eyes are molten pitch and he is possessed of one of the biggest erections she has ever seen.

No matter that this is a man so big he is almost gross, no matter that he has insinuated his fat fingers secretly, uninvited, into Queenie and is now easing them to the bottom knuckle. She needs sex and behind her is a man with a massive, ready cock. Her eyes linger on this monster tool, and she licks her lips then gives Noguchi a raunchy, droopy-eyed smile before turning her head away and lowering her chin on her hands. This body language transmits to the man all that he needs to know; the English reporter is open to him and willing to do as he wishes. His fingers slide up and down Queenie's tight, wet sheath while his other hand finds its way beneath her torso and encircles a breast, its touch almost as gentle as the girl's had been. A shudder of utmost pleasure engulfs Queenie. Bending to her, Noguchi performs a service which few men have delighted her with before. Tracing his tongue along her buttock-cleft, he pauses at her puckered little bottom hole, darting the tip of his tongue inside and flickering and probing, he brings her exquisite sensations before moving on to replace his fingers inside her pussy.

He eats her with enormous enthusiasm, burying his face in the folds of her backside, slurping, rocking his head, and as he does so he wraps both meaty hands around her upper thighs and raises her from the table, onto her knees, his face going with her buttocks until her bottom is high in the air, her head still resting on her hands. Then he climbs up behind her, kneels between her thighs on the edge of the table, handles the swollen head of his cock an inch into Queenie's vagina. He leans into her, his great belly squashing over her buttocks, his hands fold over her breasts and he heaves his cock all the way in to her. Only his grip on her breasts prevents her from being flattened onto the table-top.

Queenie's loud gasp at this penetration mingles in the steamy air with Noguchi's grunt of effort, and for the first time in several minutes Coco, deeply involved in the pleasures her blind Taiwanese masseuse is bringing her, flutters open her eyes. Her expression changes from momentary shocked surprise as she watches Noguchi almost withdraw from Queenie then bang into her again, to amusement to finally rampant lust. Queenie, she notes, has shoved her thumb into her mouth and is sucking it as Noguchi fucks her. Coco is very familiar with this particular fantasy of her girlfriend; she does it sometimes when the two of them are making love, it is a little cock in Queenie's mouth, not a thumb. Her eyes lech on Noguchi's mammoth penis as it heaves in and out of one of Coco's favourite places, his matching-sized balls slap back and forth and his buttocks, despite their mounds of flesh, tense with each thrust. It is Coco's turn to be overwhelmed with lascivious need.

Rolling onto her back, Coco reaches for the masseuse's knee then slides her hand high up the girl's thigh under her coat. There is a momentary tension in the

31

girl, a surprised stillness, but she does not try to pull away, nor to defensively tighten her thighs. Coco's almost flat hand creeps higher until the side of her index finger reaches its prize, sinking into a wisp of panties stretched tight over a warm, fleshy mound. Coco gentles her knuckle back and forth and is gratified when thighs suddenly gone hot close onto her hand, not in protest but in carnal acceptance. The masseuse stoops over Coco as Coco's dextrous fingers crawl under the edge of her panties and probe. Her hand blindly finds Coco's face and the edge of her mouth; she joins lips with her and, as Coco's green-nailed second finger worms its way inside a delightfully tight and humid pussy, the girl's tongue slips between her teeth to mingle with Coco's.

Although in full and sweaty rut, Noguchi's eyes do not miss the beginnings of lesbian sex at his side; he grunts a few words in Japanese, evidently a command since the girl responds by straightening up and, with Coco's hand and fingers busy between her legs, unbuttons her cotton coat, shrugs out of it and climbs onto the table. In moments of mounting frenzy, Coco yanks the girl's knickers off and pulls her body flat into her own, crotch to needful crotch, breasts flattened against breasts, tongues devouring tongues.

The sight of this further inflames Noguchi. He uncouples Queenie, takes her by her ankles and spins her easily around onto her back. Squatting onto his heels, he drags her thighs high up his and thus impales her; the resting place for his belly is now Queenie's own, its size completely hiding from sight the energetic pounding of his penis. Peering through her breasts along her body Queenie sees only a great mountain of flesh enveloping her from the waist down, trembling and wobbling from Noguchi's exertions. She is nevertheless filled and fired by the enormous cock as it drives relentlessly into her. She responds with buttocks wildly bouncing on the man's thighs, feeling totally, wonder-

fully wanton in this undreamt-of situation, any anticipation of which might easily have repulsed her.

Sexual contortions in a room so close to the Jacuzzi
and steam rooms quickly raise the temperature, and the
flesh of the four naked, writhing, caressing, copulating
bodies begins first to glisten, then to run with snaking
rivulets of sweat. Coco and her masseuse, utterly
immersed in the delights of one another's carnality,
reverse positions, heads to crotches. Bodies slip against
one another, tongues dive into sweet wetness, hands
clutch and kneed hot, damp buttocks, hips jerk, the
ecstasy of orgasm close, as it is with Noguchi and
Queenie grappling at their side.

Noguchi lifts Queenie off himself, moves back off the
bed to his feet, turns Queenie onto her face and slides
her towards him down the bed until her heels land on
his toes and she is doubled over the padding. Like
that he begins his final attack, grabbing her with hands
hooked around her upper thighs, dragging her onto
him, impaling her to his belly. Then he begins to jerk
and heave, faster and faster, belly bouncing and quivering, cushioned over her buttocks as her hands, knuckles
white, clench the corners of the table, and her cheek
rocks on the tiny pillow. Feeling a great, warm gush
of sperm flooding into her, followed by another, then
another, she turns her face down, bites her lower lip
and yells her own climax into the pillow.

With Coco and her masseuse in the final throes of
orgasm, heads bobbing between each other's legs,
tongues stabbing, Noguchi sags at the same rate as his
penis wilts. His knees give way and he sinks to the
floor, his hands sliding down Queenie's thighs, his fat
cheek mingling with her buttock. His glazed, sated eyes
vaguely witness the onslaught of mutual, supreme satisfaction on the adjoining massage table where thighs
clamp over ears, hips go suddenly tense amidst muffled
groans, whimpers and little shouts and then there is
left only the sound of panted, laboured breath and

Noguchi's wheezing against a background of gurgling water.

Recovering, but perspiring almost as heavily as he had been in the sauna, Noguchi, a hand on the small of Queenie's back, pushed himself to his feet. Queenie remained comatose in the aftermath of her orgasm. His eyes travelled over the sea of bare, succulent female flesh at his disposal, glinting with a mixture of lust and amusement. With a sigh, Coco rolled off of her masseuse and onto her back. Stepping to her, Noguchi ran the tip of a finger from navel to breast, then enclosed the breast in his hand, squeezing it. 'So,' he muttered. 'So far, so good. This evening is, I believe, proving to be a most positive step forward in East-West relations.' Then he laughed, a curiously deep, rumbling affair which set his flesh trembling.

Queenie slowly stood up, turned around and parked her bare behind on the top of the table. With a lazy, crooked smile she said, 'In the West we don't refer to this as relations. We call it fucking!'

Coco rolled back into her masseuse and, face buried in the girl's thigh, dissolved from head to toe into giggles.

Chapter Three

F*** of the Irish

'For a moment there last night I couldn't believe you were actually screwing the guy,' remarked Coco. She was sitting, legs crossed, in a white satin mini-slip in front of the mirror of an ornamental dressing table. Her long, lush, black hair hung thickly forward over one shoulder almost reaching her thigh, and it waved and shimmered as she treated it to its daily tonic of one hundred and fifty brush strokes.

Queenie, in a black silk dressing gown, was finishing off her breakfast with a last sip of orange juice at a table by the window of their Imperial Hotel suite as she gazed out and down at Hibya Park and the grandeur of the Imperial Palace itself beyond it. There was thin, watery sunshine on this late September day; the light appeared to be filtering through invisible remnants of yesterday's smog. She turned towards Coco with a mischievous smile. 'I got unbelievably horny in that place. The girls, the pampering – you. And he was very okay, as it turned out.'

'I was watching you. Well, Jesus, how could I not?' She pursed her lips. 'He moved incredibly gracefully for such a fat guy.'

'And I was watching you.'

Coco grinned. 'All at once it started feeling great to be back to my eastern roots.' Laying down her brush she swung her hair back over her shoulder with a swirl of her head. 'But today, work calls. It's early enough for us to get out on the street to watch the Japanese male on his way to the office.'

'Right.'

Hustle, bustle. Faces intense and inscrutable, each individual cocooned within himself yet little more than a living cell in the pulsing heart of business Tokyo. Grey suits, grey skins, black eyes, black hair, half a million of them on their way in to work. Mingling with them, ambling, observing, Queenie and Coco – Coco continually firing off her Nikon – were colourfully out of place, engulfed in a scurrying which still retained a certain grace and dignity. They were nudged and bumped, but never without an accompanied token apology. This army appeared to share a determine, tight-lipped expression which seemed to confirm what the girls had already learned: in many ways the Japanese male was a slave to his company – during the day at least.

The occasional diversion in this sea of sameness came as a cultural shock akin to the appearance of a rap group at Sadler's Wells. Twice, the Japanese equivalent of punk rockers posed extravagantly for Coco's camera. Both wore Elvis type suits; one had spiky, strawberry hair, the other had a bright yellow Mohican. Briefly, as the crowds began to thin and frenetic office life got under way, Queenie and Coco were surrounded by teenagers in brightly coloured, ancient Chinese costumes who danced politely around them, all smiles and laughter, before moving on. Later, they were to discover that groups such as these were known as *takenoko*, young rebels who considered themselves and were indeed perceived by the public in general as highly antisocial. In certain parts of other cities or in other countries such gangs might attack you; here in Tokyo they danced gaily around you. It was all most odd.

Queenie and Coco wandered around intrigued, utterly lost in the unnamed streets whose numbers went according to the age of the buildings, engrossed in the sights and smells of central Tokyo. For lunch they stopped at an attractive looking restaurant, its offerings advertised in the window by an array of replicas.

And there, squatting alone on a floor cushion at a table facing an ornate garden, was Queenie's Irish thriller writer, Sean Magee.

He looked around and up as Queenie's delighted hand fell on his shoulders. His big face creased into a surprised grin, and he clambered to his feet. Taking Queenie in his arms, he kissed her warmly on the lips. 'Unable to resist, you track me down the moment you arrive,' he said.

She broke away from with a smile. 'Sorry to disappoint. This is our third day.'

His grin melted into good-natured reproach. 'With never a phone call. Hell!'

'And who . . . ?' asked Coco.

For the first time, Magee noticed Coco. His all-seeing eyes darted over her as he raised an appreciative eyebrow. 'Bet I know who you are. Am I right, Queenie my love?'

'Absolutely. Coco, meet Sean Magee.'

'Ah,' Coco entrusted her delicate hand to his brawny one. 'The famous Irish writer and philanderer?'

'The very man. It would seem to me that your, ah, girlfriend's been telling tales about me?'

'Naturally.'

'All of them true, no doubt.' He nodded towards the floor. 'Then we shall have a very cosy lunch. Draw up a cushion each.'

A waitress in traditional dress with heavily lacquered hair that was piled high, hovered by their table. Queenie noticed the direction that the girl's slightly nervous eyes were taking. 'Oh my God, the shoes!' she exclaimed. 'And we're standing on a *tatami*.' She pulled Coco off the tightly woven matting and they both slipped off their shoes. The girl smiled and bowed her head, relieved that she had not been obliged to verbally remind them of the custom. *Gaijin*, foreigners, were anyway expected to make mistakes in observing the complicated set of Japanese etiquette rules, and this one was common enough.

The restaurant, simply decorated in classic style, was partitioned off with decorated paper walls into individual eating areas, providing intimacy and privacy. They sat around two corners of the squat, square table, which had a restful view of the sunlit garden with its big, smooth, carefully arranged stones, its fish pond with a stream running in and out of it and miniature island reached by a small, ornamental, wooden bridge.

As they tucked into *tempura*, pieces of fish and vegetables dipped into an egg and flour mixture and deep-fried, Magee gave them pointers on the Japanese style of dining. Washing it down with Sapporo lager, they learned that the esoteric qualities of the food's appearance and the type of ware it was served in were considered as important as the taste itself; the food was prepared to bring out its visual beauty as well as its flavour. The lovely, delicate ceramic bowls they were eating from had been most carefully selected as having the perfect colour and design to compliment the *tempura*. Queenie was the only one to experience trouble with her chopsticks.

Being so close to Magee in this charming setting, listening to his softly lilting voice and feeling once again the powerful presence of the man, Queenie began to be aroused by him. Memories of her single afternoon's sex with him flooded her mind; she needed more and made little attempt to disguise this in her mannerisms and the searching way in which she looked at him. As full of her as she was of him, Magee nevertheless came up with a stream of useful information about Japan and its customs. As they started on the traditionally final course of rice, he explained the reason behind the taboo of stepping on the *tatami* in shoes – it was related to basic religious concepts; shoes are in constant touch with the outside, with unclean things, and they had but one place inside a house – by the front door. It was unthinkable that they should be on its mats.

Coco, enjoying her meal immensely, also took a slightly perverse pleasure in the way Queenie and Magee were reacting to one another and found herself highly amused by the man. Besotted he might be with Queenie, but that did not prevent his eyes from falling frequently on Coco, revealing an obvious sexual interest. Mischievously, Coco steered the conversation around to sex by asking Magee about the average Japanese man's attitude to it.

'Your salaryman lives a perfectly acceptable double standard,' said Magee. 'In that respect, at least, he's a lucky fellow.'

'Salaryman?' echoed Queenie, very aware that his hand had fallen on her stockinged foot and was squeezing it.

'That's what they call a member of the grey-suited commuter army. But the standard applies to all men. The Japanese sincerely believes that he has two souls. One is spiritually bound to a higher reality than earth, the other is tied here. No matter what mischief the tied soul gets up to it cannot reflect on the spiritual one, which remains pure and sublime. So when salaryman is not working his butt off for his company he's quite often screwing it off or getting amazingly drunk while wifey sits at home darning his *tabi* or whatever. This is established behaviour which we foreigners – not I, may I hasten to add – often find disagreeably chauvinistic.'

'It all sounds dead bloody convenient,' remarked Queenie, wriggling her imprisoned toes. 'Women's Lib, eat your heart out.'

'To be sure.' He treated her toes to a final, affectionate, promising squeeze, and let go. 'Salaryman has no hang-ups in the sexual department. By western standards I suppose he is thoroughly debauched and his carnal needs are plentiously provided for. The sale of sex here is an incredibly thorough, businesslike concept.'

'Geishas?' asked Coco.

'Not particularly. The traditional geisha is highly

39

trained to entertain men, but isn't usually a prostitute. If she is, then she will be very expensive, the eastern equivalent to the western high-class call-girl, and only for the rich as she is several times the price of your normal whore.'

'Ah. That explains last night.' Queenie glanced at him through a suggestive half smile as she pushed her empty rice bowl away.

'Into mischief already, was it? I might have expected it. What in Heaven's name were you doing in the company of rich men's geishas?'

'Never you mind, Sean Magee. It was a bit of a party, that's all.' She laughed throatily. 'But tell us more about this creature salaryman – we've already learned quite a lot about one of his bosses.'

'Have you now? I think you're a wicked couple of colleens, unfit for the company of a religious Irishman such as meself.' His hand dropped to her knees. 'All right, now. The Tokyo male is serviced by an army of whores – there are probably more here than in any other city in the world. And would you believe they're supposed to be illegal? Basically they are as easy to find as pebbles on a beach. If you pick one up off the street you can whisk her away to a love hotel for a bit of a kiss and a cuddle in a tiny, garish room with lots of mirrors and maybe a vibrating bed. Or you get her from a strip club or any one of dozens of bars with hostess service. There are even Turkish baths with built-in sex facilities.'

'And you've been to these places and done all these things yourself, have you, Sean?' asked Coco.

'What me? Not me.'

His hand rose a short way up Queenie's thigh. 'Quite some city,' she said, the suggestion of a tremble in her voice.

'It changes its clothes for the evening and night. Well, most cities do, I suppose, but not to the extent of this one. Those same earnest men you see scurrying to and from the office with their grey suits and greyer faces

40

change into casual clothes and turn into whoremongers and get drunk on their nights out. It's amazing, so it is. You observe them so straight-faced and serious by day that you can hardly credit these as the same men laughing to shame the Irish, even outdrinking the Irish, would you believe, at night. Well, that is to say they throw up or pass out much easier.'

'We haven't had the chance to go properly out on the town yet,' said Queenie. 'Are you going to take us?'

'Tonight, the three of us will paint it pink – the traditional Japanese colour for sex, by the by, not blue. You agree, Coco?'

Coco tossed her head as she grinned, her hair undulating down her back. 'Yes, please.'

'You ladies are tempting me to be uncharacteristically wicked, so you are. How about we do some sleazy dives, then I'll take us to a place where there happens to be the most extraordinary sex show I've ever set eyes upon?'

'But you haven't done these things yourself,' remarked Queenie, grabbing hold of his black-socked foot. 'Have you?'

'Not I!'

That evening, they finally reached Magee's preferred sex club at ten o'clock by way of a number of bars and clubs featuring topless dancers, bottomless dancers, and even a dixieland jazz band. Tokyo by night was every bit as bustling as Tokyo by day, yet it was a city transformed; workplace miraculously metamorphised into playground. By the time the three of them arrived at the neon lit, arched doorway of the club, which displayed crudely painted drawings suggesting explicit sexual fair within, they were in high spirits.

The initial impression within the club was one of a décor which seemed especially designed to dampen those spirits: instant sleaze. It was three-quarters occupied. All of the clients were men and sat in tip-up cinema seats arranged in rows in a curve facing a small square stage. The black walls were festooned with a mixture of mirrors and posters advertising forthcoming attractions and the ceiling was rather oddly hung with clusters of dusty-looking plastic flowers. There was no bar as such, just two vending machines dispensing Coco-Cola and beer, and discarded, flattened tins littered the floor. As Magee and the girls found seats three rows from the front, a stripper, incongruously to the music of the Beatles and 'Penny Lane' and bathed in pink light, was going through the finale of her act on her knees, leaning back with wide-spread thighs as she smoked a cigarette in her vagina.

The engrossed audience was utterly silent and took no apparent notice of the two expensively dressed women who had entered this normally, performers aside, exclusively male preserve. Queenie's eyes nearly popped out as, seated between Magee and Coco, she looked up into the cigarette-puffing pussy. 'Smoking can seriously damage your health,' she whispered, making Coco titter.

The stripper stubbed out her Benson, smoked almost to the filter, on the edge of the stage. Gathering up her discarded fripperies of clothing to a round of polite applause, she hurried off through a black, backing curtain. Th bright auditorium lights came on emphasising the sleaze. There was a rustle of movement in the audience, but hardly any conversation. The music switched to Japanese as a little man in a gaudy shirt entered the stage where the stripper had disappeared, carrying a *futon* under his arm. He stepped forward onto the circular stage and, with a flourish, he unrolled the padded quilt, which was unhappily patterned with intertwined flowers.

The lights dipped again, the little man was replaced by a tuxedoed compère who rather grandly announced that the *honban manaita* show was about to begin. As he did so, men in the audience began getting to their feet and making their way to the stage.

'What's going on?' asked Coco.

'There's going to be a sort of a lottery.' Magee grinned. 'They have a colourful way of naming this part of the show. *Honban* means the real thing and a *manaita* is a chopping board for raw fish.'

'It sounds gruesome,' said Queenie. 'This is a sex show?'

'Leave now to save further offence.' Magee's hand fell on her knee. 'It's sex alright. If a little different from the average Irish version.'

A tall, buxom girl with peroxided hair and wearing a mini-skirt so tiny that it revealed the tops of her black, diamond patterned stockings and pinky suspenders, slunk through the curtain and onto the circular stage where she knelt by the *futon*, facing the audience as a number of men clambered onto the stage and gathered around her. Noisily, excited, they began extending their hands to one another, either as a closed fist, or flat, or with two fingers extended. Each time they did this one man left the group and returned to his seat.

'*Janken-pon*,' Magee informed the girls. 'The ancient papers-scissors-stone elimination game.'

'For the girl?' asked Coco.

'Well, for once with the girl. I know about her. She's an ex-American hippie from Los Angeles, would you believe, one of hundreds of foreign girls in Tokyo who make a living from live sex shows. She's even reputed to enjoy it.'

'God,' breathed Queenie, whose across-the-board sexual experience had extended only once before to a live sex show in Manila where there had been no audience participation.

The game continued until there were only two men left on the stage both in 'salaryman' suits, one grey, one blue, both minus their ties. They raised their hands, calling together urgently *Janken-pon*, one displaying a V-sign, the other an open palm. 'Scissors' had cut 'paper' and therefore won. 'Paper' returned with a resigned shrug to his seat. The show was about to begin.

Producing a small wicker basket spilling over with damp tissues, the compère gave it to the girl and disappeared as the auditorium became suddenly hushed. The man was swaying on his feet, clearly slightly drunk, but he nevertheless knew what was expected of him next; he dropped clumsily to his knees and extended his hands, palm upwards. The girl carefully began to clean them.

'Oh, wow, heavy stuff!' Coco couldn't resist uttering, and was shushed by Queenie.

The spots turned blue, bathing the stage in an eerie light. The silence was shattered by slow, heavy rock music and as the girl sunk to her knees in front of the man, the stage began to slowly revolve. Pressing her large breasts forward, the girl indicated that her sex partner should undo the buttons of her blouse. This he did with a certain amount of difficulty. Her breasts fell trembling free and she shrugged out of her blouse as the man fondled her. As he groped her, she took off his jacket, folded it carefully and laid it on the floor beside the futon. Then she pushed his hands almost brusquely off herself and had him stand.

Skilfully and with nimble fingers, the girl unbuckles the man's belt, slicks down his zip-fly and pulls his trousers down to his ankles. Supporting himself with his hands on her shoulders, lurching somewhat, he steps out of them. She folds them and they join the jacket. She stares for long seconds at the blue-tinged, white underpants, then, as the stage revolves a complete three hundred and sixty degrees and Guns 'n' Roses plays a series of raucous riffs, she takes her time stripping him of his underpants, her face inches from his genitals.

For the moment there is little evidence of arousal in this semi-drunken salaryman's penis; short, plumpish and uncircumcised it rests comfortably on commendably swollen testicles beneath a sparse thatch of inky pubic hair. The blonde slips the flats of two fingers beneath it, lifts it slightly, her blue eyes vacant of expression as she examines it. Then she has the man lie on his back on the futon beside her still wearing his shirt. She takes a tissue from the basket, pulls back his foreskin and busies herself with public, pubic ablutions.

It is a strange, clinical, yet oddly arousing affair, of which the girl does a most through job – yet salaryman's penis is stubborn and remains short, fat and flaccid.

Queenie, fascinated, asked Magee, 'What happens if he doesn't get it up?'

'Then she goes to the runner-up,' he told her.

But this, presumably embarrassing, event is not to be. The washing ritual satisfactorily completed, the girl takes the man's penis in a firm grip, cups his balls, exposes his glans and begins to flicker the tip of her tongue over it whilst squeezing his balls as if testing the firmness of tomatoes. As she runs her tongue all over his cock and balls, washing them for a second time, the object of her wanton attention begins to stir. As it rises she takes all of it inside her mouth, walks on her knees over his thigh so that she is between his spread legs and moves her hands under him to clutch his buttocks.

She is a sexual artiste, this American hippie refugee. Her cheeks indented, she sucks deeply on her Japanese cock. There is a break in the music during which the audience seems to be holding its collective breath as, revolving in front of them, she steadily moves her mouth up and down until the penis surprisingly has grown into a pole five times its original size, solid and heavy. The man's hips begin to rock, his hands are tangled in her long blond hair at the back of her rising and dipping head.

The girl is completely in charge of this lewd and bawdy public display of sex. Music booms again, exciting sounds from Elton John. She stands, unzips her little skirt and lets it drop, peels her knickers down over her high-heeled shoes and leaves those and her suspenders and stockings on. Then, picking up her basket from where she has left it on a corner of the futon, she takes two steps so that she is straddling the man's head. As he stares up between her legs, his hand straying to his cock and stroking, she completes her washing ritual, with her vagina, then sinks to her knees over his face, facing his feet.

Becoming thoroughly aroused, Queenie leans forward in her chair, rocking gently to the music of 'Ebony and Ivory', acutely sexually aware not only of the on-stage action but of her male and female lovers seated on either side of her.

The girl now performs a trick of her own. From her basket she removes a condom, strips it from its seal, puts it in her mouth, and with its rubber circle resting between teeth and lips, she ducks her head and rolls it down the turgid penis. The man is allowed only a very brief lick of his prize. Still absolutely in charge, she swings around, kneels over his cock, facing him, and lowers herself onto him, impaling herself to the hilt; she sits quietly like that, wriggling her bottom, as the stage makes two revolutions. It is almost as if she alone is the show, salaryman merely her flesh and blood dildo.

Now, as Queenie's eyes momentarily stray from the stage to Magee's trouser front, vainly seeking signs of an erection, while she wonders if there is an unraised organ in the entire house, the girl begins to bounce, her tits jiggling, hair swaying over her shoulders, biting her lips with her eyes closed as if she is truly enjoying herself. The man's hands are rifling her breasts, his mouth is open. Beneath her, he responds to her bouncing with hip-jerks of his own which grow faster and faster.

The smoky air is charged with a heavy fug of eroticism, yet the audience sits tense and still, exhibiting no evidence of their presumably mass arousal. Queenie, in mounting need, continues to rock, hands clenched together in her lap, pressing into her crotch, whilst Coco's eyes gleam as she straightens her legs in front of her, thighs squeezed together and gently rubbing.

Magee's eyes take time off from the approaching climax in front of him to roam in amused lust from Queenie to Coco and back again as his brain forms plans of how he is very shortly going to get around to showing them what a true, red-blooded Irishman is made of.

This carnal display is destined not only to be a gymnastic exhibition. The girl remains kneeling, though she leans forward so that her big tits squash into the man's chest. Her heaving bottom, suddenly pink as the spots change, presents itself big and slightly plump to each section of the audience as the stage continues to turn, full and furious copulation clearly visible as the cock slams in and out of her and the hairy balls jiggle.

It is over. The man shouts above the music, produces two climatic heaves which throw the blonde's hips higher than ever and he is still. She surprisingly, bounces a few more times as if she is actually carried away with this – who knows, perhaps she is – she arches her neck, pushes herself back into a rigid sitting position. Head back, lips open she shudders, appears to sigh, then her shoulders sag. But, almost immediately, she climbs off the man, strips the condom off his wilting penis and drops it in her basket. She gathers together her bits and pieces of clothes to a smattering of applause. The man somewhat wearily gets back into his pants and suit as she leaves through the back curtain. The house lights go on and a few seconds later the stage is empty, harshly exposed under the lights, looking more sordid than when topped with colour-washed copulation.

Queenie rocked on, eyes mesmerised on the stage as if she could still see the action, and let loose a long, slow breath as Coco, drawing her knees up, muttered 'Jeeesuuus.' Men, suddenly seemingly instilled with urgency, began to leave in droves; a few began to form a queue in front of a pink-curtained doorway off to the left of the stage.

'What's behind there?' Queenie managed, breaking her sexual spell.

Magee grinned lethargically. 'What you might call the hand-job room. For a small extra fee quick relief is provided. Most of the rest will be heading for the nearest cat-house.'

'Well, you did say quick relief,' Coco observed with a smirk as the first man behind the pink curtain emerged with a glazed expression on his face, still in the act of zipping his flies. 'That must be an all-time record.'

'A good reason for being first in line.'

'I can't say I blame him. That was a horrible turn-on,' Queenie commented. 'Is there a cat-house for girls, too?'

Magee's eyes travelled over her, then Coco, as his arms went around their shoulders and he pulled them into him. 'No, but I guess there's me,' he drawled. 'If you ladies don't mind sharing?'

'Heh, what's this? You're mine.' Queenie objected with eyebrow raised.

'Yeah, but then so is she.'

Coco smiled. She was feeling deliciously horny, but she said, 'Do I, uh, get to have a say on what is to be done with my body, buster?'

'Sure you do.' The Irishman squeezed her shoulder. 'Get it over with, girl, then what I suggest is we all three make our way post haste to the most luxurious love hotel in town.'

'But we have a perfectly lovely suite at the Imperial,' Queenie pointed out.

'The Imperial?' He took both of them by their hands and pulled them to their feet. 'You don't know what you've been missing, to be sure you don't. Let's go.'

Deciding against what would be probably a longish wait for a taxi, the three, happy and slightly inebriated, strolled arm-in-arm through the Ginza area – a remarkably different experience from joining the morning rush-hour crowds. It was eleven o'clock, turning-out time for many of the bars, and there were drunks everywhere. Their behaviour was apparently perfectly acceptable even when they were throwing up or peeing in the gutter, which was frequently. They weaved their way through this Baccanalian flotsam and jetsam for more than a mile, until Magee stopped them at a garish doorway in a high wall. It was in the shape of a massive pink heart, the word 'Hotel' in English above it together with a clumsy painting of a couple embracing on a bed. The door was unattended. Beyond it was a small, neat garden area and the love hotel itself, boasting a remarkably ornate facade with colourfully painted plasterwork in complicated patterns topped with friezes of nude statuary. Just inside the door, screened behind a small window and sitting in an area no bigger than a large cupboard, they found an ancient crone whose slate-grey face was as rugged as a ploughed field. Magee passed some money through a slot and wordlessly she slipped him a key with a number tag.

Beyond the darkish, narrow entrance hall was a foyer so theatrical it made Queenie gasp in surprise. There was a central fountain with naked, intertwined male and female figures spilling water from their mouths beneath lights that constantly changed colour, and the ceiling was festooned with tinkling glass chandeliers.

That their room had everything to do with sex and little with sleeping was obvious as soon as Magee let them in. It was dominated by a kitchy, massive, heart-shaped bed with black satin sheets, crimson pillows and a huge, circular, pink-tinged mirror centred on the ceiling above it. The walls were lined with red velvet and hung with more mirrors, this time in heavy gilt frames. There were pink rugs in place of the customary *tatamis* and two armchairs covered in fluffy white material. The room was spotlessly clean and had been freshly perfumed; a piped music system dispensed soft, romantic western music and there was a television and audio-video equipment including a video camera which was locked into a stand angled on the bed.

As he closed the door behind them, Magee smiled at the look of disbelief on both the girls' faces. 'Interior decorator's nightmare,' he observed.

'If this is supposed to turn me on,' said Coco, staring appalled at the bed, 'I'm scared it's going to do the reverse.'

Queenie laughed. 'Then close your eyes, my love.' She slipped off her shoes.

'You don't have to take your shoes off here,' said Magee. His eyes draped lecherously over her. 'But the feet are as good a place as any to be making a start.'

Thoroughly amused, horny but in no hurry, Queenie dropped into one of the candy floss chairs as Coco tested the bed for comfort, first with her hands then sitting on it and bouncing while Magee removed a bottle of French champagne from a mini-bar and stripped the wire from its neck.

'Strokes for folks,' said Queenie, as the cork came out with a slight plop to fall disappointingly to the rug and the minimum amount of champagne foamed. 'Wow.'

Magee filled three glasses. 'It's a sort of a funfair sex palace,' he observed, giving a glass to Coco then going to Queenie. 'I was here last year with a darling little girl, so I was.'

Taking her glass, sipping, Queenie said, 'What's this, a refresher course?'

'Better, I hope.'

'Are you going to write a sex thriller?' asked Coco.

He perched on the arm of Queenie's chair. 'I may put a little sex in it here and there.'

Queenie's over-active libido began to gain control. She put her hand high up on his thigh. 'Then you'll need as much personal experience as you can get.'

'You bet,' he breathed. Knocking back the contents of his glass in one, he put it on the rug. Then he cupped her chin in his hand, turned her face up to his and mingled his lips with hers. As his free hand slid down the neck of her blouse and under her bra to cup her breast, pinching the nipple, the kiss grew more fiery, tongue sliding against tongue, and Queenie filled with an anticipatory tension.

Coco curled her legs under herself on the bed and slowly sipped her drink, settling down to watch their progress with an excited gleam in her eyes. Magee left his perch on the chair arm and sank to his knees by Queenie's thigh, contriving to keep his lips locked on hers as he did. He fumbled blouse buttons undone then hooked his fingers under the wired edge of her bra and lifted it up to free her breasts, filling his hands with their softness and warmth, rolling them together, his tongue slipping deep inside her mouth as she squirmed, arching her back.

'Just pretend I'm not here,' mumbled Coco into her glass. She grabbed her breast through her thin, black sweater, squeezed, then slid the flat of her hand sensuously down over her belly, fingers rigid, moving on down until their tips found her crotch above emerald green lycra slacks.

Queenie was shamelessly hot. Pre-aroused by the live show, in desperate need of this Irishman who had performed such a thorough job on her in his Belgravia mews house, she was in no mood for further preliminaries. 'Fuck me, Sean,' she mumbled into his mouth. 'Fuck me, now, right here on this chair.'

Magee is not about to argue against something he was in any case on the point of doing. He unhooks the waistband of Queenie's skirt, unzips it and slides it all the way down and over her feet, the satiny material crackling with static against her stockings. Impatient, panting for what is to follow, Queenie raises her bottom and he strips off her miniscule knickers in one long heave then walks on his knees between hers and yanks her thighs wide apart. Folding forward at the waist he performs simultaneously the acts of diving his tongue into her coppery bush and getting his trousers and underpants down to his knees. Then he straightens, slips his hands behind her buttocks, takes a firm grip and drags her forward and onto his throbbing, desperately needful cock, impaling her to its root as a strangled gasp rattles in her throat.

Coco finds her view of the proceedings most incredibly lubricious: Magee, whilst having removed no article of clothing whatsoever, appears more shockingly exposed than had he been undressed. His shirt has ridden a short way up his back to reveal his heavy buttocks tautening and slackening as they heave and strain, his thighs are slightly apart and his hairy balls jiggle heavily between them, and his thigh muscles bulge above the untidy pile of pants and trousers. Coco feasts on the sight, tense, her need swiftly rising as Queenie's stockinged feet wrap themselves around the back of Magee's thighs and she is offered a perfect view of her girlfriend's penetration. Queenie's fine buttocks are flattened on the edge of the chair as Magee's thick member plunges in and out of a pussy fringed in reddish shadow. Tension rising all the way up to the back of her throat, Coco produces a moan which is in odd harmony with Queenie's own. She fumbles with her zipper, frees it and unfolds her legs from under her. Swinging her feet to the floor, she lifts her bottom and peels her slacks down over her knees. Leaning forward, she spreads her thighs while her black eyes are glued on Magee's now pounding buttocks and heavily bouncing balls. She digs the tips of three fingers into herself through her satiny white panties, taking their tiny, embroidered flowers inside her damp pussy as her thumb slips under the waistband and flickers on her erect little clitoris with extreme urgency.

This fuck promises to be an event briefer even than Queenie's first tumble with Magee. The two of them are so incredibly turned on there is no question of sampling the delights of different positions or of slowing down to delay the final pleasure. They are screwing in all the lewdity of their disarranged clothing, doing it with the singular objective of bringing the quickest possible relief to an almost unbearable horniness, to climax, to come. A vague realisation of what a ribald picture they must be presenting to Coco adds sauce to this gluttonous dish. Queenie climbs her feet halfway up Magee's back, her toes curl and her heels drum on the Irishman's arching spine as she wails her orgasm at the same time as Magee's buttocks go taut as iron and his load begins to gush into her. His buttock muscles slacken then tighten again while semen pours out of him. Coco is coming right along with them; her whimpers mingle with Queenie's wail and the fingers under her knickers give a final jerk and go still. She collapses back on the bed, draws her legs up, closes her eyes and, with her fingers still rammed inside her, curls into a foetal position.

Their heavy, regular breathing steadily grows quieter. Queenie became vaguely aware of romantic background music – Sinatra, bringing her violets for her furs and it was spring for a while, remember? – and her eyes flickered open. In the mirror above the bed she saw, reflected from a wall mirror, Coco curled in a ball, her lower clothing in disarray, her fingers still cosily lodged inside herself. Her eyes swivelled to the top of Magee's head which was resting between her bare breasts with her bra crookedly flapped over his thick, grey, mussed hair. Over his shoulder she had a view of his bare buttocks poking out from under his shirt tail with her thighs splayed on either side. Her feet were treading down the shaggy pile of the outrageously pink rug and her skirt and panties were in an untidy heap near her left foot. It was as if she were awakening from a powerful, erotic dream, so intense had this copulation been. Several minutes drifted by and Queenie became aware that Magee's flaccid penis was still within her and that she was awkwardly uncomfortable, cramped in her lumber region and with pins and needles in one foot. Wriggling and flattening her hands under the fronts of his shoulders and pushing, she grimaced at the author's head and grumbled, 'Get off me, Sean Magee.'

Magee grunted and turned his head up to present her with a deliciously languid smile. 'I'm somewhat of a heavy brute, I'm told,' he muttered, and leant his weight back and off her onto his knees.

Queenie rearranged herself in the chair, banging her tingling foot on the carpet and for no particular reason pulling her bra down to cover her breasts. 'God,' she breathed, smiling back at him and brushing a stray lock of hair from her face. 'We seem to have got just a little carried away.'

'Bet your sweet life, baby,' came the voice of Coco as she disengaged her fingers and uncurled. She pulled up her knickers but removed her shoes and slacks – dropping them on the rug – and sat up, cross-legged.

Raising his eyebrows in mock horror, Magee glanced down at himself. 'I am,' he said, 'it would seem, some-what shockingly exposed, and in the sight of two lovely ladies.'

'So why don't you therefore get naked?' Queenie suggested. 'It would be rather more aesthetic.'

Magee grinned. 'Well, since I wasn't exactly planning on an early night.' Turning sideways to Queenie, he sat on the rug and pulled off his shoes, his trousers and his underpants, leaving them in more or less a tidy pile to which he added his shirt. 'Is nobody joining me then?' he asked.

'We shall drink bubbly in the buff,' Coco said with a grin and stripped nude through the final few bars of 'Violets for Your Furs' and the opening ones of 'It was Just One of Those Things'.

'We shall, we shall,' agreed Magee, as Queenie's bra once again parted company with her breasts. He got to his feet and topped up the glasses. Taking one to Coco he handed it to her as his eyes swept briefly over her nakedness. 'Holy mother of Jesus,' he remarked. 'I must be the luckiest man alive at this moment. I find myself in a situation which before today I would have sworn could only be the stuff of wild erotic fantasy.' He went over to Queenie, gave her a glass and knocked his back in two gulps.

'Material for your next book, perhaps?' suggested Queenie, her eyes strayed to the dangling instrument which had just brought her such a high of pleasure.

'Were I Harold Robbins, perhaps.' Demonstrating the legendary capacity of the Irish, Magee refilled his glass and once again drained it. He poured the remains of the bottle in it, dropped the bottle on the rug and went to the mini-bar to get another. Untwisting the wire, he said, 'We are going to have ourselves a little party to remember all of our lives, so we are.'

'Bragging in advance, is it?' said Queenie.

'You bet, missie. Not all Irish boasts are invention.' This time the cork came out with a satisfying bang, sailing across the room to bounce off the TV screen as Moët's finest – or a passable Japanese imitation – gushed into his eagerly awaiting glass.

'As it happens, I read your last book, Sean,' said Coco. 'It was tough and fast, but there was hardly any sex.'

'*Captive Bay*. Did you enjoy it?'

'Very much. Even with the missing sex.'

He laughed. 'They were English criminals. Maybe they don't do it.' More champagne went down his throat, this time not quite so thirstily. 'Now I'm about to write about Japanese gangsters. They do it all right, so I am reliably informed.'

Queenie, feeling comfortable in her nakedness, happy to chat for a while whilst knowing that the fires of her lust would shortly rekindle from still glowing embers, took her champagne to the bed and stretched out next to the squatting Coco. Piling one crimson satin pillow on top of the other, she reclinedinto the softness. 'What's a Japanese gangster like?' she asked as Magee perched on the bed next to Coco.

'Awesome bugger,' he said. 'What I find truly amazing is the massive role they have in everyday business. They're sort of like the Mafia with knobs on – they've apparently muscled their way into almost every company. Enormous corporations are scared of them to the point of conspiring with them. For instance, a fellow called Susumi Ishii is head of one of the country's three largest and most feared crime syndicates, the Inagawa-kai. You remember a . . .'

'Funny,' interrupted Coco.

'What is?'

'Hanging around here bare-arsed listening to you getting serious.'

'Shut up, Co, I did ask,' Queenie complained.

'You want me to finish or not?'

'Shoot,' said Coco, as yet untouched by the Irishman, but raring for action.

'Right.' He sipped more champagne. 'There was a massive scandal a year or so back which made world headlines.'

'Stockbrokers, no?' remembered Queenie.

'Right. Nomuri and Nikko. They were found to have lent Susumi the equivalent of about a hundred and fifty million pounds for use in manipulating the markets. That was only the thin end of a massive wedge. Japan's attitude to corporate manipulation began to change because of it but I don't see how they're ever going to get rid of the gangsters.'

'More pasty-faced little men in drab suits, are they?' asked Coco.

'Not at all. Curiously enough they're usually flamboyant – as if they want to advertise themselves. It's part of the Jap's love of uniforms, of identifying with his group. They kind of swagger, like the image of the Twenties Chicago hood. Flashy dressed, oodles of gold, that sort of shit. And they're usually disfigured in some way, a deliberate infliction, sign of allegiance to their first boss.'

Queenie's eyes widened. 'Perhaps, for instance, a missing top joint of a little finger?'

'Sure. Pinkie castration is the commonest. What makes you ask?'

'I think we might have met a gangster last night. We were invited by Makita Noguchi, the president of Nippon Petrochemicals, to a small party in his penthouse. There was a character there who stood out because of his clothes and his gold – just the way you described it. The top joint of his little finger was missing.'

Magee raised an eyebrow. 'You didn't exactly come to Tokyo without important introductions, did you? Noguchi's one of Japan's top men.'

'Courtesy of *Time* magazine.' Queenie finished her champagne, declined the offer of a refill. 'He must be one of Japan's biggest men physically, too.'

'That would almost certainly have been a gangster at your party. And he could only have been one of the bosses, on a par with Susumi Ishii. Therefore Noguchi, whether he likes it or not, is most probably doing business with him. What was his name?'

'Ankoku something or other,' said Coco. 'Remember, Queenie?'

'No way. Unless I write them down on the spot, I find their names totally confusing.'

'I'll try and find out,' said Magee. 'Ankoku. Shouldn't be difficult. It might add an interesting dimension to your copy.'

'We had quite enough of gangsters the last time we were in the Orient,' Queenie remarked. 'We got mixed up with a Chinaman and a Cockney who were using a gambling boat to run drugs. We came bloody close to being killed.'

'Bloody close,' affirmed Coco. 'About a pube's width.'

Magee grinned. 'Must have made a great story.'

'Nah, we didn't use it.' Coco moved close to him, leaning her shoulder into his muscular upper arm, her first physical contact with Magee since their arrival at the love hotel. 'It wasn't part of our brief. We were writing a story for *Madame* about life on a gambling junket. It kinda didn't fit.' Her hand fell to his thigh as her eyes dived into his crotch. 'This don't fit either.

Here we are sitting around nude and chatting away like this is some dinner party.'

Magee's eyes danced in amusement tinged with lust as her squeezing hand sent a shockwave up his leg into his belly. 'Would you be having us do something else then, kid?' he asked.

'You bet.' She stuck her chin out at him and with a defiant little smile on her face slid her hand between his legs to cradle his limp penis. Her voice dropped half an octave into huskiness. 'Like, what we came here for, what you and Queenie have already done.'

Magee's grey eyes swept lustily over Coco's pert breasts. He knocked back his champagne, leant forward and carefully put his glass on the floor at the foot of the bed, by the heart's point. Extremely aware that his penis was in the palm of a girl whom he had not yet laid a finger on, he said, 'Well, I was just, er, resting up.'

Queenie propped herself on her elbows but hung her head back to watch the two of them in the mirror. 'Recovered now?' she asked.

His penis stirred in Coco's hand. 'I guess.' He glanced down at himself. 'I could do with two of those.'

'We'll make out,' murmured Coco. For the first time he noticed the tiny, tattooed rose at the top of her thigh. He touched it with the tip of a finger, indenting the soft flesh.

'Nice,' he said. 'Kinky.'

'A rose is a rose is a rose,' quoted Queenie.

Coco rubbed Magee's cock, watching it grow to full size in the warmth of her hand. 'And a rise is a rise is a rise,' she muttered, moistening her bottom lip with her tongue.

Billie Holiday began singing 'Crazy He Calls Me' as Magee wrapped Coco in his arms, locked his mouth on hers and they keeled sideways together on the bed. She lost her grip on his cock but trapped it between the tops of her thighs as he rolled onto his back, taking her comparatively slight frame with him as she ended up on top of him, and with the back of his heels he shifted them up the bed until his head rested on a pillow next to Queenie's. More than ready for additional action Queenie draped an arm over Coco's back and wormed her tongue into Magee's ear as he and Coco's kiss lingered on. They nestled cosily together for long moments, the Irishman lazily moving his cock in the hot, silken, fleshy grip, then he suddenly titled Coco off him.

'Don't let's waste the facilities,' Magee said, almost breezily. He sat up, rolled over the bed, dropped his feet to the floor and went to the video camera. His erect cock swayed before him as he adjusted the machine and got it going. Then he pressed a button in a small panel at the side of the bed and, quite silently, it began pleasurably to vibrate gently.

Coco rolled into Queenie's arms, they touched quivering tongues and rested a hand on one another's curvy flanks. Giggling, Coco said, 'This isn't a funfair sex palace, it's a porno king's bedroom.'

Pinching her erect nipple, Queenie muttered, 'I like porn.'

Magee was standing above them by the side of the bed. 'Maybe you two don't need me?' he said.

'Oh, we need you alright.' Queenie reached for him, cupping her fingers under his balls, lifting them as if testing their weight. 'Get down here and prove your Irish boasting.'

'To be sure,' said Magee, clambering onto the bed. 'And, since we're on camera, let's make it like it is in the filthy movies.'

Queenie grunted assent deep in her throat, following it up with an extraordinarily long and dirty chuckle.

Magee kneels over Queenie's head and with Billie singing '. . . sure I'm crazy, crazy in love . . .' Queenie runs her tongue up the underside of the Irishman's cock then sucks it inside her mouth while Coco, getting very happily and lustily into this threefold act and raunchily aware of the camera, leans her nose into Queenie's cheek and flicks the top of her tongue over Magee's scrotum. Staring down across his taut, hairy belly, the author can hardly believe this is happening to him. Two dreams of young womanhood, one with shiny black hair, the other thick red, are simultaneously spoiling his genitals with busy, hungry mouths and tongues. He arches his back with a groan, beginning to very slightly rock his pelvis. Coco wraps thumb and finger around the root of his cock, slides it from Queenie's mouth and swallows it into her own, relishing it, making little slurping noises, while Queenie takes the skin of his scrotum between her teeth and gently nips it. Magee's neck stretches, his head falls back and he faces the ceiling where he is now presented with the image of his delight in the mirror. Queenie's hands, he sees, have begun to get busy with both her own and Coco's pussies, the scene is lubricious in the extreme. He groans again and for some reason mutters in a strained voice. 'They'll never believe this back in Killarnie.'

Coco unmouths him and lazily, wickedly, mutters, 'They will if you show them the video.' Then she angles the head of his cock back between Queenie's lips and runs her tongue down its side.

The Rabelaisian trio leches on, the bed steadily vibrating; the music switches to Sade. Magee moves away from the eager mouths to kneel between Coco's knees, and spreading wide her thighs, he lowers his belly to hers and penetrates her sweet pussy. Queenie gets it into her inventive head to straddle the two of them, rubbing her copper-thatched mound against Magee's rocking buttocks and groping between sweaty thighs to clutch his balls. The Irishman is suddenly unsure if he is having them or they he, then decides it matters not a tinker's cuss – they are all three having each other.

It is a rising, libido-consuming tide of lust and passion which threatens to devour them. Their snaking, perspiring limbs slip and slide against each other, hands greedily grope and clutch, fingers penetrate every available orifice. As Magee withdraws his penis from Coco's vagina to the tip of his glans, he hovers teasingly for another plunge but she wriggles out from under him. 'Do me like an animal, Sean,' she gasps, climbing to hands and knees, presenting a lipstick-smeared, mascara-streaked, droopy-eyed face to the camera and a delectably trembling rear end to Magee. 'Fuck me like a fucking dog.'

As Queenie says, 'Yeahhhh!' she rolls from Magee's back, moves her hand from his balls to his cock and goes with him as he kneels behind Coco. As Magee gets a firm grip on Coco's buttocks, Queenie guides the head of his penis into Coco's wet pussy and he lurches into her. Queenie unhands him so that the full length of his big cock rams all the way into her friend's tight little hole, all the way up until his heavy mass of grey-sprinkled pubic hair bangs into her buttocks, his weight knocking her forward from resting on her hands to her elbows, her nose bumping into a pillow. He goes quite still, eyes closed, savouring the heat and tightness of this delightfully full penetration as Queenie contrives to crawl on her back beneath Coco's torso. As he slowly withdraws the length of his cock until only its head rests in Coco's pink-lipped vulva, Queenie makes herself thoroughly sexually comfortable, opening her thighs on either side of Coco's face on the pillow, her knees indenting the velvet wall. Reaching behind and up for Magee's buttocks, she raises her face to the interlocked genitals. As the Irishman plunges again into Coco the engorged vein beneath his penis slides over Queenie's tongue on the way in and when his cock is completely buried once more he shudders and gasps with the additional thrill of Queenie taking his balls completely inside her mouth.

The three become integral parts of the identical sexual tiger, a beast surely destined to reach mind-blowing orgasm in three parts of its wild, heaving body simultaneously. As, faster and faster, Magee fucks Coco, Queenie feasts on her close-up view of the heaving, plunging genitalia. Her tongue laps over the jerking cock and the slapping balls, while Coco buries her face in her friend's crotch, the tip of a finger jerking on her clitoris as she eats her with greedy gusto.

One of Queenie's hands strays from Magee's buttock to Coco's bouncing tits whilst the index finger of the other penetrates the Irishman's bottom hole to the first knuckle. The tiger erupts. Magee's body goes rigid, he roars through gritted teeth as Queenie sucks his balls into her mouth where they pulsate, emptying into Coco's pussy which clenches and unclenches as she moans in orgasm into Queenie's climaxing vagina.

The bed remains in ignorance of the beast's explosion. It rocks on, and the still, silent, sated sexual tableau rocks with it, and slowly keeling over onto its side, it is shaken apart into its three separate beings.

Magee crawls an exhausted hand over the damp, black satin sheet, fumbles for and finds the rocking mechanism switch and he and the bed slumber.

Minutes later the Irishman opens his eyes to the back of Coco's swanish neck. Her lank hair is in a tumbling mess all over the pillows; her cheek rests comfortably on Queenie's thigh, and her nose is inches from Queenie's glistening, coppery pussy. Very gently, she is snoring.

Magee's eyes swivel to the ceiling mirror where he studies the entire picture of the aftermath of sexual excess before wandering on to the video camera which continues to record. Idly, he grins to himself. 'Should I be fool enough to be caught with that film in dear old Ireland,' he mutters, 'they'll lock me up and throw away the key, so they will.'

CHAPTER FOUR

Whoresplay

Naturally enough, I've seen that video. I assure you that that steamy evening in Tokyo love hotel was, if you will excuse the pun, blow by blow exactly as described.

I'm Frannie, and I find myself most happily writing up a second adventure of my two very good friends and sometime bed-partners, Queenie and Coco. As, previously, when they got into an awful lot of trouble and even more sex on a gambling boat on the South China Sea, I was supplied with Queenie's sketchy notes and some dead horny photos from Coco to help guide my pen. To receive the bonus of a video was a wonderful surprise – apart from giving Lord Ballington and myself an incredible case of the hots when we watched it together, it showed me for the first time with just what utter abandon those two horny young ladies wallow in their sex.

Forgive me this indulgence, it seemed to me an opportune moment to briefly interrupt my narrative. The girls have begun their article plus they've had a riotously sexual introduction to Tokyo, but so far there is no sign of anything even remotely dangerous looming on the horizon. We'll, however catch up with them two days later when they are arriving at a party in the country house of Ankoku Nangi, the gangster . . .

Late afternoon sunlight filtered through the windborne, foamy mists that the Kegon waterfalls created.

Within the drifting, watery haze and disjointed rainbow patterns, hundreds of twittering sparrows swooped and dived. Observing this from a viewpoint a short way down the twisting steps at the side of the falls, Queenie and Coco, dressed in jeans and light woollen sweaters, were spellbound. It was that sublime, soul-cleansing beauty discovered only on rare occasions, and Coco was trying hard to capture it with her Nikon.

Awaiting them in the carpark above was a limousine and chauffeur, courtesy of Ankoku Nangi, in which they had an overnight case with evening clothes. When inviting them to his house on nearby Lake Chuzenji – from where flowed the stream and cascading rivulets of Kegon Falls – Nangi had suggested that they enjoy a full day over the trip. It was over two-hundred kilometres from the city of Tokyo to his house and there were some wonderful sights on the way, he had told them, particularly in this area of Honshu. They had spent an enchanting, sometimes astonishing three hours in the Nikko National Park, exploring its renowned collection of extraordinarily ornate shrines, temples and mausoleums scattered amongst four-hundred-year-old cedars, as well as spas, lakes and rivers and surrounded by mountains. They had a late lunch there, wandered for another hour, until the chauffeur, who hardly spoke any English – and had instructions to bring them to Nangi's house by early evening – had hurried them along to the magic and soothing Kegon Falls.

Coco finally ran out of film, despite the fact that she had brought along six rolls of Kodak asa 100. She rewound the last roll, put it and the camera away in her case and leant on the wooden rail next to Queenie. She could feel the slightest touch of water, lighter than a fen mist, on her face, and she was supremely content. As the sparrows endlessly, noisily, flitted in and out of the wet rainbows she murmured, 'What a hell of a bloody terrific day.'

Queenie smiled at her. 'Wonderful,' she agreed. 'And

one now begins to wonder what special delights the evening may have in store.'

'Yeah.' Coco reluctantly turned her back on the water-fall and propped her elbows on the rail, bringing her mind into clear focus. 'You know,' she said slowly, 'now I give it thought, I find myself just a touch apprehensive. Sean told us all about this guy Nangi, how he happens to be one of Japan's most notorious gangsters and here we are about to stick our butts inside his private house.'

'We are, aren't we? And on the line, I should think.' A sparrow whisked close enough to Queenie's face to make her draw her head sharply back with a laugh. The sudden breeze from its wings matched the strength of the wind.

'Of course, fatso Naguchi has obviously told him in great detail about our little episode together with him in his sauna. Now Nangi sends us the politest of invitations and treats us like a couple of princesses for the day. You bet we're being treated to this sort of hospitality with but one thing on the guy's mind.' She sighed and raised an eyebrow. 'Oh, well.'

'Is there ever anything else on a man's mind?'

'And of course we never encourage such thoughts, do we honey?'

Queenie grinned. 'Man has his will – but woman has her way,' she quoted. 'Oliver Wendell Holmes.'

'There you go again, professor.' Laughing, Coco took hold of Queenie by her upper arm and tugged her away from the rail. 'Let's move. The evening beckons its mysterious finger – Coco Qua Min Baker!'

Ankoku Nangi's house was at first sight incredible and on further investigation even more so. Perched on the banks of Lake Chuzenji it was on several levels. It might have been a pagoda, so ornate was it, except that it was not as high and it was spread over a far broader area than any usual temple. Its many different, green and red, shiny-tiled roofs elegantly curved and rose to tipped-up points like a mandarin's hat. When their limousine came to a whispering halt in a carpark the size of a castle's, Queenie and Coco were slightly taken aback to see that, amongst several luxury cars already parked there, was a white Rolls Royce Silver Spur with gold trimmings. Floodlights were on, though the sun had only just begun to sink over the lake.

One of a pair of high, elaborately carved, mahogany front doors swung quietly inwards as they stepped up to it and they were greeted, oddly, by a swelling crescendo from Pink Floyd. They walked into a cavernous entrance hall with a startlingly coloured spherical painting in a cupola twenty-five feet above their heads where flying dragons chased each other in an eternal circle, flames belching from their mouths. Awestruck, they were contemplating this, unsure of what to do since their chauffeur had vanished and the robed servant in charge of the door was neither saying nor indicating anything, when their host appeared.

Nangi was dressed entirely in black and white. His suit, exquisitely tailored, was in shiny white silk as was his tie. His shirt and pocket handkerchief were black – all was in fine silk, and his leather shoes were both black and white. A huge gold broach affair served as a garish tie clip and a thick gold watch and strap hung loosely amongst the heavily bunched hairs at his wrist. He was short and very broad. As she shook his hand while he briefly bowed his head, Coco had the impression that with a blackened face and white gloves he could fall on his knees and do a creditable take-off of Al Jolson singing 'Mamie'.

'Then you here are. Good,' he said. 'Prease?' he added enigmatically. Like many Japanese, he had difficulty with the letter 'L' which is not a part of their alphabet.

'We had a super-cool tour. It's sensational around here,' Coco told him, to which his only response was again, 'Prease?' His broad, flat face registered little expression. Then he waved a vague hand, 'Come.'

He escorted them through a labyrinth of passageways

66

and rooms which, all of them exquisitely furnished, had little to do with anything they knew so far about traditional Japanese interiors. Whilst the outside of the house could not have been anywhere in the West except perhaps Disneyland, the inside was a tasteful mixture of cultures, owing much to India, China, Italy, even to France as far as many of the modernist prints were concerned. Nangi, meanwhile, uttered not a single word until he led them into a bedroom with a view over the lake, to which their suitcase had somehow appeared before them. Then, producing one of his sharp little head-bows again, all he said was, 'For you to stay,' and he was gone.

'Taciturn little bugger, isn't he?' remarked Queenie as she glanced admiringly around the charming room. The floor was an inlaid pattern of Italian marble scattered with colourful throw-rugs – no *tatami* mats here in what would most certainly be a twelve *tatami* room at least. The walls were hung with the palest of pink silk and the large four-poster, canopied bed matched the walls.

'He very rittle Engrish speaky,' said Coco, imitating Nangi's accent as she swung the suitcase from the floor to the bed and unsprung the locks. 'Didn't you notice the other night? He was the only one who never joined in the English conversation.'

'I can't say I'm exactly wild about the man.'

'Me neither. But he is one of Japan's biggest gangsters, that's supposed to be some sort of a romantic image, don't y' know?' Coco pointed out.

Queenie grunted and wandered to the window. She looked out at Lake Chuzenji; it was serene, a deep blue which was tinged with orange from the setting sun, which had started to slip behind far-off, misty mountains. A rowing boat, strangely and eye-catchingly fashioned in the shape of a shark, was passing the bottom of Nangi's tailored gardens. A girl in it was taking photographs. In mid-distance, backdropped by the fiery orange sun, a tour boat trailed a rippling furrow.

'Joe Bananas Nangi,' said Coco with a giggle as she unfolded her silver-spangled, Lacrois evening dress from the case and held it up in front of her. 'Do we get changed for him right away?' she wondered aloud. 'It seems a little early for partying.'

With coincidental timing, as if in answer to her question, there was a rap on the door. Coco opened it and a servant in a short white jacket and a bow tie wheeled in a chrome trolley bulging with food, enough for at least four. There was even champagne buried to its neck in ice in a silver bucket. The complexion of the man's round face was sallow enough for him to have been Chinese and when he spoke it was in a sing-song Chinese fashion. 'You eat, misses, you enjoy,' he said. 'In one and a half hour I shall call for you.' His slanty eyes ferreted around the room. 'Ah, yes, and see here,' he went on, leaving the trolley and crossing the room to an inlaid wooden coffee table.

The man opened a small slat in the table. Beneath this was revealed a panel of buttons, one of which he pushed and a section of silk wall slid aside. Behind the wall was a mini-cinema-sized TV screen which flickered to life on – yet another surprise in this houseful of them – the satellite Sky Movie Channel and the middle of the film *Bonnie and Clyde*.

'I must say,' remarked Queenie, inspecting the contents of the trolley as the servant exited and while a good citizen leapt on the running board of the Bonnie and Clyde gang's accelerating getaway car to be blown away for his trouble, 'we are being done most proud by.'

'The idea being, I guess,' Coco suggested with a wicked grin, 'that we should be most proudly done a little later.'

Queenie laughed. 'Which remains to be seen.' She picked up a small square of warm toast from under a serviette. 'Amazing – there's even caviar,' she said,

'. . . and knives and forks.' She spread a thick layer of the caviar onto the toast and popped it into her mouth.

By the time they had eaten the food, polished off the champagne, and dressed, it was quite dark outside and a large half moon, starkly white, was bouncing its ghostly reflection on the waters of the lake. The same Chinaman who had brought the food arrived to escort them through the house to the party.

The sheer opulence of the room which was the party's venue was breathtaking. When Queenie and Coco wandered in, the first object to grab their attention, suspended from a high, vaulted ceiling, was a crystal chandelier of such massive proportions it must have weighed a ton. It was centred beneath a round painting of tigers chasing each other's tails, of similar dimensions to the one in the entrance hall, and this gaudy chandelier was the only evidence of shocking bad taste that they had come across in the house. Like some great glass globe over a ballroom, it slowly revolved. Surrounding spotlights reflected off it to throw multi-coloured dots over the forty or so people beneath it.

The room was hexagonal, each of its six walls twenty-five feet long and entirely mirrored, offering a confusing panorama of revolving chandeliers stretching off in all directions towards infinity.

Nangi, still sporting his black and white silk outfit, had a willowy young Philippino girl on his arm, who was a head taller than him. He greeted them with that disconcerting, childish grin which must have hidden a soul carved out of rock. He undraped the girl from his arm, waved fingers at her dismissively, and linked arms with Queenie and Coco to escort them across the room and up two steps to a bar housed in what appeared to be an out-of-place gazebo. There was no marble here, unless it lay beneath a rich, fitted, cream carpet which gave way pleasantly underfoot and was liberally scattered with thick rugs and animal skins.

The bar had six sides, like the room and a pagoda-type roof supported by fine, filigree-worked columns.

With slight shock, as she elected for more champagne while Coco switched to whisky, Queenie realised that the columns and the latticed roof were entirely of hand-carved ivory and must therefore be worth an enormous amount of money. Nangi left them without having said one word.

'Weirdsville,' commented Coco as, sipping her whisky, she gazed wide-eyed around the room, trying to get her head in gear with it. The only actual furniture in the room, unless you counted the bar, was a collection of sofas and coffee tables. The sofas had little to do with the normal western variety with their seats somewhere between the size of a single and double bed; they were a mere nine inches off the floor and they had elegantly curved backs with carved wooden tops and arms. There were more than twenty of them in a pleasing mixture of plain, subdued colours but heavily sprinkled with bright, lively-patterned silk cushions. There was a lacquered wood coffee table for each sofa, also low to the floor and with short, bowed and stubby carved legs.

The overall impression of the area from the raised point of view of the gazebo bar and staring above chattering heads and around the mirrored walls, was of a somewhat eccentric and enormously expensive hotel foyer which stretched on and on for ever and was populated with thousands of gaudily dressed men, the majority middle aged or more, and thousands of glittery young women, all of them sprinkled with constantly moving coloured dots. To add to the strangeness, yet somehow almost appropriate with the chandelier, waltz music filled the room from no visible source, though it was inspiring no one to dance. Queenie and Coco's overall impression was of having trespassed into some vast, esoteric cult gathering.

'You have, by now, taken stock of the women?' asked Queenie quietly, trying to keep her eyes from being lured into the confusion of the mirrors.

'Sure,' said Coco. 'No wives. Dolly birds. Guys and dolls.'

'Gangsters and molls,' Queenie suggested, which was, indeed, exactly what the scene suggested. 'I reckon the doll-molls are a bunch of high-priced whores. What say you, my love?'

'Could be, honey, could be.' Coco took a sip of whisky and pursed her pretty lips. 'Some party. So where do we fit in?'

'I think we're about to find out.' Queenie nodded towards the only break in the mirrored walls, the single door which was itself mirrored on the inside. 'Here comes the fat man.'

Dwarfing most other people in the room, Makita Noguchi was striding across it, making his way directly for them.

'I am pleased to see that friend Ankoku was quick to extend you an invitation to one of his renowned parties,' he said as he reached them. He bowed his head briefly to them; their previous sexual intimacy had not dulled the edge of famous Japanese manners. 'Nevertheless, I find myself surprised that you choose to mingle amongst such women. It hardly enhances the reputation of the West's top journalistic team.' He produced a bland smile. 'Unless this is in the name of serious research, of course.'

Queenie shrugged. 'We were invited, so we came – with open minds as always, of course. In any case, it would have been rude to refuse an invitation from one of your friends.' She paused, gazing out over the floor. 'Ladies of the night, the girls, are they?'

'Whores, naturally. And *yakuzi*, the men, or most of them – as you can tell by their attire.' He adjusted the knot in his sober, spotted tie, as if to bring attention to the difference between himself and the rest. His eyes did their usual job of piercing their clothes, roaming over Queenie's curve-hugging, red satin Balenciaga evening dress. 'It's going to be an orgy.'

'Oh,' said Queenie flatly, her mouth remaining in the shape of the word.

'Oh,' echoed Coco.

'Ankoku failed to explain that little fact?' He seemed amused.

'Yes, he did rather,' said Queenie.

'Lapse of memory, I expect. Shocking of him.'

'Yeah, well.' Coco swallowed back the remains of her whisky, gave a little gasp as its heat hit her stomach and turned to the barman for another one. 'Then I guess we'd better get pissed, hadn't we?' she said.

However, before Coco had time to match her words with her actions, just a short while later, as she and Queenie were wandering through the gathering where no sign of sexual activity was yet in evidence, her eyes fell on a newcomer to the room. She found him so instantly attractive her insides gave a lurch.

Slightly taller than the average, he was slim to the point of almost being skinny and soberly dressed in an extremely well-cut, dark blue suit. His black hair, neatly cut and styled, appeared soft to the touch; he was very handsome in a way which almost transcended the oriental idea of good looks. And he was very young, no more than twenty Coco guessed as his dark, broody eyes caught her stare and held it for seconds, a question forming in their depths.

Moments later, the magnetism of mutual attraction having inevitably brought them together, they were talking. His name was Tanaka, his English was a little muddled but acceptable, and he had the problem with his 'Ls'. As they chatted Coco felt a power emanating from him which added to his charm, a self-confidence rarely found in one so young, and soon she discovered what might at least have been a part of the reason for this; Tanaka was Nangi's son.

Tanaka was completely fascinated by Coco from the outset. He was intrigued to discover that she and Queenie – who had hooked the interest of a pair of the flashier gangsters and was gushing to them – were journalist and photographer and nothing remotely to do with what the other girls in the room were about.

'But, my father, the reason for this party he not exprain when he you invites?' he asked.

'No, he didn't,' Coco told him.

'Incredible how he is acting sometimes,' he said.

'Oh, it's okay, we don't mind.' Coco smiled into his eyes. 'At least. I don't think we do.'

'You don't?' He sounded, and looked, quite shocked. 'But, then, do most western chicks this attitude have?'

'No,' said Coco, her eyes wandering over his face. 'But there are a lot who don't who'd probably be less uptight if they did.'

He was bemused. 'In this country only a prostitute such a meeting as this would attend.' He studied her carefully, his eyes trying to penetrate her mind in the same way Noguchi's did her dress. He clearly fancied her, and his longing was written all over his face. 'Well, we see, I see,' he said enigmatically. 'But first, a show comes.'

'What sort of a show?' asked Coco.

'A sex show. But this you don't have to see if you not want.'

Coco shook her head and managed an artless look. 'It's okay, I'm a big girl, I am,' she said.

Shortly after, the lights dimmed and Tanaka took Coco's hand in his and led her to a sofa. Coco noticed for the first time as she folded herself awkwardly almost to the floor and into the surprising comfort of the seat that the sofas were arranged around the room in roughly three-quarters of a circle. There was general movement as everybody sat down around them; Coco had just time to notice that Queenie was still with her two flash gangsters and that she appeared to be enjoying herself before the rest of the lights went out and they were plunged into complete darkness.

The black air was permeated with the noise of a rising, whistling wind; the sound of rain grew louder, and there was a sudden, loud, thunderclap followed by

73

a long, scary, female wail of fright – this clearly, unlike
the sound effects, was real and in the room. A broad,
pale blue spot cut a swathe of light from the ceiling
down into the carpet; into this light wringing her hands,
moaning and shaking in simulated fear staggered a
young, pretty girl in a brightly-coloured kimono. She
fell to her knees as there was a gruff, masculine bellow,
a peal of evil laughter, and another spot, this time red,
split the air to pour over an extraordinarily belligerent
looking creature who, as he laughed, swished a cat o'
nine tails menacingly through the air.

He was made up as a demon, wearing a hideous
mask with the features contorted into a menacing snarl,
and he was wearing the battle uniform of a samurai
with a plastic sword thrust in the sash. Adding to the
evil effect, the mask was topped by a great, tangled
mane of flaming red hair. As the background of wind,
rain and thunder played on, this gruesome vision strode
to the girl; The red spot followed him and mingled with
the blue one as he reached her. He took hold of the
girl's hair, twisted it viciously and lifted the whip high
above her as she shook her head and begged for mercy,
her hands in the attitude of prayer. As she struggled –
or, rather, pretended to struggle – against him, the
demon produced a short length of rope from his tunic
and tied her hands behind her back. This accomplished,
he forced her head down to the carpet, her cheek
squashed against it, and he planted a foot on her neck
and yanked her bottom high in the air.

Briefly, he glanced around the spookily lit room, eyes
glinting behind the horror mask. There was a roar of
encouragement from the men, Tanaka included.
Intrigued, eyes hooked on the scene, Coco leant forward on the sofa as the demon hiked the girl's kimono
up over her hips to reveal white cotton knickers. To
further, enthusiastic, male yells, he dragged these down
her plump thighs.

Her fearsome attacker brought his cat-o'-nine-tails
down across his poor, cringing victim's bare backside

and she screamed. But this was no real sadistic act of pain; he pulled his arm up fractionally before the moment of impact and the knotted rope thongs caught her hard enough only to make the faintest of marks. The next blow looked as if it was to be far more punishing as he raised the whip high above his head and brought it down with slashing force – managing to just miss her flesh and bite into the carpet behind her. In this way the performance progressed. As the girl screamed above the storm she was thoroughly 'flailed', the weak blows merely stinging her, the hard ones missing until, after thirty or so, the whip was discarded for more horrifying sadistic simulation.

The villain now roughly shoved his victim over onto her side with his boot, crouched above her, yanked off her knickers, throwing them into the darkness, then tore off her kimono. The dress must have been specially doctored for this because it jaggedly ripped from neck to hem. The kimono went the way of the knickers and the girl was naked, flesh bathed in a cocktail of red and blue light. The demon stood, dragged his plastic sword from his sash, whirled completely around once with it firmly gripped in two hands and slashed its tip across the girl's stomach in a long, sweeping blow.

Coco gasped, feeling slightly nauseous, as blood appeared to curtain down from a wound. She grabbed Tanaka's arm, clinging to it with both hands as if it offered her protection from the bloody spectacle.

'Don't worry,' he muttered, excitement in his voice. 'Is pig's brood from the inside of the sword coming.'

Coco was relieved but as turned off by this part of the show as she been on by the thrashing; blood was most definitely not on her sexual agenda. 'How, how can you enjoy this?' she whispered as the sword sliced across the girl's quivering breasts and more pig's blood streamed across them. 'It's, it's – obscene.'

Tanaka shrugged, his eyes filled with voyeuristic arousal as the demon cut and slashed and the girl was covered with more and more blood. 'Obscene, no,' he argued, squeezing her hand. 'Is game only. Soon the sword empty will be. Then, better even to come there is.'

The demon rolled the girl over onto her face with his boot. The storm raged on as he slashed her buttocks and she stayed still and silent, as if she had lost consciousness. Final drops of blood trickled from the tip of the sword, and the demon stuck it back in his sash and then produced several lengths of thin, white rope from his tunic. Clearly extremely practised in the next stage of his 'torture', he proceeded to truss the bloody figure up with speedy, nimble fingers, concentrating on her torso, her arms pinned to her side by the cords. He criss-crossed her body diagonally, forming diamond patterns through which red-stained flesh bulged as if through the bindings of a too-tight, lace-up corset, a well-known S&M technique designed to stimulate rather than injure; when she was released the girl's only damage would be rope marks which would fast fade away.

Coco was still clinging on to Tanaka's arm with both hands, watching him out of the corner of her eye. He was enrapt with the performance, his eyes narrow, a muscle occasionally twitching at the corner of his fine jaw. Coco was experiencing a mixture of emotions; the tendency towards nausea had disappeared with the end of the flow of pig's blood, her prurient interest, but not her libido, was aroused by the bondage and her sexual attraction towards the boss mobster's son remained intense despite his worrying tastes. As the demon secured his final knot, she peered through the gloom for Queenie and saw that her two gangsters had closed in on her. One of their gold-ringed hands was on her knee, another on her breast, and Queenie seemed to be raising no objection. Ah well, Coco mused fleetingly, smiling to herself. The upper class Brits do have a strong reputation for being thoroughly aroused by a spot of punishment.

Sliding back to the performance, Coco's eyes latched

onto the demon. His legs parted astride the girl's trussed torso, he was stripping off his uniform. Wriggling against her bonds, her charade of fear ceaseless, she stared up at him with wide eyes, not forgetting the occasional moan as the background storm began to fade away.

Naked except for his horror mask and his frightful wig, the male protagonist of this harmless exhibition of mock violence sported a singularly impressive erection, thick as his sword handle, which brought a flurry of applause and a medlee of muttered comments from his oddball audience. But he was not quite yet ready to put this machine to the purpose for which it was designed. Once again he took up his cat-o'-nine-tails and proceeded to pretend to inflict more violence on the struggling, protesting girl, darting around her with peculiar little hops and lashing the thongs at her body, but cutting the power of the blows short just before they connected.

Her shock at the brutal pretence of the performance had by now dissolved and the sight of the muscular, naked man with his swaying hard-on had the effect of making Coco feel suddenly very, very horny. Looking forward to what was shortly about to happen – clearly mock rape – she let go of Tanaka's arm and leant forward, her hands, backs together, gripped between her knees. Although she was unaware of it since her attention and libido were firmly held by demon-man and his hapless victim, all around her pockets of sexual activity were beginning, female bodies were groped and plundered as their owners' hands raided male crotches. One of Queenie's companion's was high beneath her dress, the other man was undoing buttons to get at her breasts as her eyes, enrapt as Coco's on the show, narrowed and she bit her bottom lip.

The whip was flung aside, the finale was about to begin, but not before two last S&M refinements. The girl's tormentor reached into his bundled tunic and took four items from a pocket: two wooden, sprung clothes

77

pegs, a candle and some matches. He put the candle and matches on her belly and knelt astride her, his cock hovering over her blood-stained navel. Then, taking his time, he applied the clothes pegs to her nipples which were squeezed up like the flesh of her crushed breasts through their diagonal bindings. With the pegs trembling upright on her nipples she gasped and screamed, and then she screamed louder, twisting her torso beneath him as her torturer lit the candle and dripped molten wax over her. Neither of these actions hurt more than minimally nor did they do any sort of damage, but they gave the impression that they did and the audience loved it.

From the hips down, the girl was not bound. Satisfied that he had created his effect, the villain blew out his candle and kneeled to one side of her, lifting her knees and spreading wide her thighs. Making sure that most of the crowd had a clear view of his actions, he slipped the candle into her vagina and, using it as a dildo, briefly masturbated her with it. Then he got between her knees, picked her up with hands cupped under her buttocks, so that her shoulders were on the floor and her back arched; he worked his glans inside her and held still, which afforded a clear, sideways view of his beginning penetration.

The demon starts to heave his pitiful, trussed, tortured, blood-smeared victim up and down on his pole of a cock as her nipple pegs flop around, and throughout the room there is a gathering sexual frenzy. Few of the audience's clothes are actually removed as yet, but many skirts are rucked up high on thighs with male hands at work beneath them and a number of zips are undone; the demon's cock is no longer the only one on display as slender fingers excite turgid male flesh.

The girl is turned onto hands and knees and breached from the rear and her 'raper', who has retained commendable control for a considerable time over his needful hard-on, begins to slam into her faster and harder, his heavy balls bumping solidly into the backs of her thighs with each thrust.

Queenie's gangsters are now in full invasion of her body. One of their hands is inside her knickers, two fingers slipping in and out of her wet pussy; the other man has her breasts free and is rubbing them together as he tongues an erect nipple. Aroused beyond coherent thought by the orgiastic atmosphere in this room, by the performance she is watching, by the groping, gold-ringed hands, Queenie fishes out a stubby gangster cock and ducks her head to it, but her eyes remain fixed on the copulating couple as the demon suddenly goes very tense. He is motionless for seconds then grunts loudly, withdraws and, holding onto his cock, with a roar he directs a stream of semen over the girl's buttocks and back.

The show is over; the main attraction is only just beginning. Only the red and blue spots remain. The demon swiftly untrusses the girl in their suffused glow, and they gather up their bits and pieces and, clothes in hand, flit through the room and out, the only sign of their act some pig's blood stains on the carpet. Music of a samisan replaces the sound effects of the storm, and blends in with the rustling sounds, low laughter, moans and sighs.

But Coco and Tanaka, the only couple in the room to have experienced an electrical, sexual magic between each other on first sight, are in awe of its power. Neither knows the other's thoughts, but they have so far not touched in any flagrantly sexual way and both have unspoken reservations about spoiling this special thing in the company of an orgy.

Tanaka took charge of their situation. Standing, he took Coco by her hand and pulled her to her feet. 'Come,' he breathed, as the spots went off and the room was filled with a red glow from hidden sources. 'We down to the lake go, the two of us.'

He led them quickly through the room, Coco's eyes

popping at the ribald activity taking place all around them. At the door she turned for a last glimpse of Queenie giving enthusiastic head and then they were in a corridor which turned sharply around three outside walls of the hexagonal room. This took them to a small games area where they went through a glass door into the garden.

Tanaka, for the moment, suppressed whatever sexual urges the combination of the show and his desire for Coco had aroused in him. It seemed strange to Coco who was aching for intimate contact with him, as they wandered hand in hand down a gentle slope towards the lake and the two moons. He explained to her about formal gardens and how his people liked them to be a direct reflection of nature, thus he said, there were no flower gardens and manicured laws, but sand, rocks and pebbles with plenty of streams and ponds, with everything carefully laid out in symbolic ways. They followed a meandering path of large, flat, well-worn stepping stones whilst he told her how this tall, elegantly standing stone represented a waterfall and that pleasantly rounded shrub signified a far-off mountain whilst she, more aware of the heat of his hand than the beauty of the gardens, floated along beside him on a cloud of sexual desire.

When they arrived at the tranquil lake, he put his hands on her shoulders and turned her to face him, and she waited tensely for the first kiss. But he went on about gardens, saying, 'Some of the most beautiful gardens very tiny. Prants to make music when falls the rain are so arranged.'

She managed an intelligent comment. 'You relish beautiful things, lovely gardens,' she said, 'so how come you go for that beating and blood and rape stuff?'

He studied her gravely. 'I not know, but us men we all do. Maybe is Japanese history of beauty and viorense side by side.' He paused, his broody eyes searing into her, yet looking almost sad. 'You very rovely chick. To hurt you I not want.'

'It never occurred to me that you would.' And it had not, despite his love of violence. She took his hands. 'How old are you, Tanaka?'

'Nineteen,' he said. 'But much I know.'

Nineteen. Hardly more than a boy. She noticed something strange in the way he held one of her hands and she turned it to look at the fingers. The little one came to a horny, rounded top above the second knuckle. 'How did that happen?' innocently she asked, knowing full well.

'A sign of respect in honour of my father. But of this we not talk.'

'No? OK.' Coco had had enough of talking anyway. She was very aware of her heartbeat. Leaning towards him, her face raised to his, she murmured, 'Are you never going to kiss me?'

'In the house I wanted not to. Those others, hookers they are. You not.'

'Nor is my girlfriend Queenie.'

'No.' He looked momentarily puzzled. 'Yet she is with . . .' He shook his head. 'I understand not this,' he said. Then he cupped her face in his hands. 'You most beautiful are and yes, kiss you I am going to. But just for the sex, the rust not, you understand? To use you as a whore, no.'

'Yes,' Coco murmured. 'I think I like that very much. Thank you.' Losing herself in his eyes she melted into him. His lips met hers with such a depth of tenderness, with a softness and a sureness unexpected in so young a man, that they had her heartbeats turning into hammer blows.

In a similar situation many a man – having been sitting with a lovely girl through a live performance of sex and sadism and the beginning of an orgy and now finding himself alone with that female in a deserted garden – would have laid her down there and then and had sex with her. But this was exactly what Coco's whole being screamed for. There was a chill in the night air but with Tanaka's body heat burning through her

81

spangled dress and his lips hot on hers, Coco was unaware of it. His hands slipped to the small of her back, touching the swell of her buttocks but, maddeningly, dropped no lower. As she wriggled tighter against him, feeling the hardness of his groin, the hands crept back up to her shoulders and he bent her slightly away from him while his eyes met hers.

'Like this with other girls it has not been, I swear it,' he muttered. He seemed a touch perplexed. 'This, this something different is hitting me.'

'Yes,' said Coco. 'Me too.' The boy was hardly her idea of her dream man, yet more than merely her body was crying out for him. Perhaps it was the combination of youth, beauty, and the Oriental half of her reaching out to him. Had she not been the wise and experienced young woman she was, Coco might have convinced herself that this was love at first sight. Slipping a hand inside his jacket, she flattened it on his tight, silk-shirted belly. 'Well, mister?' she whispered.

'We perhaps to my room go?'

'You bet.' The green-nailed tips of her fingers slid beneath the waistband of his trousers and her eyes flashed fire at him. 'Like, now – please?'

As Coco and Tanaka, filled with consuming need, hurry with their arms round one another towards the massive house, the orgy within it – a multi-faceted celebration of unbridled lust – is hotting up.

Queenie's gangsters are stripped to socks and shirts, their loud suits lying across a coffee table, their shoes side by side on the carpet. One man is sprawled in a corner of the huge sofa, propped on a pile of cushions with his legs parted and his hands resting on top of Queenie's red, bobbing head. His eyes feast on her actions as she slides her mouth slowly up and down his rigid penis. The other gangster is kneeling behind her.

The only items of Queenie's apparel so far to have come off are her gold-strapped evening shoes which lie on their sides at angles to each other by a pair of brown and white male brogues. On her knees on the sofa, performing her fellatio with great and skilful gusto, Queenie has her bottom raised high in the air and is happily aware that it is in the process of being lewdly exposed as her other sexual partner crumples her red satin dress above her hips. Beneath it she is wearing white, lace-edged camiknickers which he eases down over crimson suspenders and black stocking tops, letting them fall in a loose heap around her knees; Queenie may not have been certain that sex was the objective of Nangi's invitation, but she had been fairly sure and had selected the underwear with that in mind.

The man behind her sinks back on his haunches to lust over the sight of Queenie's deliciously curved, naked buttocks framing the swelling lips of her pussy. The mat of coppery hairs around and below it burst against the creamy tops of her slightly parted thighs. Coaxing her legs wider, he runs a hand up the inside of one of them, over silky stocking and smooth, firm, inner thigh until it is flat on Queenie's belly. He draws it slowly over her bush, his fingers mingling with the crinkly hairs, exploring, then further down until the tips of two of them pause at her damp opening before plunging.

Queenie unmouths the cock and gasps, swaying forward, head tilted back, eyes closed as the fingers inside penetrate all the way and twist and turn inside her. Then insistent, greedy hands urge her head back to its former position and she closes her mouth over the stubby penis once more, taking hold of the heavy balls beneath it, jiggling them together in her hand, squeezing.

Throughout the huge, red-lit room, to the totally unfitting background music of the Beatles, the great god Priapus holds salacious court. Queenie is too engrossed in her own lascivious pursuits to notice that, not far from her, Makita Noguchi has stripped his massive bulk nude and is flat on his back with an equally naked, tiny girl astride him. With his huge hands almost meeting around her waist he is bouncing her up and down on his pole of a cock, her long black hair flying, her little tits quivering as his great belly wobbles and shakes.

Even closer to Queenie is Nangi, being paid bawdy attention to by the same willowy beauty he had so off-handedly dismissed earlier. Fully dressed, she kneels on the carpet between his knees with his cock, which pokes through the open zipper of his black silk trousers, comfortably between her lips. Nangi has removed no item of clothing. Whilst wallowing in the delights of the professionally administered blow job – this evidenced by the slackness of his mouth and his protruding tongue-tip – he is not watching it; his eyes are leching on what is happening to Queenie. Likewise, Noguchi, whilst contentedly jumping the girl up and down on his cock like some doll, using her rather as a woman uses a dildo, is paying a great deal of prurient attention to Queenie's sofa. Both these powerful Japanese men have designs on this ravishingly beautiful example of British journalism at its best who has so miraculously appeared at one of their regular, whores-only orgies – and who is clearly enjoying the libidinous time of her habitually raunchy life.

The man who invades Queenie from the rear has been slow to get it up. His reluctant erection finally grows, rising above his thick thighs and poking through the open flap of his shirt. He slips his fingers out of her. He replaces them with his tongue which he pushes as far up inside her as it will go as he creeps a hand up her torso to plunder her breasts through their satin covering. Queenie is overwhelmed by a tidal wave of lust. With her head bobbing fast on the throbbing cock in her mouth, her tongue flickering over its underside at the same time, she is willing it to come; in her perversity she longs for the spicy taste of warm sperm, her craving exacerbated by the onrush of orgasm as the hot tongue works busily in her pussy like a delightful little cock. Seconds later, groaning through her mouthful of

penis she shudders with her first climax of the evening
– and goes on avidly sucking.

Once in Tanaka's bedroom, Coco had eyes only for him,
the room was a blurred background. He started to say
something and she stopped his lips with her finger,
then loosened his tie, murmuring, 'May I take your
clothes off?'

He was startled. 'This then is the way in America?'
he said. 'The woman, she does so?'

Swiftly, she undid his tie, and with it draped through
one hand, she started on his shirt buttons. 'No,' she
said very quietly. 'Not often. I just want to, that's all.'

'Well, is okay, I guess.' He allowed her to slip off his
jacket and hang it over a chair. 'Japanese man shy not.'

She pulled his shirt from his trousers, then, as she
opened it over his chest she stopped still in amazement.
She was faced with the most startlingly beautiful tattoo
she had ever seen. Spread across Tanaka's hairless chest
and stomach was a series of small, colourful pictures,
their exquisite linework was of a young man and
woman in traditional dress. They seemed to be in a
sequence as they walked through gardens, took a boat
across a lake, had tea, kissed; each picture was divided
by japanese writing. In a graphically detailed picture at
the bottom right of his stomach, they were making love.

'You rike?' he asked, the merest trace of anxiety in
his voice.

'It's very, very lovely.' She planted a kiss on a nipple
which broke through the waters of an ornamental
garden pond like an island. 'Dig it.'

'Is an old story, most famous.' He paused. 'But in a
moment my back you see.'

She folded the shirt over his shoulders and stripped
it off him, laying it over the jacket. He turned around
and she gasped, sexual desire almost forgotten as she
found herself presented by – almost completely covering his back – a family of lions so real they looked as if
they might spring right off him. There was a magnifi-

cently maned father, standing proud and tall, and a sprawling lioness surrounded by gambolling cubs. They were in a jungle clearing, lush vegetation all around them and with brightly coloured birds swooping and diving over their heads.

'It's, it's . . . sensational. Jesus!' Coco exclaimed.

He let her run her fingers over it, then he faced her. 'One year's work to make,' he told her. 'But for rife is, and now is done, I wonder . . .' he shrugged and produced an almost rueful grin.

'Mad kid, huh?' Her eyes ran admiringly over the story on his front and as she kissed two of the pictures, her desire came flooding back. 'This is too wonderful to ever regret. You're beautiful, Tanaka.' Dropping to her knees in front of him, hands nervous, she fumbled undone the buckle of his black crocodile belt and the buttons at the top of his trousers. 'Are there any more tattoos?' she breathed, tugging at his zipper, remembering the man a friend had told her about who had one on his penis.

'No more, no.' His fingertips tensed on her shoulders, he suddenly went very still, the surging excitement within him communicating itself to Coco as she took off his shoes and slid the trousers down off his legs.

Tanaka was wearing a pair of yellowish, silky briefs which were filled with an erection which belied his slender frame. Coco's eyes lingered on this welcome sight. She longed to enclose the bulge in the heat of her mouth, but something about the very special feeling sizzling between them warned her to delay those sort of games for later. Right now was reserved for the gentle, innocent pleasures of first time lovemaking. She freed his hard-on and stripped off his pants sitting back on her heels to admire the bounteous erection pointing at her above tangerine-sized testicles without succumbing to the temptation of taking it between her lips, or even touching it. Then he gripped her shoulders so tightly that he was clearly expecting something of the sort.

She stood, closing in on him, wrapping her arms around his neck, his hard-on snuggling and digging between their bellies; she felt it throb. Their lips mashed together, their tongues mingled then Coco, trembling, wet between her legs, murmured. 'Are you ever ready, man.'

He pulled her tighter against him, his naked erection half buried in her silver spangled stomach. 'And waiting too much longer I cannot be,' he said.

Breaking their embrace, hands impatient, he clumsily got her out of her evening dress, then her shoes. Like Queenie, she had selected her underwear with sex in mind; a skimpy bit of lacy bra with nipple holes, panties hardly large than a G-string, a suspender belt with tiny, embroidered flowers, and shiny, sheer, white stockings. Most men would have left this arousing gear on, except for the knickers, but Tanaka, in no mood for fripperies, needing this gift from the gods to be naked, quickly had it off, leaving the titillating items spread over the soft, white carpet.

Weak with anticipation, already keyed up close to climax, Coco was led to the bed, picked up and laid on her back on it. There were no more preliminaries. Tanaka did not touch her, the understanding that she was as ready as he. He eased himself down. Her legs opened and welcomed him as she guided his penis with one hand and sunk it slowly, deeply within her, pausing when it was fully impaled as she dragged in her breath and held it, her eyes drowning in his, her vaginal muscles tightening on him.

His eyes close, his buttocks tauten and he begins to slowly rock his hips on her, his cock sliding in and out of her pussy as if the two organs had been expressly made for each other while her nails passionately rake over his family of lions.

This first time fuck, born of instant, mutual desire

and therefore long-awaited, even if it has in fact been little more than an hour since they met, cannot contain itself within a cocoon of control for any length of time. As the heir to a gangster fortune jerks his groin faster and faster, the product of GI lust and Philippino wantonness beneath him matches his hip movements with her own, thrusting up at him with increasing, overpowering need, panting, gasping, her arms tightly wrapped around his rocking lions, her cheek crushed against his.

Orgasm swoops over them with mutual suddenness, they soar together in a mingling flood of juices, he shouts something in Japanese and she sighs into his cheek. They move into one another, two, three more times and are still, both panting for breath, for the moment fulfilled.

And so far they have laid not one sexual finger on each other.

Queenie had achieved such a degree of carnal abandonment that her body in its salacious entirety had swamped her mind which was observing each new act in prurient glee. One of her gangsters, still attired in a rumpled shirt, was reclining on the sofa and she was kneeling astride him, her hands propped on the sofa back. Balenciaga-clad tits wobbled in his face as she heaved her bottom wildly up and down, impaling herself on the man's cock. As she fucked, her head was rolling around, her loose, red hair flying and her fire eyes darted over the room to devour as much of the ribaldry which surrounded her as they were able. In a parallel performance to Noguchi's, who continued to bounce his tiny girl on his cock, she was masturbating with this man – not simply having sex with him, but the entire roomful of people.

Her other partner-in-excess was kneeling on the sofa next to them holding Queenie's dress high on her hips, his other hand squeezing Queenie's buttock as it rode up and down, leering at this act of copulation. Letting the dress fall, he clambered off the sofa, shrugged out of his shirt and let it drop over his shoes. Naked except for his white socks, he padded around the sofa. Standing to one side of Queenie's bobbing head he found the zipper in the back of her dress and opened it all the way. Happy to get rid of the encumbrance of Mr Balenciaga's not-quite-so-latest, she made the effort to still herself on her cock as the dress was dragged off and flung onto the sofa by her side. Her bare breasts with their fine erect nipples began to flop over her impaler's face as she again heaved herself up and down on him while he stuck out his tongue to lick them. The other man took his cock in hand and offered it to her over the back of the sofa.

Noguchi's eyes narrowed into lustful slits as he watched Queenie rock herself with total abandon and, at the same time, suck this cock into her mouth. Lifting his little whore off him as easily as if she were made of feathers, he sat up and dumped her in a corner of their sofa. Abandoning her he went to Nangi who, now minus his suit but still attired in his black silk shirt and white tie, was lying on top of his willowy beauty with his weight on his elbows, his tight little bottom moving slowly, regularly as he fucked her almost nonchalantly while he watched Queenie's ménage à trois.

Stooping to Nangi, Noguchi muttered something to him and with an eager nod the mobster rolled off his girl and sat up. Standing, he took her hand and the three of them crossed to Queenie's sofa; there was something curiously listless about the girl's manner as she did so, as if her mind were totally divorced from what was happening. She had thick, shiny black hair cut short to hang neatly around her neck, large, dark, vacant eyes and small, firm breasts and a heavy pubic thatch matching the colour of her hair.

With her mouth and pussy stuffed with cock, Queenie observed the approach of the fat plutocrat and the gangster boss – both with unflagging, swaying hardons – and the unenthusiastic whore with eyes drooping and hazy with lust. Noguchi barked a couple of words to Queenie's partners and she found herself instantly disengaged. Without protest they left her and wandered across to Noguchi's little girl.

Queenie sank to her haunches and rolled herself into a sitting position as the other three walked to the front of the sofa. She was by now so worked up that her libido, her entire self – she had been poised on the point of her third orgasm when the penises were so abruptly withdrawn – was ready, willing, eager for any type of diversion. The girl, she noticed, was a beauty.

With a leer, Noguchi thrust a hand between the girl's thighs and took hold of her pubis as if he were about to pick up some furry animal, to which she made no response whatsoever. 'This is Akiko, Queenie,' he said. 'Apparently she prefers women to men.'

Nangi murmured something to him and he translated. 'My friend complains she is as cold as a fish under ice.' He let his handful of pussy go and traced a pudgy finger tip between its owner's breasts. 'Remembering our delightful evening in my sauna it has occurred to me that you may, like your lovely partner Coco, be partial to female flesh – and could therefore warm our fish up?'

Queenie nodded, running a tongue over her smudged lips. Saying nothing, eyes travelling lustfully over the sensuous curves presented to her, she reached for Akiko's hand and pulled her down beside her. Pressing her flat palms on the girl's cheeks, Queenie kissed her gently on the mouth. The lips were indeed cold. Without breaking the kiss, Queenie moved her hands to Akiko's shoulders and laid her on her back. Spreading her legs she rolled on top of her, her knees and thighs pressed together so that they were pubis to pubis, tits flattened against tits, as the kiss went on and on.

Slowly, voluptuously, like a man's first breaching of a woman, Queenie rocks her hips, smoothly sliding her copper mound against the springy black one, clitoris moving against clitoris, bringing herself gradually back to the brink of the orgasm she had just been cheated of. Akiko's lips begin to warm against hers, Queenie's tongue forces its way between them and she is delighted as Akiko's greets it with a responsive flicker and her own hips begin to move.

The sofa creaks with Noguchi's massive weight as he deposits it close to the girls' knees, eyes pigging on Queenie's rutting bottom, a hand enclosing his massive cock. Nangi decides to plant all of his stockily diminutive self on the huge sofa at the girls' heads. Queenie, whose eyes have been closed, senses his presence as the sofa indents, and she opens them to a close-up of Nangi's genitals. He leans back into a corner, stuffing a cushion behind him, his legs stretched out, his erection, untouched, pointing at the revolving chandelier.

Akiko is heating up. Her feet with their black-painted toes hook around Queenie's calves and her hands slip down and around Queenie's buttocks, urging them into further movement, and nails, matching her toes, dig into the soft flesh.

Noguchi interferes in this lesbian fuck. As he had done on the evening of the sauna, his initial approach to Queenie is to slide two fat fingers into her heaving pussy. Not realising just how wound up she is, with a few fast thrusts he brings her to her much needed third orgasm and she squeals.

But Queenie is not about to rest. She is floating in that rare, delicious, priapic heaven which will permit her to experience a whole string of minor climaxes before culminating in sated explosion. Having thoroughly aroused Akiko she craves to bring the 'cold fish' off, to show these lusty Japanese men just how it should be done. She reverses her position on the girl, nose to cunt, opening her thighs around her face. As Akiko's mouth and tongue avidly explore her, Queenie finds the girl's clitoris and sucks it while her fingers slide into the warm, damp depths beyond.

Unnoticed, the Beatles warble and strum on. They are singing 'Lucy in the Sky with Diamonds' as Akiko, grunting into Queenie's crotch, moves her hips more or less in time with them. With lips slack, and his leching eyes, Noguchi is masturbating. Nangi, however, not content with onanistic activity, aroused to the point where he thirsts for contact with the flesh he has been ogling, performs something as new to Queenie as it is welcome. He kneels between her wide-spread knees, behind Akiko's head, drops his weight on one hand to the side of their intertwined bodies and lowers his girth above Akiko's head towards Queenie's pussy and – the first moment that Queenie is aware of what he is doing – his hairy balls hanging on Akiko's nose, he guides the tip of his cock and thrusts it deep into Queenie.

Akiko, who most assuredly does not normally achieve sexual satisfaction with men, is hovering close to orgasm with Queenie's tongue slipping in and out of her pussy. Queenie's cunnilingus falters with Nangi's initial penetration but then it continues with renewed fervour as Nangi begins to fuck her and the added thrill of the extreme close-up of male and female genitalia locked together next to her licking tongue brings Akiko all the way to orgasm. She fiercely bucks her hips, flickers her tongue from Queenie's clitoris to Nangi's bouncing balls, the lower half of her body goes rigid and she lets out a groan so long that in other circumstances it might have been one of pain.

These two Japanese kings of very different, highly specialised industries are possessed of a stamina to match their business prowess, which Queenie is about to discover. Akiko rolls out from under Queenie and into the back of the sofa, where she all but flakes out, and Nangi drags Queenie up to her hands and knees as his copulation heats up. No longer content with masturbation, Noguchi kneels in front of Queenie and offers her mouth his penis. She sucks the huge glans eagerly in and, now riding what is certainly a high to rival any

92

others in her bawdy young life, gets ribaldly into her second three-way swing of this lewd and lovely evening.

Not far away, in Tanaka's room, Nangi's son and Coco were lying side by side in naked contentment on his bed. Tanaka was mildly amused at Coco because she was puffing on one of her infrequent cheroots and he had apparently never seen a woman smoking a cigar. Admiring her body, he discovered the little rose tattoo on the inside of the thigh and softly traced its outline with his finger.

'So, you tattoo have as well,' he said. 'Is very pretty.' His fingertip moved up to the diamond-shaped mole on her groin. 'This, too.'

'I used to hate the mole as a kid,' Coco told him. She took a final draw on her one-third smoked cheroot and killed it, figuring that Tanaka must entertain frequently in his bedroom since there was an ashtray by his bed and he didn't smoke himself. She smiled at him. 'Then, when I got into sex, I found out that boys liked the bloody thing. So I had the tattoo done to sort of compliment it. She smoothed an admiring hand over his chest. 'I never thought I'd ever see anything like this though.'

For the first time since entering it she looked around the room, discovering it exhibited traces of the boy who had not quite grown into the man; western, page-three type, pin-up posters, all knickers and overblown boobs, vied for silk-lined wall space with elegant coloured wood-block prints, *ukiyo-e*, by modern master Masami Teraoka. The tasteful furnishings were stream-lined and modern, but overpowered by a wall full of TV, video and computer apparatus, a music centre and a large library of CDs and computer games.

Tanaka rolled off the Indian silk bedspread, selected a CD and put it on. For some peculiar reason which had nothing to do with the prevailing mood, it was Guns 'n' Roses and as soon as their heavy rock filled the room Coco covered her ears and objected. With a

93

grin, he switched it off. 'Is perhaps a bit noisy, no?' he
said. 'Rod Stewart you like, maybe?'

'Rod Stewart I like, yes,' she said gratefully.

Next to the ashtray was a small pile of comics. Coco
picked the top one up as Tanaka rejoined her on the
bed while Rod Stewart sung a lie about not wanting to
be a millionaire. She raised an eyebrow at the lurid
cover and the title. Splashed across its front in bold red
letters were the words 'Rape Man'. 'What the hell is
this?' she asked him, opening it somewhere in the
middle.

'*Manga*,' said Tanaka. 'In English, I not know.'

'Comic. But comics are supposed to be for kids, not
nineteen-year-old young men.'

'In Japan, not,' he told her. 'Here *manga*, comics, for
every age there is. *Rape Man* is man's comic.'

'Christ – you're not kidding, are you?' Flipping a page
she came across a vivid drawing, the graphics superb,
of a muscular man in a mask and cloak and costume
top swinging on a rope from one apartment block to
another, rather like an oriental Batman except that this
hero was naked from the waist down and sported an
impossible-sized erection. Over the page, he went sailing through an open window into a ladies toilet into
which, in the next frame, came a pretty teenage girl in
school uniform. In a further page and a half of highly
explicit drawings, Rape Man trussed the struggling girl
up, ripped off her knickers and did to her what his
name suggested.

'Amusing, no?' commented Tanaka.

'Strokes for folks.' Coco kept turning pages, hardly
believing what she was seeing while Japan's anti-hero,
with fiendish glee, attacked girl after girl, woman after
woman, from cover to cover. 'Jesus, Tanaka,' she said,
dropping *Rape Man* on the floor, '. . . this is awful.'

'Oh.' He looked at her without understanding, then
dug into the pile and handed her another *manga*.
'Maybe this better you rike.' Nonplussed, Coco glanced
through this one. It was called *Erotopia* and featured

94

graphically, skilfully illustrated sex, sadism – and once again, rape. In one of the most lurid sequences a lovely, smartly-dressed, young woman was trapped in an alley-way by a gang of punks, stripped naked, beaten with short chains and then, bruised and bloody, raped by each member of the gang in turn as the others held her across an open, overflowing dustbin.

'But, for God's sake, why, Tanaka?' asked Coco, dropping *Erotopia* on top of *Rape Man*, nauseated.

'Why what?' Tanaka was genuinely puzzled.

She looked at him in worried amazement. 'What do you get out of those? Does that sick rubbish turn you on?'

'It does job, yes. Is meant to.'

Coco's amazement turned to horror. 'Do you do things like that?'

He matched her horror with his own. 'Me? Is that what of me you are thinking? Of course not. Nobody does. It is madness of which you speak. The *manga*, pure fantasy they are.'

'Flying through the air with a hard-on, yes. But rape, back-alley gang rape – this happens, Tanaka. In New York it happens all the time, but they certainly don't allow comics showing it.'

'They don't? Strange people, the Yankees. In Tokyo, this never happens. But I told you, everybody the rape comics read, sometimes even woman.'

Coco shook her head. Reassured that his choice of literature was no personal aberration but a national one, she managed a twisted smile. 'Me, I'm half Oriental,' she said, 'but understand the Japanese . . . ? Brother, forget it!'

'I shall not rape you!'

Grinning, she lifted her knees and spread her legs. 'Just try me, boy.'

'You must some minutes more give me.' He raised a smile which made him look no more than fifteen. 'After tonight, some other time you will see me?'

She closed her knees, studying him. The grim revelation of the *manga* had done little to lessen her powerful attraction to this boy/man. Not enjoying more of him would be just a little painful. 'I hope so,' she told him, 'but you're way out of Tokyo and me, I'm working.'

'On photographs, no? Maybe some of me you take?'

'I don't have my gear with me.'

'A small apartment in the heart of Tokyo I have. You will perhaps some shots of me there take?'

Finding herself delighted with this news, Coco laid a hand high on his thigh. 'You bet,' she said, 'and while I'm about it I'll have a go at unscrambling your English.'

'This "unscramble", what it is?'

She giggled. 'Never mind, you're cool. When will you be in Tokyo?'

'In two or three days I am there.'

'Ring me when you know. Leave a message if I'm out.'

'Okay.' His eyes roamed over her, pausing for a moment in the region of her tattoo. 'Me, very young I am, sure,' he said to the tattoo, then raised his eyes to hers. There was a mature amusement there. 'But in my apartment certain things sexual I have to deright the woman. Things maybe you have seen not. My father, much since I was sixteen he has taught me.'

Coco's heart skipped a beat. 'What things, Tanaka? Not things like in the comics or that performance? Not whips and chains? Not canes and ropes?'

He laughed. 'Why things like that about me you keep on thinking? A pervert I am not, you will see. I have, devices for the woman very, very exciting and therefore for the man.'

She squeezed his thigh. 'I'm sorry. Okay, I guess I trust you honey,' she said. For the first time, her hand strayed to his penis. She enclosed its soft, silky warmth in her palm. As she felt it stir, she was overcome with temptation. Cocks were usually hard before they reached her lips, so she was filled with a craving to seize this opportunity to have her new lover's penis grow to full size in her mouth. Stooping over his body she took it between her lips, watching his face for a reaction as she did so, and she was rewarded by his sharp intake of breath and ecstatic expression.

Its slightly musky smell and salt-spice taste, the product of their mingling juices within Coco's pussy, added to her pleasure. She sucked the whole of the semi-flaccid, fat, growing organ into her mouth, curving her tongue on its underside, and using it as she might have done the palm of her hand. Within seconds it had swollen to its full size.

He mumbled something guttural in Japanese and she lifted her head off him, flicked her tongue all over his glans then ran it slowly up his folk-story body and his neck to his ear as her fingers cradled his testicles, his hard-on resting across her wrist.

'You liked that, right?' she whispered.

'Of course.'

'You, you don't think it dirty – something perhaps that only a whore should be doing?'

'Why such a funny question you are asking?'

Propping herself on one elbow she took a firm grip of his cock. 'Because I find everything about the Japanese very strange. You're an oddball lot, different, weird sometimes, witness those terrible comics. I want to be making love with you, right? I don't want to be doing things which maybe only whores are expected to do in this country.'

Smiling, he put his hand over hers on his cock. 'In Japan, in sex and love all is permitted. You will see.'

'In sex, I've already seen. But love?'

'A dangerous word.'

'Sure is.' Idly, she massaged his cock, his hand going with hers, her mind mostly elsewhere. 'But, whatever it is, there seems to be something kind of special between us, you know? Hell, I come to an orgy, then this happens.'

He ran a hand over both her breasts, gentling them, then fiddled with a nipple. 'Whatever this is,' he said.

Renewed sexual need suddenly and unexpectedly

swamped her; her belly was full of fire. 'Fuck me, please?' she murmured.

'In the West a dirty word this is not?'

'It's a lovely word.' She jerked his cock. 'Fuck me.'

Tanaka rolls Coco flat on her face, his passion matching hers. He moves onto her back, weight on one hand, the other on his erection and slips it, hard and solid, between her buttocks. For a moment she thinks he is about to bugger her, not her favourite dalliance but for this gorgeous young man she will allow anything. Penis nestling comfortably, he reaches under her beneath her belly and runs his hand down between her legs, all the way and past her pussy. Raising his hips to free his cock he takes hold of it from below, manoeuvres its head into her cunt and rams it home with a shudder, bringing a delighted squeak to her lips.

Like that he sets to steadily fuck her with long, even, hard strokes as she luxuriates in this rear penetration by the highly experienced screwing of this very young man who has already lost any clumsiness or inhibitions as far as sex is concerned. Each time he plunges fully in her pussy she receives the added pleasure of his thick pubic bush colliding with her buttocks and his heavy balls banging into the inside backs of her thighs.

Coco slips her hands down to her crotch to find Tanaka's jiggling scrotum and clings to his balls, crushing them gently together, holding on for a few strokes and going with them as they bounce up and down. Then, her cheek and breasts flattened into the India silk coverlet, she performs the contortion of reaching her other hand up and over his smooth buttocks. Adding yet more spice to his fuck, she explores the cleft of his bottom, the tip of her index finger with its neatly manicured, emerald-painted nail teasing its way into his anus.

Thoroughly used to cohabiting with whores as his upbringing from early maturity has included them as a matter of course, Tanaka has, however, little experience

98

of girls who are not for sale. He finds that Coco is driving him sexually wilder than any transaction with a hooker, which unavoidably is often somewhat mechanical. But he exerts iron control; his ability to prolong copulation, to delay orgasm for as long as possible, is something of which he is justifiably proud. The first time with Coco was excusably short, now he intends to protract their enjoyment.

Feeling climax building up, he slows his strokes down sufficiently to enable him to hover at its glorious brink, prising Coco's fingers from his balls because that intimate contact, above all, threatens to send him over the top. Without breaking the sexual union, he heaves them over so that she is on her back on him, and he pushes her upright into a sitting position. Folding her feet back under her thighs and making herself supremely comfortable, she is urged on with little, coaxing pushes on her buttocks and letting him lead her, she rises and falls on his cock. Head drooping, her eyes are mesmerised by the view of her penetration.

After a while he has her turn around to face him, her knees splayed on either side of his colourful belly. His control has communicated itself to her libido; she is riding the gut-crunching feeling of an extended approach to orgasm, and she sits happily fully impaled on his strong cock, their equally black pubic bushes intermingled, his eyes languishing on her body above him and a thumb indenting her rose tattoo.

Closing her eyes, she wriggles her butt and starts to rise and fall, but he stops her. 'No, without moving we remain,' he murmurs, the words sticking in his throat. 'You, still, me, still and then you discover a thing. On the sensations between our legs and deep in our insides we concentrate. Utterly, our minds we compose until we are no thing but our genitals.'

'Compose!' thinks Coco, who desperately needs to bounce herself to a climax. But, going along with his wishes, she rests her hands flat on his picture-book chest and sits absolutely still, forcing herself into complete awareness of the hot pole of a cock on which she is impaled. She tightens her vaginal muscles on it with a sudden twitch and he surprises her by saying very sharply, almost as if he is annoyed, 'No! This, not. No movement.'

As Coco squats in exquisite torture, Queenie is discovering just how much stamina Noguchi and Nangi are possessed of and how incredibly agile for one so large and fat the head of Nippon Petrochemicals can be. Whilst the lovely Akiko remains comotosed, wedged on her side in the sofa, oblivious to the sexual gymnastics taking place next to her, Queenie is being fucked in an ever changing variety of positions. At the moment she is kneeling on the carpet, the top of her head indenting Noguchi's grand stomach as she fellates him while Nangi is going at her steadily from behind with enthusiastic powerful thrusts which are transmitted through her head into Noguchi's trembling belly.

Noguchi mutters to Nangi who withdraws from Queenie and takes her by the shoulders, lifts her to her feet and turns her back to Noguchi. He coaxes her into standing astride Noguchi's flabby, hairy thighs then sits her on him as at the same time Noguchi guides his cock into her. The fat man's hands slide under her buttocks, he bounces her up and down on him with urgent little movements, while Nangi takes her head and pulls her mouth onto his hard-on.

All around them, the air is suffused with a medley of richly sexual sounds, the orgy is in full swing, the whores are being passed around, copulation celebrated in every conceivable fashion and combination. The steamy atmosphere is so arousing that whenever a man does come, something that Nangi and Noguchi seemed determined not to do, within minutes he is hard again and ready for more action. The main attraction of the orgy is non-stop sex until satiation and exhaustion take their toll. The background music continues to be incongruous songs from the Beatles, a CD is on shuffle and several numbers have by now been repeated, but the orgy is too intensely involved with itself, too frenzied, too wallowing to care or even notice.

Yet again Nangi and Noguchi exchange brief words. Nangi takes his cock, glistening with her saliva, from Queenie's mouth and Noguchi lifts her off him, turns her to face him and impales her once more. Dropping to his knees behind her, Nangi folds her forward over Noguchi's belly. Lips slack, eyes heavy with sexual greed, he clutches with both hands at Queenie's red suspender-framed buttocks. He kneeds them, then stretches them apart to open her bottom hole into which he works the stub of his ritually mangled finger. Queenie's hips respond with a powerful little jerk and she grunts into Noguchi's shoulder.

The gangster boss has a somewhat specialised penetration in mind. Extracting the symbol of his profession from Queenie's rear end he moves forward, stills her rocking buttocks, positions the head of his cock and begins to cram it into her pussy on top of Noguchi's.

Queenie is not totally sure what is happening to her at this moment. She is aware of a sudden tension in Noguchi, an attitude not evidenced before, his eyes narrow to tiny slits and his cheek twitches. She feels her pussy being stretched in a way it has seldom been, but seldom is not never and she realises with a surge of almost unbearable excitement what is going on down there. She slides an exploratory hand over her thigh to touch Noguchi's testicles and, a second later, Nangi's as his cock slides all the way into her and his balls squash into Nangi's.

Nangi bends forward over Queenie's back until his chin is against her hair and she is hotly sandwiched and engulfed in sweaty male flesh – thoroughly stuffed with two cocks buried and still, all the way in her, she fondles the two, unmoving, sets of balls and is in screwing paradise.

Midst more guttural mutterings, Queenie notices a heightened tension in Nangi as well as Noguchi, then

Nangi begins to rock his buttocks, slowly at first with the speed steadily building, his cock sliding tightly, warmly in and out of Queenie's wonderfully pampered pussy. Its underside slips against the length of the underside of Noguchi's monster machine with a friction which cannot be bringing anything other than homosexual pleasure to the two men.

This is the moment when control will finally be lost, Queenie senses as she climbs unstoppably towards her sixth orgasm of the evening. Noguchi begins to heave his hips, the two cocks reach a pounding rhythm within her, moving faster, faster, each tight within a male/ female sheath. The men begin to pant and gasp, getting enormous, perverse gratification from this ultimate threesome act. Queenie is so crushed between the bullishly rutting men that she herself cannot move. One of her hands clutches Noguchi's heaving buttock flesh, the other is down there in dreamland plundering the pounding cocks and bouncing balls as an incredible orgasm takes hold of her. It begins in a groin which is on fire and shudders up within her to her throat where it escapes in the form of the loudest shout of the evening, followed by another, and yet another as, with massive grunts of their own the two Japanese erupt, and erupt, and erupt inside her aristocratic British cunt, gushing in there, filling it with a cocktail of sperm that the delicious sensation adds to the power of her orgasm and Queenie almost faints away.

Then suddenly, so suddenly, the two men go utterly still.

In Tanaka's room, he and Coco are also unmoving, but for a very different reason, and their self-induced sublime torture has now become almost unbearable. For the entire duration of Queenie's orgy room sandwich, Coco has remained sitting motionless astride Nangi's son, hands flat on his tattoos, his cock buried in her belly. She is vaguely aware of his heartbeat, strong and steady, beneath her right palm, of his eyes which have melted unblinkingly into hers, of Rod Stewart beating out his old standard 'Maggie May', but there is an over-riding sensation which threatens to consume her, the fire of which burns between her thighs and rages around their interlocked genitals, spreading throughout her entire body even to her brain; Coco's sweet pussy has the habit of taking her over, but never has it achieved such utter domination as now.

At last there is movement. Tanaka's hips tremble; he arches them, momentarily raising Coco, holds her like that for seconds and lowers her again. 'Enough,' he muttered. 'Such a thing as this abused must not be.'

He sits up and folds his feet back under himself then straightens Coco's legs so that, still with his penis deep within her she is straddling his lap, her legs stretched out on either side of him. 'Now,' he mutters, cupping both hands around her buttocks and supporting her bottom as he stands on his knees. 'Now, with the speed of the tortoise, I fuck you.'

Toppling her onto her back, he lets go of her buttocks and rests his weight on his elbows on either side of her stomach with his hands on her breasts. For the first time in what has seemed to Coco an eternity of full impalement, infinitely slowly he withdraws his cock until only the glans remain inside her.

'Move you may not,' he blandly informs her as he holds himself steady at her entrance. 'When we reach the final moment, when to come you are going to, only then is okay.' He crushed her breasts together. 'Prease, not to move.'

More exquisite torture follows as Tanaka commences to fuck Coco with the slowness of a boy pushing a stick of rock in and out of his mouth whilst thoroughly savouring each flavourful moment. 'The speed of the tortoise' means long, long seconds as his cock slides fraction by fraction into her tight pussy until it is all the way in with his balls resting on the underswell of her buttocks. Then, at the same controlled, agonisingly slow pace, his fingers and thumbs pinching and twisting her nipples, he withdraws to his glans to hover for a moment before slipping back in again.

Coco closes her eyes tightly. She can hardly believe what is happening to her. This handsome, exciting Japanese man, little more than a boy, is bringing her pleasure which few, far older and more sexually experienced men have. Somehow she manages the feat of again remaining extremely still. It is even more difficult than previously because his tantalising, slow-motion screw has her pelvis pleading to rock with him. Incredibly, he goes on and on and on, without the slightest change in tempo. After minutes she opens her eyes to discover that his are closed. His face is a mask of concentration, sweat beads his forehead; a tiny rivulet trickles down his cheek.

Her eyes slide over his tattoos and into their groins and Coco watches, almost mesmerised, as his fleshy pole creeps all the way within her then almost completely out again. Each thrust is a full minute while her body is filled with the need to have him bang it into her, to pound it, to give her a proper fucking, but her mind persuades her to cool it. This extended hovering at the edge of the ultimate pleasure is sublimely delicious.

Time is standing still, but libidos are not. An orgasmic explosion begins to gather low down in Coco's belly. At the same time Tanaka, whilst not changing his pace in the slightest, starts to tremble. Abruptly, the quivering ceases. His entire body goes steely rigid within its limited movement, muscles stand out on his arms and thighs, a vein bulges in his forehead. More sweat runs down his face to drip on Coco's shoulder, a sudden, massive shudder takes hold of him and all outward movement comes to a stop. It seems for moments, as his seed streams out of him and into Coco, as if he is carved from granite.

The sudden flood within her releases the safety catch on Coco's climax. Now at last, she moves. With a great gasp of relief she heaves her hips, her vagina contracts one, two, three times on Tanaka's penis, further milking him. She jerks one more, massively, almost throwing him off her and then goes still, mouth wide, eyes closed, fingers clamped on Tanaka's relaxing, collapsing buttocks. In a motion as slow as this fuck has been he keels sideways off her. She flops her arms out as if crucified, and then her only motion is the steady rise and fall of her breasts.

They sleep. So demanding, so fulfilling has this act of copulation been that they doze right away.

Coco's eyes are the first to flicker open. They focus on a colourful family of lions and stray down to Tanaka's milky, hairless, tightly-rounded buttocks. Her mental clock must be perfectly tuned to Tanaka's because the lions stir and are flattened under the man as he awakes and rolls onto his back.

The young man turned his head towards her with a supremely languid, self-praising smile. 'How it can be, you now understand?' he asked her.

Coco smiled at him as she shook her head in wonderment. 'Dig it, yeah. That was quite, quite . . . something.'

'A whore, a lovely lady maybe thirty, by my dad paid, such things when I was only sixteen me she taught.'

'Sixteen, huh?' Coco raised an eyebrow. 'Well, hoorah for daddy!'

He glanced at his watch; he had not yet arrived at the probably inevitable solid gold Rolex or similar statement stage in his life; it was a Mickey Mouse watch with a multi-coloured plastic band. 'More than two hours here we have spent,' he said, sitting up. 'We must return.'

Coco frowned. 'You want to go back to the orgy? After what we have enjoyed here? I certainly don't.'

'Perhaps not.' He put a hand on her belly. 'But, you see, for us not to most impolite it is.' Swinging his feet off the bed he reached for his underpants on the carpet.

'Impolite?' she echoed. 'Not to go back to an orgy?'

'Most, yes. Without a word to my father we were reaving. Not to return, unthinkable it would be.' He pulled on his pants and stooped for his shirt. 'Come, crothes be putting on. The orgy in any case almost finished will be. To fuck more you won't have to.'

She gaped at him for seconds. Then she sat up and slid her feet to the carpet, stretching down for her knickers. 'To fuck more I won't have to,' she muttered to the knickers as she slipped her feet through them. As she wriggled into them, she said on the verge of annoyance. 'You do realise that there has been something between us, and still is, that has nothing to do with orgies?'

As he zipped himself into his trousers he looked at her with an enigmatic expression. 'Something, yes, sure,' he said. 'We spoke earlier of rove. You believe that this with such a thing has to do?'

Standing there in her knickers, she thought briefly about that. Blinking her eyes, and chewing gently on her lower lip, she stared at her new, terrific lover. There had been an enormous sexual current between them, a compulsion which was, for the moment at least, appeased. 'Yes, we spoke of love,' she said. 'Well, perhaps it's not quite that.'

Disconcertingly, he grinned. She had once said similar words to a man fifteen years her senior and he had almost wept. 'No. But dressed you must get. However, your crothes in there will stay on. This I promise.'

'And yours?'

'I guess.

There was little need for Coco's slight apprehension because the orgy had more or less screwed itself to an exhausted halt. She and Tanaka entered the room hand-in-hand to discover that half of it was asleep, but only two couples were still actually at it.

Everyone was naked, or almost. Discarded clothes lay in a sordid shamble. There was a heavy sweet atmosphere, the tangy smell of decadence throughout the room. The Beatles interminably played on, only now backing snores instead of copulatory grunts and moans.

Tanaka, hanging on to Coco – like fresh pictures of

young innocence, wandering through some Fesscenin-
ian garden – searched in vain for his father. Both he
and Noguchi had disappeared. But they found Queenie
– comfortably snuggled in Akiko's slender arms.

'Well, there you are at last, darling!' exclaimed
Queenie. 'You missed a simply wonderful party.' Her
gaze travelled over both of them. 'What are you doing
dressed, for God's sake?'

Grinning, Coco squeezed Tanaka's hand. 'Staying
that way. We, ah, we had a great time.'

'I believe it. Me, I've had an unbelievable. . . . Well,
I'll fill you in later. And just look at the gorgeous girl I
ended up with.' She cupped Akiko's breast and planted
a kiss on her cheek.

The Philippino was the one female Coco had particularly noticed early in the proceedings. She was the sort
of girl they both went for. 'She has a name?' she asked
Queenie, smiling at her companion.

'Sure, Akiko.'

'Hi, doll,' said Coco, feeling slightly peculiar making
introductions under the ribald circumstances. 'I'm
Coco.' The girl managed the faintest of smiles.

'Akiko's come out from Tokyo, too,' Queenie said.
'Maybe she can visit us some time at the hotel.' Her
eyes flickered amusingly on Coco's face. 'How about
that?'

Coco, never too sated to not be thrilled by the prospect of three-way lesbian sex, looked admiringly over
Akiko's luscious body. 'That's cool,' she muttered, with
a particularly wicked grin.

Chapter Five

Hooking for Trouble

With unspectacular climaxes from the last two copulating gangsters, the orgy came to an end and a general lethargy filled the room. There was almost no conversation as the whores, as if a mutual understanding had passed between them, got into their clothes and shuffled from the room within a period of five minutes.

Most of the men were dressing; the majority quaffing the inevitable sake but without much obvious enjoyment; spirits seemed to have seriously flagged along with penises. The remorseless Beatles had finally been silenced, and no new music took their place.

Queenie, now dressed and very tired but contented, gave Akiko their hotel details before she left, and Akiko promised to call. Coco, rather expecting to spend the rest of the night in Tanaka's bed, was surprised when he escorted her and Queenie to their room and said goodnight with a boyish kiss and the promise to call her as soon as he arrived in Tokyo.

'I don't understand the bloody Japanese at all,' remarked Coco puzzled, as she closed the door. 'I mean, you'd think he'd . . .' she paused.

Queenie voiced her unspoken thoughts. 'Whisk you back to the bed you've no doubt been messing up together all evening? Sour grapes is it, my love?'

'He's such an incredible lover.'

'What? That slip of a kid?'

'Yeah, and how.' Coco sank wearily onto the bed. 'I guess the guy wore himself out.'

'Makes three of us.' Stifling an enormous yawn, Queenie kicked off her shoes. She inspected one black stocking which had a run from top to toe as a result of the evening's activities, and unclipped it and rolled it off. 'What a hell of a night,' she said. 'How do you like Akiko?'

'Sensational. A real doll.'

'And quite a bit more than just bi – she's almost all gay.' She unclipped her other suspender. 'But there's something funny about her. Something wrong I can't quite put my finger on. My reporter's nose tells me. And there's a sort of deep-rooted sadness in her. I just don't know. I managed to bring her to life for a while there, but she was totally turned inwards most of the time.'

Coco watched her peel off the other stocking. 'Nothing that unusual in a whore, honey,' she told her. 'Protective shell, I guess.'

'No. It was much more than that. Just before you came back, after we were left alone together, we were chatting. When I told her what I do for a living, I'm sure she wanted to tell me something, to open up, but she didn't have the guts. I'd almost swear that that girl's in some sort of bother.' She unzipped her dress, which was crumpled beyond belief, and got out of it.

'Jesus, I sure as hell hope not,' said Coco.

'Why? What's it to you?' Suspender belt and knickers came off and for the first time that evening Queenie was actually completely naked.

'To us, Queenie, to us,' Coco answered. 'You've given her our telephone number, remember? She's going to get in touch and if she's in trouble you – we – are going to get involved. Christ, didn't we have enough aggro last trip?' She sighed. 'We're on an assignment, in case you'd forgotten.'

'Aren't we just.' Queenie smoothed her hands over her breasts and tossed her head, her thickly tousled red hair bouncing on her shoulders. 'But that girl's too much of a peach for us to ignore if she's got problems.' She grinned and added archly. 'Aside from that, what an assignment this one's turning out to be!'

'True.' Wandering to the window, Coco looked out onto the moonlit lake. Below her, where the carpark encroached slightly onto the back of the house, a tour bus was being started up. The lights were on inside, and Coco saw that it was full of the evening's prostitutes. 'That's almost beyond belief,' she exclaimed. 'Take a look at this.'

'What?' Queenie joined her just a fraction before the tail-lights of the bus disappeared around the house.

'Godfather Nangi just busses 'em in and busses 'em out. A regular, stream-lined operation.' Coco laughingly put her arm around Queenie's waist. 'I'm delighted to report that sex is very much alive and kicking in the land of the rising sun.'

'You can say that again.' Queenie briefly hugged her. 'I'm for a long, hot shower. Join me?'

'Okay,' agreed Coco as they broke away from one another and turned from the window. 'But no funny business, right? Huh?'

After breakfast in bed, the girls were escorted through a house so still and silent it might have been empty apart from themselves and the servant. The same limousine which had brought them was waiting to whisk them off along the side of Lake Chuzenji into a gloomily overcast day.

Some three hours later they were in bustling, lunch-time, smog-ridden Tokyo being dropped in front of the Imperial Hotel by the chauffeur who made no move to help them with their case or even to open a door for them.

'We seem to have lost a day and a half's work,' Queenie pointed out over a noodle lunch.

'And gained something like half a lifetime's experience,' said Coco. 'For that I'd skip the work any time.'

110

'No doubt. Me too. But now we need to get on with the job – there's barely half of the article in the bag.'

They started right away after lunch, putting in a useful afternoon watching salaryman – *sarariman*, to give him his correct title – at work and at play. First they took advantage of an open invitation of Noguchi's to a conducted tour of the labyrinthine Nippon Petrochemicals building where an army of grey and blue suited men was regimentally labouring.

Late in the afternoon they paid a visit to a multistoreyed driving range where hundreds of executives were sending thousands upon thousands of golf balls into space. Securing an interview with one of them. Queenie discovered that this was the closest he had ever been to actually playing the game; his company would not afford him the massive membership and annual fees of a club until he had moved a couple of notches higher up the corporate ladder – but he was determined to be competent at the game by the time that happened.

When, satisfied with their afternoon, they arrived back at the hotel, there was a message for Queenie from Akiko. She was going to be in the area at eight, she would stop by to see them.

'I'd guess,' commented Queenie after reading the receptionist's note aloud, 'this means trouble.'

'You don't know that,' said Coco. 'Perhaps she's coming around for a bit of a kiss and a cuddle?'

'Trouble.'

No one would have reached the conclusion that Akiko was a whore from her appearance, as, five minutes after eight, she walked smartly into the Imperial bar where Queenie and Coco were waiting for her with aperitifs. She was wearing a simple, well-made, black woollen sheath dress which covered her knees and had a crew neck that was offset by a single row of pearls. The only, slight mar to her loveliness was the tiny lines of tiredness around her eyes. 'I am so happy you could

111

see me,' she told them with a fleeting, sad smile as she sat down. She crossed one leg elegantly over the other, showing very little thigh as she did so.

Memories of their lovemaking, of how soft and responsive her body had been, even the sweet taste of her lips, flooded through Queenie's mind. She leant forward to drop a hand lightly on Akiko's. 'We're pleased you came,' she said, then she caught the waiter's eye.

While Queenie ordered a Martini for Akiko, Coco, seething with curiosity about the purpose of the whore's visit, remarked, 'That was quite a party last night, wasn't it?'

'Party?' echoed Akiko. 'For me that was no party. Me and the girls were just doing our job.'

'Oh dear,' said Queenie, blinking at her. 'I rather thought you and I . . .' she paused. 'That it was, you know, good. Sort of special.'

'Yeah, well, with you it was different,' Akiko admitted. 'Then you weren't paying – and you're not a man.'

'You don't like men at all?' asked Coco.

'Hate the bastards.'

'That's a pretty strong generalisation.'

'You bet.' Her drink arrived and she took a long sip of it. 'But I don't understand what you two were doing at such an affair? Me, I get paid for feeding these pigs' filthy appetites. Did you get paid – is that a sort of a sideline for you?'

'Christ, no,' exclaimed Queenie. 'We weren't filled in beforehand. We had no idea what we were getting into.'

Akiko gaped. 'So why the hell didn't you leave?'

'You don't know us, baby,' remarked Coco.

'You mean you actually enjoyed it?'

Coco wetted her throat with Tio Pepe. 'Well, I wasn't there,' she pointed out. 'At least, not for the main action.'

'But Queenie was.' Akiko raised a thin, black eyebrow

at Queenie. 'That stuff you went through with the men, the way you were reacting – it was for real?'

'I'm afraid so, yes,' she confessed with a smile of utmost innocence.

'You swing both ways all the time?'

'She swings,' said Coco.

Queenie decided it was time to change the subject and find out what it was the girl wanted. 'You didn't come here for sex, did you?' she asked.

Akiko's eyes momentarily hooked hers, the merest trace of longing in them belying my answer. 'For sex, no.'

'Then I'd guess you're in some sort of trouble?'

'I am in the trouble of being what I am,' she said, 'which, in the first place, is only my own fault.'

. 'Then pack it in?'

'I want to, but they, they have me trapped, those swine.' She took a long, nervous slug of her Martini.

'Who does?' asked Coco. 'Nangi?'

'Yes. Well, not exactly Nangi himself. A partner of his, Okiwa. Okiwa runs the prostitution racket.'

Queenie frowned. 'I don't get it. You have your freedom or you wouldn't be here with us right now. If you really want to quit being on the game, what's there to stop you?'

Akiko lit a cigarette, her hand slightly shaking. 'They, they have my sister,' she told them through a cloud of smoke. 'She is just sixteen and a prisoner in Okiwa's brothel. He, he has told me some of the very nasty things that will be done to her should I stop working.' Her face dropped, etching the weariness lines deeper; she inhaled a lungful of smoke. 'I suppose it's crazy of me, Queenie, but I thought you were very nice. And then, when I found out you're a reporter . . .'

'A journalist,' interrupted Queenie.

'Well, a journalist. I thought perhaps you have some influence? That you could maybe find some way of helping me get poor Kiki out of there? She is, she is

113

forced to go with different men all the time, day and night.'

'God, I'm so sorry, Akiko,' said Queenie. 'But, Jesus, I don't see that there's much we can do. We've been in this country just a few days, and it's the first time. We really don't have any influence with anybody.'

'But you are invited to Nangi's private house. And there you are made love to, not bought by the powerful Makita Noguchi and by Nangi, both at the same time. These are people with great influence.'

Coco glanced sharply at Queenie, amusement dancing around her eyes, her lips pursing, because Queenie had not told her that little fact. But she did not comment. Instead she said, her eyes still on Queenie, 'How come Kiki came to be a prisoner in a cat house in the first place?'

'The *yakuza* kidnapped her six months ago when she was only fifteen.'

'And the police?'

'Hah! Don't even think about it. Like all men, they are also bastards. You imagine I haven't tried? Forget it. Besides, we aren't even Japanese, we are Philippinos.' She took in more nicotine and crushed the half-smoked cigarette out, mashing it in the ashtray as she continued. 'I, I had sent Kiki a ticket to visit me. They saw us together – she is very pretty – found out who she was and . . .' Her eyes began to water and her shoulders trembled, but she took a hefty slug of Martini and got hold of herself. 'Sorry.'

'It's okay.' Queenie again laid her hand on the back of Akiko's. 'Let's have the whole story?' she asked. 'You're from the Philippines and yet you become a call-girl in Tokyo. How did that come about?'

'You have the time?'

'We have as long as it takes.'

'All right,' Akiko began. 'I was born in a poverty-stricken slum village in the south of the Philippines, on Mindanao . . .'

She described in painful detail the life of a child grow-

114

ing up in harsh poverty, with starvation and disease. Then she told them how by the time she was twelve she vowed that no way was she going to spend the rest of her life like that. At fourteen she made the journey north from Mindanao with virtually no money at all, arriving in Manila where she searched for work, lying about her age. She was picked up by a self-styled 'talent scout' and promised work as a model in Tokyo. A visa, on which she was described as an entertainer, was arranged for her, and her passage was paid. But when she arrived in Tokyo she discovered that the 'talent scout' had close links with the Japanese gangsters, the *yakuza*, and that the only talent they were interested in was her ability to lie on her back with her legs open. She tried to evade them, but she was in a strange, hostile country with no friends and no money. They locked her up and then, incredibly, she was put up for auction in a prospering white slave market. In a sleazy, backstreet night club near Uen station, she was sold for a million and a half yen, then she was forced by her buyers – Okiwa's gang – into prostitution. It didn't take long for her to harden herself to this life – at least she had plenty to eat, a comfortable place to sleep, and fancy clothes. She decided that she would put up with being on the game for three or four years, save hard, and break away when still young. And she had been almost ready to achieve that ambition when she made the fatal mistake of having her sister over to visit . . .

'So now you know,' she finished. She shrugged hopelessly, looking terribly sad. 'I need help, if only for Kiki.'

Queenie and Coco had listened to this lengthy horror story with hardly an interruption. Now, taking a deep breath, Queenie said, 'Christ – no wonder you loathe men.'

'I get nothing but trouble from bloody men ever since I started growing up. An uncle raped me when I was eleven.' Finishing her Martini, she hooked a finger to a passing waiter, indicating with the same finger a repeat round. When it arrived, Queenie told him to put it on their tab.

'Hell, kid, I really don't know what to say to you,' said Coco. 'It's a lousy story, I feel for you.'

'Just one amongst thousands. This Tokyo is one crazy city. And when that fucker Okiwa he threatens to hurt Kiki, what he means is that she will be made available to certain sadist punters. And when a Japanese is a confirmed sadist, believe me, that means blood – not pig's blood like last night, but the real thing.'

'If those nutters like to do for real what I've seen in their comics . . .' Coco left the rest of her thought unspoken. 'Shit, what a bastard mess you two are in.'

'The samurai are just the popular example of the Jap history of cruelty. They'll do what they threaten to Kiki if I disappear, for sure.' She lit another cigarette. 'I have to somehow get her out of there and us out of this fucking country.'

'I want to help,' Coco decided. 'I'm half Philippino, and besides, I think I like you. We'll both do what we can.'

'You bet,' agreed Queenie. 'What you just told us makes me sick to my stomach.'

Coco sipped her sherry thoughtfully. 'Listen, I've got a bit of a thing going with Nangi's son Tanaka,' she said. 'I'll be seeing him in a couple of days, I'll talk to him about this.'

'We can have a word with Noguchi, too,' Queenie suggested. 'Where is this place that Kiki's locked up?'

Akiko told her with wide eyes, taking little, nervous puffs on her cigarette as she did so. 'It's a big, rambling old house in the Ginza district – the most fashionable area of Tokyo. It has a high wall around it and appears totally respectable. But it's an exclusive, and illegal brothel – they all are but nothing much is done about them – which caters to rich executives and the like.'

Smelling her untouched sherry but not putting the glass to her lips, Queenie said, 'We have an Irish friend here who knows Tokyo quite well. He might come up with some ideas, too. I'll tell him the story.'

'You're serious? You really will try for me?'

'No way we'd say it if we didn't mean it. It isn't our style.' Looking at her as she said this, Coco could not help thinking, but you sure are.

'We'll try whatever we can,' Queenie said adding a word of warning, 'but, more or less woman of the world that I am, I visualise it being far from a piece of cake to get one of their valuable girls away from a gang of Japanese gangsters.'

'I know it.' Akiko laid her hand on Queenie's forearm. 'It means, like, life or death to me.' She moved her fingers in almost a caress, her dark, sad eyes softly hanging on to Queenie's.

'We'll get her out, baby, you can count on it,' Coco unexpectedly said, forcefully, almost with anger. 'Whatever it takes.'

A few minutes later, with Akiko gone to the ladies, Queenie said, 'Jesus, Co, why did you promise her? You don't seriously think all you have to do is to ask Tanaka nicely to have his dad's partner let Kiki go, and bingo?'

'I get mad when I hear a story like that. I get real mad. We're going to get that kid out of there Queenie – however.' The ire on her face changed to a twisted smile. 'Your doing, this situation, getting involved with a hooker. I was brought up on old American comedies, so for once I can out-quote you. "Another fine mess you've got me in" – Oliver Hardy.'

Queenie laughed. 'I did, didn't I?'

When Akiko rejoined the table, Queenie asked her to stay and have dinner in the hotel.

'I'm allowed a free night, believe it or not,' she said. 'This is it. Yes, thanks, I'd like that.' Her hand touched Queenie half-caressingly again, this time on her knee.

Here we go again, thought Coco, happily.

Chapter Six

Buff Stuff

It was, perhaps, inevitable that, after a delicious dinner accompanied by endless *sakazuki* – tiny cups – of sake, the three young women should end the evening in Queenie and Coco's suite. Lingering glances, frequent touching and sexual innuendo had been on the increase as the meal progressed and the wine flowed; there was no doubt in any of the girls' minds now that they had come to the suite that they were going to enjoy an evening of sex.

Akiko, sipping a glass of the potent *shochu*, had lost her mask of unhappiness at last and brought the subject of sex to the fore in an oddly blatant manner. With a giggle, her dress hiked on her thighs and her feet tucked beneath her on her chair, she dug a hand in her bag to produce, to Queenie and Coco's surprised delight, a remarkable, exquisitely carved dildo. Displaying it to them showily, she held it by the bulging testicles with its fine leather straps hanging over her forearm. She said, 'Meet my personal *harigata* – the closest I wish I would ever have to be to a fucking man!'

It was ivory coloured; its fine detail included bulging veins and a tightly stretched foreskin. Akiko told them it was made from buffalo horn and that if it was soaked in warm water before use it achieved a degree of texture indistinguishable from the real thing.

Coco, sitting on the arm of Akiko's chair, took the dildo from her and examined it with a twisted grin. 'A gas,' she commented, holding it by its oversized glans, turning it around. 'But I thought you hated men?'

'Like I hate rats,' Akiko said. 'But one thing a man's got that I happen to need from time to time is a cock. With a woman on the other end of that thing, for me it's the best fuck there is.'

Queenie got up from her chair by the window overlooking the floodlit Imperial Palace gardens. Swaying slightly, the whisky from her overfull glass spilling onto her hand, she went to Coco and relieved her of the dildo. 'Soaked in warm water, you said?' she mumbled. 'I think I just, just might do that!'

She wandered off to the bedroom, stopping in the doorway to turn her head as Akiko said, 'Be careful, don't get the straps wet.'

'Right.' Raising an eyebrow suggestively and licking her lips, Queenie slid half the thing in her mouth and jiggled it there.

Coco exploded with laughter, 'Don't make it come, kiddo, Akiko wants it saved for later.'

Taking the dildo from her mouth, Queenie winked lewdly. 'And I intend to be the woman on the other end of it,' she said, and disappeared towards the bathroom.

Cupping Akiko's chin in her hand, Coco tilted the whore's head back and leant down towards her so that their faces were only inches apart. The sight and feel of the artificial penis had caused a rising tide of lust to break through her alcohol-induced fuzziness and she muttered, 'Queenie's going to fuck you, doll. And, boy, is she good at it:'

'She really goes for women, uh?' said Akiko. 'I found that out last night.'

'Me, too, honey.' Coco's fingers slid from Akiko's chin, around her cheek and into the thick hair at the back of her head. She pulled the girl's face to her and crushed their lips together, insinuating her tongue deep into Akiko's responsive mouth and sliding her free hand all the way up under her dress.

When, a minute or two later, Queenie returned from

119

the bathroom, it was to discover Coco and Akiko, squashed in the armchair, passionately kissing. Both their dresses were hitched high on their hips, fingers at each other's pussies through their panties.

'Christ!' exclaimed Queenie. 'A girl can't leave the room for two seconds.' She stopped close to them, amused, hungry eyes raking over them, a tipsy leer on her face.

Coco broke the kiss to mumble. 'I'm warming her up for you, darling – while your cock warms up.'

'Be my guest.' Queenie found the dimmer switch and turned the lights down low, then went to the piped music controls and flipped through three bands, stopping it on romantic music. With Coco and Akiko's lips firmly locked again and their fingers jerking between one another's legs, Queenie began a slow dance, kicking off her shoes, lurching a little. Swaying around their chair, she performed an impromptu strip-tease, hardly an art in which she was an expert but she managed it with almost as much elegance as the average Tokyo stripper – that is, not a great deal – as Coco and Akiko's caresses hotted up.

When she was naked, her clothes spread all around the chair, Queenie asked, 'How long should that thing soak for?'

Akiko grunted something unintelligible into Coco's mouth and Queenie bent over the back of the chair. 'What did you shay, say?'

Pulling her face away from Coco's, Akiko muttered in a throaty voice, 'A few minutes more, then it's ready.' Stretching her neck, she offered her damp, lipstick-smudged mouth to Queenie who hungrily kissed her. It was the first taste of the delights to come.

'Oh, boy – are we chicks going to have ourselves a party,' said Coco. She crossed her legs on Akiko's hand, trapping it between her thighs as she stretched the girl's pantyhose and knickers with two probing fingers.

With rising euphoria, Queenie undulated her nude body in rhythm to the slow beat of the music, her eyes eagerly following each move of Coco and Akiko's lovemaking. With Akiko's index finger slipping and sliding inside her panties, Coco pulled the whore's tights and knickers down to her mid thigh and pushed two fingers into her pussy.

As both girls squirmed on one another's penetrating fingers Queenie dragged her eyes off of them and went to the bathroom. She took the dildo out of its sink of warm water and dried it on a towel. Closing her fist around it, she discovered with delight that it truly felt like the real thing; the water had softened the exterior of the buffalo horn so that it had the exact heat and surface flexibility of an erect penis. Excited with the anticipation of what she was about to do, she took this formidable weapon back into the lounge.

'Ready, willing and able,' said Queenie, rolling the imitation cock against Akiko's cheek.

Akiko laid a hand over it, her eyes sweeping over Queenie's body lustfully, tongue curling over her top lip. Breaking her embrace she twisted sideways and sat up, Coco's two fingers still firmly inside her. 'Let me strap it on,' she breathed.

Nimble fingers untangle the leather straps, Akiko works the base of the dildo into Queenie's pubic thatch then has her get hold of it. She takes two straps up around Queenie's waist, buckling them tightly into the small of her back and, reaching between her legs, brings the third strap between her thighs. Pulling it snugly up into the crease of her buttocks, she buckles it with the other two. Queenie turns around, pleasured already by the kinky sensation of the soft leather biting into her vulva as the dildo sags marginally when she lets go of it. Taking Akiko by her hands, she urges her to her feet as Coco's fingers slip out of her.

'Get her tights off,' mutters Queenie, the words half sticking in her throat, the glans of the contraption digging into the Akiko's pubis.

Coco, titillated by the sight of Queenie's massive erection, is more than eager to lech on the sight of her girlfriend giving buffalo horn to this gorgeous leggy whore. She drags her tights and knickers off, then she stands to unzip Akiko's dress at her back. She puts the row of pearls inside its open collar, eases the dress over her head and Akiko, except for the pearls, is as nude as Queenie.

The upper-class English journalist takes the Philippino whore-slave by the hand. Her ivory-coloured cock, leading the way, is as huge as that of Makita Noguchi. It is a splendidly erotic contrast to the thick red pubic carpet which curls over its base. Queenie hurries Akiko into the bedroom. Coco follows close behind, her rumpled dress collapsing to the knees. Her head is slightly dizzy with pussy pleasantly a-throb. She strokes the fingertips of both hands simultaneously upwards on both the tempting, naked bottoms in front of her; for a second before she shakes her head, they swim out of focus.

They reach the foot of the bed and Queenie envelops Akiko in her arms and crushes her lips against hers. She is slightly taller than the whore. The dildo is squashed upwards between their tight, tense bellies, and she can feel that the buffalo horn has magically retained its warmth and the almost rubbery texture of its surface. For a moment her enjoyably sake-and-whisky-muddled mind almost convinces her that she has turned into a man, that this bawdy, artificial appendage is for real.

There is a soft, deep-piled blue rug at their feet. Falling to her knees on it, Queenie grabs Akiko by the buttocks and dives her mouth and tongue into Akiko's heavy, black bush. She explores its sweet wetness for long seconds, Akiko's hands at the back of her head urging her on. Then she pulls away, and taking her by the hips, she sits her on the bed.

'Now the fucking begins,' she says. She opens Akiko's thighs wide around her own, takes hold of the dildo by its thick middle and leans forward to position the realistically carved glans at the entrance which her tongue has just vacated. Coco sits on one corner of the bed, scrunching her dress into her groin with probing fingers as she watches Queenie thrust her hips forward. Akiko, leaning back on straight arms, stares down between her fine tits and shudders as the dildo disappears inside her. She sways forwards, throws her arms around Queenie's neck, presses her mouth against hers with a strangled sob, jerks her knees up and crosses her feet over Queenie's buttocks.

Queenie's generous helping of male genes – which no man, without intimate knowledge of her would dream existed within so spectacular a body – take over her libido. Suddenly, she is male. This is *her* cock sticking it to the delicious bit of oriental crumpet wrapped so tightly around her. Tongue flickering avidly in Akiko's mouth, she bangs the dildo in and out of her with almost savage masculine enthusiasm, imagining that the friction of the soft leather strap between her pussy lips is the same sensation a man gets from a penetrating cock.

This sexual position is rather too limiting and too much of a strain on Queenie's knees and back to keep up for long. She pulls the horn phallus out of her and has Akiko lay back on the bed, knees raised and parted. Queenie climbs over her and plunges greedily all the way in her. Teasing her with tiny, fast hip jerks, Queenie sucks Akiko's erect nipples, first one, then the other; her hand steals beneath the girl to her buttocks and she runs her fingertips up and down the sensitive cleft.

Watching Queenie in her rutting, masculine role – a salacious sight which occasionally blurs out of focus – does enormously arousing things to Coco. As Queenie's bottom gets into a regular, heaving rhythm and the dildo dips and plunges, Coco unzips her skirt and quickly slips it, together with her knickers, down her silk-stockinged legs. Eyes glued to her girlfriend's bobbing buttocks, she rubs her hands, flat and hard, fingers spread, slowly up and down her legs then slips them inch by tantalising inch up her thigh. Scarlet tipped hands meet back to back; the sides of her index fingers press together and find the softness of her vulva. She buries them there and begins to rub back and forth as she folds her belly over her wrists, sensually masturbating, rocking in time with Queenie's hips.

Queenie turns into a tigress, or rather a tiger. With her weight supported on straight arms, hands on either side of Akiko's shoulders, she gazes down at their slender, milky bodies and beautifully rounded tits, her tits bouncing, Akiko's shuddering. With head rolling and copper hair flung about, Queenie rams that slab of buffalo horn in and out of Akiko's wet pussy, slamming it home, ribaldly immersed in her role as the savagely rutting male.

Coco is carried away. 'Do her, baby,' she moans. 'Fuck her, honey. Fuck the life out of her!' She shoves two fingers deep inside herself, the wrist of that hand remaining trapped between thighs and belly as its knuckles jerk up and down with a masturbation which is becoming increasingly urgent. Stretching out her other arm, she creeps her fingers along Akiko's thigh and finds the whore's hard little clitoris and rubs it in time with the fingers in her pussy as Queenie's bush bangs on and off them.

Eyes rape and plunder. Three pairs: two black, one green, all sultry and smoky with lust and all focused on the area between Queenie and Coco's bodies where the buffalo horn and Coco's fingers are doing their lubricious work. Three libidos together soar towards orgasm. Coco is very close to bringing herself off, Akiko moans and gasps and Mr Queenie imagines his cock is about to perform the impossible feat of eruption while Miss Queenie's onrushing climax is induced by a combination of mental arousal at the sheer, wonderful lewdness of what she is doing and the physical stimulation from the leather in the lips of her pussy and on her clitoris.

The three of them come almost together: Akiko draws

124

her legs back and high with a whimper, Queenie squeals and goes suddenly rigid and Coco, her fingers buried all the way in her, silently heels over, eyes shut tight.

In a while, limp, with perspiration slowly drying on her body, Queenie withdraws the dildo from Akiko and rolls off her onto her back with a sigh. The artificial cock is most un-penis-like in its impressive hardness.

Coco's eyes flickered open to focus on the dildo. With a crooked smile, she reached out and waggled it. 'So now I know what they mean by horny!' she remarked with a giggle.

'Hands off – it's resting,' said Queenie.

'Doesn't look like it.' Coco studied it speculatively. 'Know what I'd dig doing in a little while?'

'Surprise me – you haven't managed to in years.'

Sitting up, wrapping her arms around her raised knees, Akiko said, 'Surprise? You two are the biggest surprise of my life.'

Coco smiled impishly at her. 'I'm pleased. We wouldn't want it any other way, would we, Queenie?'

'No. Like knights of old we come galloping in shining armour to rescue and succour a lovely damsel in distress.'

'Come again?' asked Akiko, puzzled.

'Take no notice of her. She comes out with nutty things like that sometimes.' Coco watched Akiko as she reached for her bag and took out a packet of cigarettes.

'We are going to rescue Kiki, you know.'

Akiko lit a cigarette, inhaling. 'God, I hope so. I somehow really believe you're going to try.'

'Every bit as hard as I'm going to use this on Queenie.' She again waggled the dildo.

'You still haven't surprised me,' said Queenie.

Coco rolled from her bed and padded to the door, bare buttocks wiggling. She was wearing her satin suspenders and silk stockings and her white blouse. The combination of clothes racily emphasised her lack of panties. 'I'll fix us some fresh drinks. *Shochyu*, Akiko? Whisky, Queenie?'

Akiko nodded and Queenie said, 'Just a tiny one.'

When Coco returned with three glasses in her hands, Queenie was standing by the bed, a figure of transvestite-like beauty, her dildo poking huge and hard before her; one hand was wrapped around it as Akiko fiddled with the buckles. The thing looked so lifelike that it was almost shocking to see it part company with Queenie's pubis as the straps fell loose and she lifted it close to her face. 'I bet you could tell a story or three,' she told it.

'It sure can,' said Akiko. 'But not half as many as I would like.'

'You should give it a name,' suggested Queenie.

'I should?'

'Right on.' Coco grinned. 'We have a friend in England called Frannie who's got a big black rubber one she christened Othello.'

Akiko laughed. 'Okay, let me see . . .' She thought for a few moments, then she said. 'Got it. I'll call it Uma.'

'Which means?' asked Coco.

'Horse!'

Coco clapped her hands. 'Terrific. It sure is almost as big as a horse's.' She nodded at the dildo. 'Why don't you put Uma back to soak, Queenie? Get him warmed and ready for his next ride?'

Queenie again went into the bathroom, chuckling to herself. Any swing towards sobriety that her recent sexual exercise might have brought about was nullified by the fact that she knocked back her not-so-small whisky on the way. There was the sound of a sink emptying and being refilled as Akiko's eyes lingered longingly on Coco's nakedness and she murmured, 'You and I have a little unfinished business, no?'

Pulling her down next to her, Coco ran a hand over her breasts. 'Ready for more so soon?' she purred.

Queenie ambled back into the room. Akiko's gaze

flitted from Coco to her and back again. 'With two such as you, I'll be ready all bloody night!' she exclaimed.

Moving in close to Akiko, as she toyed with her breast Coco pushed her tongue into the girl's ear, making her squirm. Queenie crawled onto the bed and made herself comfortable on the whore's other side, taking possession of her free breast with her mouth and sucking on the nipple. Coco withdrew her tongue, trailed it down Akiko's cheek to her mouth, kissed her lips and whispered, 'You can watch me fuck Queenie – then we'll finish our business, okay?'

'Okay.' The three intimately caressed, kissed – and giggled together – for a little while. The sensuous, steamy atmosphere was softened by a gentle playfulness, but as Coco muttered, 'I guess Uma must be good and ready by now,' there was an immediate increase in sexual tension between them, as if this hand-carved piece of buffalo horn was truly flesh and blood.

It is Coco's turn to have 'Uma' strapped firmly into place. While Akiko busies herself with buckling it on, Coco undoes her blouse, but does not take it off, and her lovely breasts tremble free. She stares down in wonder at this great cock which wobbles between her legs as Akiko secures the second buckle and its white strap deliciously tightens on her labia, making them bulge on either side of it. Unlike Queenie's experience, the wearing of the thing does not have the odd effect of actually making her feel like a man. Seized with a raunchy sense of unreality, she grips it tightly in her right hand, surprised at the warmth and elasticity of its surface which makes it feel exactly like an erect penis. She moves her fist up and down on it in an imitation of masturbating, then finds that in a sense she actually is because the dildo's base, fitted snugly into her pubis, works the strap on her clitoris.

Queenie, sitting on her hands on the bed, observes Coco's actions with jaded amusement. 'What's this then?' she asks.

Sticking her tongue out and pretending to pant, Coco says, 'I'm a naughty young boy having a wank at the pictures in a one-handed-magazine!'

'More like a young queen in that gear.' Queenie's amusement transforms to an urgent, lustful craving to have Coco do to her what she had done to Akiko. She clambers onto her hands and knees on the bed and implores, 'Give it to me like this, Co, please? Now? Like a dog?'

Coco's nostrils flare. She kneels behind Queenie without another word, eases the tip of the dildo inside her, takes a firm grip on Coco's hips and watching her action with prurient fascination as this is exactly how it appears to a man when he screws a woman from behind – she shoves it all the way in Queenie, filling her, stretching her, bringing a sharp gasp to her lips and not stopping until all Coco can see is a bunch of her ebony pubes squashed in the cleft of Queenie's buttocks.

Akiko parks her behind in a chair near the bed, sips *shochu* and lights a fresh cigarette, content at least for a moment, to be a randy witness to this lesbian coupling.

Holding 'Uma' fully buried in Queenie's pussy for moments, Coco reaches under Queenie's belly in search of her clitoris. Finding the hard little nub she gentles it with the ball of her middle finger while she withdraws the dildo about three-quarters of its length, pauses, shoves it back in then repeats the process, again and again. Building up into steady, pounding fucking which has Queenie biting her bottom lip and closing her eyes, she is rocked back and forth on her hands and knees.

The straps securing the dildo are so tight that Coco's hip flesh bulges over them, and this has a strong erotic effect on Akiko – particularly the strap which cleaves Coco's buttocks. Knocking back her *shochu*, she leaves the cigarette smoking in the ashtray and gets to her feet.

Queenie's swaying nose bumps into something warm and soft and hairy. She opens her eyes to see Akiko kneeling in front of her. Akiko's fingers lewdly spread her labia to offer Queenie's mouth her pussy. Queenie's nose dives back into the luscious bush with Coco's next thrust and this time Queenie is ready for it. With her tongue out, curling upwards, she laps the open pussy before her face is again rocked away.

As passions heat up, Queenie's mouth and Akiko's pussy yearn for closer contact. They lock together and the three young women become a sexual whole. Akiko has her hand under Queenie's neck and with her eyes resting on Coco's tits which bob and sway beneath her gaping blouse, Akiko pivots her hips back and forth in mirror image of Coco's vigorous screwing action.

The lesbian beast rides out of control. It trembles and shakes as it approaches orgasm; it moans and squeaks and whimpers; its three manes of hair bounce and float with each surge of orgiastic movement. Finally it is seized with a mighty shudder which starts at Coco's hips, travels along Queenie's body and into Akiko's pussy and thence her pelvis and on through the rest of her.

For the moment the beast is still, as if frozen, a pornographic *tableau vivan*. In slow motion it keels onto its side, breaking into three happily sated female components.

Yet, a mere half an hour later, after another injection of *shochu*, Akiko was turning her extraordinary dildo in her hands, admiring its perfect workmanship as a familiar glint reappeared in her eyes. She handed Uma to Coco. 'Why don't you, ah, give him another warm bath?' she suggested.

Taking it with a smile, Coco said, 'The unfinished business, right?'

'You've got it. And it's my turn to play bad boy.' Akiko ran a hand over Coco's buttocks as she happily got up to take the dildo into the bathroom.

Treating the contraption to a lop-sided grin. Coco told

it, 'You're sure having a whale of a time for a chunk of dead buffalo named after a horse!'

Chapter Seven

No Go Noguchi

Makita Noguchi swivelled comfortably a few inches from side to side in his oversized, specially tailored chair, puffing cigar smoke across the maroon-lacquered desk. His coal-black eyes pierced the air to where Queenie and Coco were sitting in the low, black visitors' chairs. He fiddled with the diamond-studded clip on his dark blue, silk tie as he keenly observed that the chairs were causing their usual, satisfying show of female thigh.

Watching him watching them, Queenie reflected that her two previous contacts with the enormous man had resulted in sex, the second of which, her sandwich with he and Nangi, was shamelessly wanton. Now, confronted with Noguchi attired in one of his immaculate, two-hundred-thousand yen suits in his spacious, tasteful, European-style office, she felt off-balance, like a whore might feel up before a magistrate who has secretly purchased her favours. Suddenly their mission seemed less simple.

'Well?' asked Noguchi, as Queenie struggled to gather together her words. 'Why are you here today? Is it for business – or perhaps for pleasure?' There was a heavy degree of sarcasm in his words.

'It's, uh, eleven o'clock in the morning,' Queenie pointed out.

'So it is. Business then. But you've had a comprehensive interview with me. You have been escorted over my entire building. You've chatted with a number of my executives – what more can you want?'

'Yes, and we're obliged to you.' Staring at the man, Queenie chewed the inside of her lip. Could she really have done such a bawdy things with him? At this moment it all seemed so unreal. 'Actually,' she told him, gathering her courage, 'we've come on a fairly delicate mission.'

'Ah.' His eyes drifted to Coco. Her above-the-knee Chanel suit skirt had risen high over crossed legs. He had a view of the soft underside of her thigh which was pleasingly white above a dark brown stocking top and, hardly paying attention to Queenie's words, he regretted not having taken his pleasure with Coco, too.

'There, there was a girl at Ankoku Nangi's party the other night,' Queenie went on. 'A very pretty girl. She, ah, joined us. That is to say, you and Nangi and she joined *me*.' It all felt most awkward.

'The girl? Yes, I seem to remember something of the sort.' He was being deliberately vague, as if such females happened to him every day. His eyes left Coco's legs, travelled to Queenie's which revealed almost as much thigh, then lifted to her face. 'She was called Akiko, was she not?'

'A super-nice chick, as a matter of fact,' said Coco, her first utterance since greeting Noguchi.

'I wouldn't know.' Noguchi stopped swivelling, laid his cigar in an ashtray and crossed his hands on the desk.

'She's in desperate trouble. We, we thought perhaps you might be able to help her,' Queenie blurted.

'Trouble? Is she? But she appeared perfectly all right to me. That is especially when you and her,' his eyes invaded Queenie's legs again, 'got together.'

Queenie fidgeted, as uncomfortable with this situation as she had been comfortable with the sex to which he alluded. 'She's far from all right.'

'Money, is it?'

'If only it were so simple.' Queenie uncrossed her

legs, aware that in doing so she unavoidably flashed her knickers. 'She, she badly want to stop leading the life of a whore. But it seems that Nangi has her trapped.'

Noguchi's eyes hardened the merest trace. 'Come now, what's this?'

'Well, that's not quite true. It's not exactly Nangi himself who's responsible but a partner of his who runs a brothel. Someone called Okiwa.' She looked anxiously for his reaction. 'Do you know him?'

'I might do.' He picked up his cigar, puffed a heavy cloud of smoke in the air, then mashed out the remaining two thousand yen or so worth of cigar in the silver ashtray. 'What are you accusing this Okiwa of, precisely? What is it that the foolish Akiko has been telling you? Obviously some wild tale or other.'

'It isn't wild, Makita. It's perfectly true, and it's dreadful.' Somehow, calling him Makita even after their many intimacies seemed all wrong, but 'Mr Noguchi' would be ridiculous. 'It's real shitty.' She could see by Noguchi's hardening stare that her words were not being well received.

Coco got into the act, raising her voice. 'Akiko has a sister, Kiki, who is sixteen. Okiwa has her locked up in a brothel where she is forced to prostitute herself,' she said, words tumbling fast. 'Akiko was about to go off the game when Okiwa had her sister kidnapped. The bastards threatened Akiko that if she did stop whoring for them they would turn Kiki over to the sadists. The whole situation is downright bloody disgusting!' Fire burnt in Coco's eyes; telling the story had made her genuinely angry.

'I see.' But Noguchi was unmoved. 'Akiko goes to you and you come to me.' His cold eyes wandered from Coco to Queenie and back again, but did not lose their propensity for staring through female clothing. 'And just what is it you expect me to do about it?'

Annoyed and fed up with his eyes on her legs, Coco got to her feet. Queenie was rather relieved that she seemed to be taking over. She strode to the huge desk and planted her bunched fists on it, leaning forward, not in the least in awe of this legendary giant of industry. 'With respect,' she fumed, 'what the hell sort of a question is that? I've just told you something that would make any decent man want to throw up. Do about it? Get the poor kid out of there, that's what!'

Unflinching, ignoring, or not noticing the 'decent man' taunt, Noguchi commented flatly, with a dismissive wave of his hand, 'This is hardly my concern. What Ankoku Nangi's partners do or do not is entirely their own business. And what Nangi himself does, except where it concerns me directly, has nothing at all to do with me.'

'And you can find no sympathy for this poor girl? These girls?'

'It is not my affair. There are thousands.'

Queenie's touch of nervousness dissolved as she too got riled. She joined Coco in front of the desk, containing her anger, pleading. 'Thousands there might be, but we happen to know and like Akiko. We promised her we'd do whatever we could to help her.' She was trying to look her most provocative. 'You could help, Makita. I'm sure you could. One word from you and . . .'

Irritated, he interrupted her. 'One word from me and I will be in danger of threatening relationships which you being western have no way of comprehending.' He got to his feet with that surprising ease and agility which did not belong in a man of his size.

'So your answer is no, then?' asked Coco.

'At this moment, the answer is no.' The irritation had been momentary. Now there was a slyness in his manner, and his eyes, probing her curves, were almost insulting in their sexual insinuation. They slid to Queenie, resting on her breasts. 'However, perhaps if the three of us were to discuss the problem together in my sauna . . . ?'

Coco gasped. 'You bastard!' she flung at him. She simply could not help herself.

Noguchi's jawline hardened and his eyes turned deadly. No woman, or man for that matter, had ever dared to speak to him like that. 'Leave this office this second,' he spat.

'Now, you see here, you c . . .'

'Enough. No more.' Queenie hurriedly interrupted, grabbing her by the arm. She pulled her in the direction of the door. 'Goodbye, Mr Noguchi,' she said, sickly sweet. 'Thank you so much for your help!'

'You are both completely off your pretty rockers, so you are!' Sean Magee opined in amazement as Queenie finished her tale of their quarrel with Noguchi. The three of them were lunching, that same day, in the restaurant where Queenie and Coco had first bumped into Magee in Tokyo a few days before.

'Why do you say that?' asked Coco through a delicious mouthful of tiny *ebi* – cooked prawns. 'Hell, all we did was ask the guy if he would help.'

'Thereby bruising his pride by daring to suggest that his associate and pal Nangi is involved in criminal things.' Magee sipped his Japanese lager as his growing longing for a glass of draft Guinness grew by the day.

'But Nangi's one of the biggest gangsters in Tokyo!' objected Queenie. 'You told us so yourself.'

'It's all very well, but Noguchi would never admit such a thing. He'd lose face to himself. Some time in the past, you see, Nangi muscled into Nippon Petrochemicals. Noguchi will have doubtless tried to justify this by convincing himself that their relationship is straightforward business.'

'Anyway,' put in Coco,' it wasn't actually Nangi we were accusing, it was a partner of his, someone called Okiwa.'

'Same thing. Guilt by association. Noguchi will have regarded your request as a personal attack, certainly most rude.'

'Yet still the bastard suggested he might change his

mind if we shared a sauna with him. The fat slug!' exclaimed Coco.

Queenie juggled sashimi – thin slices of raw fish – on her chopsticks. She was beginning to long for a good old English roast as much as Magee was for his Guinness. 'If the man had a decent bone in his body he would have reacted with horror about a poor fifteen-year-old kid forced into prostitution.'

Magee tutted. 'Haven't you yet realised how the Japanese regard their womenfolk? The only truly respected ones are the ones at home, looking after it.'

'So what's all this trumpeting in the media about modern-day female emancipation? And women in business, politics?' the slice of sashami was almost at her lips when it fell off Queenie's chopsticks and she sighed.

'Hah! Surface show, the male giving in with reluctance and only ostensively to the thrust of modernism. As journalists you should by now have learned about the two, officially accepted side to these people. They even have names so they do. *Tatamae*, the public face, how they act in society, and *honne*, the private face, what they really think. Your average salaryman, it's my belief, wants the woman at home to respect, the whore, who he disdains, to give him the sort of sex he does not get from the wife, and nothing in between. The working woman is a new phenomenon which he distrusts and secretly he dislikes.' Magee washed a piece of raw fish down his gullet with a copious draft of his cold Sapporo lager. 'When you ask help in the case of a whore from someone of Noguchi's standing – a Philippino whore, yet – you're talking to him about the lowest of the low. Help her? Forget it!'

'Well, we certainly found that out.' Queenie gazed into the garden where the gravel path was being raked over. Admiring the incredibly fastidious fashion in which the gardener performed this duty, she said, slowly, 'The question now is, what's our next step?'

'You don't have one. You tell this, uh, lady, you're sorry, you tried, no go. And then you back off as fast

136

as you can run if you've an ounce of sense in your pretty heads.'

'Oh, no,' exclaimed Coco with fervour. 'We made a promise and we're damn well going to keep it. Kiki gets freed!'

'You're mad you are, but then I've suspected as much for quite a while. You're foreigners in a weird country with a dichotomy of impeccable manners and rife corruption and you think you can do battle with a gangster controlling prostitution. Worse than fighting city hall, is that!'

Queenie glared at him. 'Now, you listen to me, Sean,' she insisted. 'All right, we were wrong to assume we might get any help or even sympathy from someone like Noguchi. But you at least I expected to feel sorry for the plight of these poor girls.'

'To be sure, I never said I did not.'

'Well – do you or don't you?'

'I do. But it's a hopeless position they're in.'

'Nothing is ever hopeless,' said Coco. 'We're going to find a way to get Kiki out of her prison, and you, Sean Magee, are going to help us.'

'The devil I am!' The Irishman appeared most alarmed. The glass of beer which was again travelling towards his face stopped halfway, hovering, as his wide eyes took in the two girls' determined expressions. 'I am?'

'You are,' said Queenie, most firmly.

'Holy mother of Jesus!' Magee muttered. The glass shakily finished its journey and he tipped the rest of its contents down his throat in one long guzzle.

Queenie opened her handbag and dug around inside. 'Akiko drew us a map of the area where the brothel is.' She produced a folded piece of paper and opened it out on the table. 'Here.'

Magee glanced warily at the roughly drawn map of a part of the Ginza district. On a street away from a railway line, close to the Nichikegi theatre, Akiko had made a thick ballpoint ring with an arrow pointed at it. 'Wonderful,' said Magee. 'And what about it?'

'You can find this place?' asked Queenie.

'And why should I be wanting to do a thing like that?'

She dug an elbow sharply in his ribs and he winced. 'I asked you, can you find it?'

'You should be Irish with that temper and red hair to match,' grumbled Magee. He put a finger on the paper. 'It's not far from your hotel.'

'That's what she told us.' Queenie managed to get some fish in her mouth, chewed it briefly and swallowed. 'Right. As soon as we've finished lunch, the three of us will go and take a look at this brothel.'

'Will we now?'

'The *three* of us, Sean.'

The Ginza was fairly close to the restaurant, and since the morning's smog had cleared and thin sunshine was beginning to break through the clouds, they walked. When, after twenty minutes, they reached the bustling Eki Station with its abundance of tiny food stalls, Magee, who was far from relishing anything to do with the girls' plans insisted they stop for a glass of sake for his 'jangling nerves'.

The Nichigeki theatre with its colourful pictures of all-girl revues performing Japanese burlesque was nearby, and they paused outside for Magee to have another look at the map. Akiko had drawn little squares, touching one another; one of them was adjacent to the theatre, the other to the circle which Akiko claimed was the brothel. 'We are more or less there,' Magee grunted.

They walked past two commercial buildings then came to a private house set well back from the road. Only the top of it was visible because it was surrounded by a high, brick, ivy-covered wall broken by a large set of hefty wooden, studded doors. There was no indication whatsoever of what this building was, not even a number.

'Now what?' asked Magee.

Queenie glanced across the road to where there was a small café. 'I suggest we sit over there in that window, have ourselves a tipple and case the joint, as they say.'

Magee protested. 'Don't you know I have work to do?'

'Don't we all? Come on. Don't let the man escape. Go.' Flanking him, they linked arms with him and marched him across the road.

From the vantage point of the café window, they could see more of the building. It seemed to be four storeys high and was draped with ivy like its outer wall. Many of the squarish windows were closed with sliding, freshly painted, red shutters. There was an air of old-fashioned, city comfort about the place, certainly nothing gloomy or sinister.

Queenie and Coco sipped *co-cha*, a dark tea, and Magee drunk more sake as they watched the bustling street for half an hour or so during which time the author offered several lines of protest and was roundly set upon and shut up each time. The doors across the road remained firmly shut.

Just as they were getting a little weary of this, a chauffeur-driven Toyota cruised very slowly past the wooden doors, so slowly they thought it was going to stop. But it didn't. It went on, disappeared around the next corner and a minute or so later was back again, travelling at no more than walking pace.

This time, as the tail-end of the dark blue car vanished again around the same corner, one of the wooden doors opened just enough to let someone out. A tubby little middle-aged man in a silken suit of exaggerated cut peered out. He glanced furtively up and down the road as if scared of being spotted, then hovered in the shelter of the doorway until the car made its third trip past. This time it stopped. The man hurriedly crossed to it, climbed in the back and it accelerated away as the wooden door banged shut.

'That performance,' commented Magee,' would indicate that that is most probably your place.'

'Our place,' said Queenie. She pursed her lips, staring thoughtfully at him. 'Then it's time to take our investigation one step further. There must be some sort of bell on that gate. Why don't you go over and ring it, Sean?'

He stared at her as if she had gone mad, but her expression was unrelenting. 'Are you serious for God's sake?'

'Never more. You're a fine, sporting swordsman who knows his way around practically every flesh pot in this city. Now's the chance to add yet another to your list.'

Consternation ravaged Magee's handsome face. 'You would have me stick my head, of which I happen to be passably fond, into a noose? If that place is what we suspect then it's strictly out of bounds for Joe Public.'

Queenie smiled flatly at him. 'You're a friend of Ankoku Nangi. He invited you to drop by.'

'Absolutely not, girl. Should they hold me there while they check, I'm a dead duck.'

'Come on Sean, where are your balls?' goaded Coco.

'That you already know, my pretty.'

'We only need to be absolutely certain that's the place,' said Queenie. 'You don't actually need to go in.'

Grumbling with a face the picture of doom, Magee got to his feet. 'Very well,' he told them. 'Sure, I'm crazy as you, that I am, but I'll ring the bell. But I'll not be mentioning Nangi's name.'

He could not at first find the bell, then discovered it on the right hand side of the doors, almost buried in ivy. He pressed it, holding it in for a couple of seconds, hearing nothing. Glancing across the road to where Queenie and Coco were watching him through the window, he glowered at them donning a fierce expression which did not quite come off, swore to himself, then turned around only to hear a scraping noise. A small, barred window, the size of a CD cover, slid open and he found himself scrutinised by hooded, unfriendly eyes.

'What do you want?' asked the owner of the eyes, in Japanese.

'*Wakarimasen*' – I don't understand, replied Magee, using approximately one-tenth of his Japanese vocabulary.

'Who are you? Why do you ring our bell?' asked the man on the other side of the doors, this time in English.

'I am looking for a woman,' Magee stated with what he imagined to be a suggestively raised eyebrow.

'What woman?'

'You know . . .' The Irishman stood back a pace so that the man could see him more clearly, clenched his fist and jerked it up from the elbow. 'A woman for bed? Is this not such a house?'

'Where you hear this thing?'

'I don't quite remember. At a party somebody told me. Three buildings down from the Nichikegi theatre he said, a high-class house.' Magee became cheerfully certain of himself in typical Irish fashion. 'I understand that there are certain, special pleasures to be had here?'

The eyes swivelled back and forth on Magee's face. 'You have wrong house. Go away.'

Magee heard a car door slam behind him and he found himself joined at the entrance by a wiry man whose satorial elegance was crowned by a cream Homburg. One of the doors swung open and the man slipped inside without so much as a glance at Magee who caught a glimpse of a manicured garden with some cherry trees before the door was slammed in his face. It banged into the tip of his black leather shoe which he had been tentatively starting to move in through the doors.

'Ouch!' complained the author. 'Heh, that is not friendly, sir, so it isn't.'

The hooded eyes were back at the bars, hard as black diamonds. 'Go away, mister,' said the voice. 'Now.' There was a finality about the window being slammed shut with which Magee was not disposed to argue. He made his way back across the road.

'Well?' said Coco as he joined them. 'A jerk in the Japanese equivalent of a Roller gets in but not you. Charm slipping, is it?'

'Enough, wench.' Magee downed an unfinished beer. 'I did what I was press-ganged into and my verdict is that the place is indeed what is sometimes referred to as a house of ill repute. Famed student of the human rat race that I am, I would not make a mistake about a thing like that.'

Queenie looked across the road. 'And locked up somewhere up there, being abused, is Akiko's sister.'

'Where the girl is very likely to stay, I'm afraid. I can tell you, it's not a friendly place.'

'No,' said Coco emphatically. 'There she is not staying. Tonight I'm seeing Tanaka, who happens to be Nangi's son. I'll ball him, get him nicely relaxed and off guard, then I'll go to work on him.'

'Are you never going to understand a thing about the Japanese, lassie?' asked Magee, a trace of impatience in his voice. 'The son of a gangster father is going to help you? You haven't a chance.'

'We'll just have to see, won't we? He does have a terrible case of the hots for me.'

'To be sure. And don't I myself?' He shook his head at her. 'You may try, my dear, but don't say I haven't warned you.'

'Yeah, well,' Coco responded. 'If that fails there's always plan C, isn't there?'

CHAPTER EIGHT

The House of the Rising Son

The evening air was chilly when Coco, in a heavy, jersey wool coat with a camera case slung over her shoulder, arrived at the door of Tanaka's flat, high in one of the towering blocks in Tokyo's Shinjuku district. Dressed in designer jeans snugly fitted on his slim hips, a hand-made, white silk shirt and snowy Reeboks, Tanaka let her in to a delightfully decorated, spacious room which must have been ten times the size of the average Tokyo shoe box.

They were in each other's arms as soon as the door closed. Youthful passion surged as they kissed, and Coco's mission to liberate Kiki was for the moment the last thing on her mind. When they broke their embrace and Coco took off her coat, what she had on underneath drew a gasp of admiration from Tanaka. She was wearing an oulandishly sexy jump suit by Katherine Hamnett. A dark tulle body stocking on which huge green lycra leaves overlapped and clung to her like a second skin. The leaves rose up from short, heavy black boots to halfway up her belly and over her buttocks where they ended in jagged edges. A second bunch was intertwined over her breasts. The rest was fine mesh; a scooped neck and wrist-length arms culminated the tantalisingly effect. Coco looked a million dollars and she knew it – this was one outfit which was aired for only the most special of occasions.

Tanaka feasted his eyes on her. 'Superb,' he breathed. 'Much beautifurrer than I remembered you are.'

'Thank you,' said Coco, glancing appreciatively around the room. Ten, light orange *tatami* mats covered the floor and two of the walls had misty, pastel-coloured, countryside murals over them, giving an illusion of space. An impressive bank of hi-fi and TV equipment surrounded the door. Several bean-bag seats, loosely enclosed in rich fabrics, were spread around and – apart from a tubular aquarium the size of the stove-pipe housing a colourful array of tropical fish – there was no other furniture.

'Nice,' said Coco. 'Very nice,' she repeated enjoying the feeling of warmth the place brought to her as Tanaka poured the tradition welcoming cups of sake.

'With such a father as mine I am rucky,' he said, handing her a little cup with a delicate, flying bird design both inside and out.

'Are you?' asked Coco, touching cups with him then sipping the rice wine. She wondered fleetingly how true this was.

He went back to the hi-fi. 'Some music, no?'

'Sure.' As he glanced along rows of a selection of at least a thousand CDs she added, 'How about Japanese music? All I seem to hear in this country is western pop.'

He turned a surprised smile on her. 'Mostry older people to traditional music risten,' he said. 'We, ones my age, rock and roll we rove.'

She giggled. 'Your English is okay,' she told him. 'But you should try and sort your "l's" out. It's listen, and love. Have a go – it's easy.'

Pulling his mouth into an odd shape he repeated, painfully. 'Rove. Rove. See – is no good!'

'Oh, hell what's the difference?' she said. 'So we'll make rove!'

'Here – some music Japanese.' But he put on a Tokyo version of rock which was cacophonous, even more horrendous than the French or Spanish efforts and she had him switch it off. Finally, the haunting, twangy sounds of the samisan filled the room. Coco's cup of sake was replenished and she sank into a bean-bag, feeling that here she was in a truly Japanese flat. Admiring the lithe, clean good looks of Tanaka as he sat near her, she brushed aside an intruding thought of her mission for Akiko, sex was imminent, very much in the air, and she didn't want to spoil that atmosphere with questions which, according to Magee, were at the very least going to be awkwardly received. She remembered Tanaka's promise of 'things sexual to deright the woman' and wondered what manner of thrills lay beyond the flowered paper screens where undoubtedly his bedroom was.

With Coco attired the way she was, virtually no man alone with her, never mind a new lover, would have been able to keep his hands off her for long. Within minutes Tanaka was sitting on the mat at her feet with his cheek resting on her thigh, one hand flat across her netted midrift and the other fondling her lycra-leaved breasts as she rang tingling fingers through his short, black hair. His mouth replaced his hand on her belly. Breathing heat into her navel, he ran a series of kisses down over the pelvic leaves. Closing her eyes, she sighed and opened her legs to him as his lips reached her pubis and he nipped her pussy through the thin, stretchy lycra.

'Owwww,' moaned Coco deliciously. Both hands on his head, she pressed it down as his fiery breath surged through the material and her skimpy panties to burn at her pussy. But he did not pamper her in this way for long. Raising his head against the pressure of her hands, he looked up at her, grasped both her breasts and muttered, 'Such a shame, but these crothes so beautiful must now come off, no?'

'Come off . . . Yes,' Coco managed, opening her eyes.

His hands slipped round her sides to search behind her back. 'But, no zipper I find,' he observed.

145

'No,' she said. 'First take off the boots.'

He knelt back on his heels and she offered him her feet one at a time as sexual desire surged through her. When the boots were off, she stood above him, stretched the tulle over her shoulders and, hands crossed over one another, rolled it down over her breasts and arms. With a sensuous snaking of her hips she wriggled the jump suit over them, and stepped out of it. Not waiting for her to do the same with her panties, he dragged them to her knees and plunged his face into her bush and his tongue dove into her already damp pussy, clutching her buttocks greedily at the same time.

The pussy-eating went on, Tanaka sliding his entire tongue in and out of her for long enough to bring Coco – head rolling and tilting back – close to orgasm. Then, undoubtedly sensing her imminent sexual explosion, young sexual artist that he was, Tanaka treated her to a last, slow, wet lick from pussy to navel. He finished the job of removing her knickers, stood, took her by the hand. He led her through the sliding paper doors and into his bedroom, as Coco's pussy begged for more.

The only obvious contrast to the late-adolescent style of his room at his father's house on the lake was that the all-boobs-and-bum pin-up posters were replaced by a wall full of neatly framed, exquisitely executed, pornographic prints. There was a similar pile of *mangas* – Rape Man comics and so forth – and another collection of audio-video games.

Coco had little time and less inclination to study her environment. She found herself dumped on a bed similar in size and style to Tanaka's other one. Fleetingly she noticed a pulley arrangement on the ceiling above, but then she turned her eager, needful eyes on Tanaka as he said, 'No, an orgasm you I give. To come I make you. Is good for to rerax.'

He knelt in his jeans between her shins, parted her thighs, slipped his hands under her buttocks and, lifting her pelvis towards him, he crouched into her to find again her pussy with his mouth and tongue.

This Japanese boy performs cunnilingus on Coco with as much expertise as the practised and wonderful Queenie. Without changing position or moving any part of him but his probing, darting, licking tongue, he gives her the most delicious head. He brings her speedily back to the orgiastic state she had been in in the other room; then he takes her beyond it. Her legs bend slowly until the back of her heels touch the hands on her buttocks and her libidinous excitement soars to crescendo. Coco comes with such a tide of sweet, soul-wrenching pleasure that for seconds her thighs have Tanaka's ears pressed tightly into his head. Then they slowly part. She lets loose a heavy, contented sigh. With his lips glistening, he sits back, his eyes looked lasciviously on her pussy and his hands still cradling her bottom.

'Such a pretty *momo*,' he murmured.

Coco opened her eyes with a lazy smile. '*Momo*?'

'Peach. That.' Letting her buttocks down onto the silken bedspread, he ran two fingers up between her legs and over her pussy.

'That's a nice word for it. Do you have many others?'

'Dozens at reast.' He traced the same two fingers down the inside of her thigh, indenting the soft flesh.

'Such as?'

'Oh, *kai*, a shell,' he told her. '*Hamaguri*, a cram, *nekko* which is the same as pussy.'

'By cram, you mean clam,' she said. 'Yes, I see why.' Her smile was invaded with wickedness. 'No dirty words for it – like cunt?'

'Of course. *Omanko*.'

'Which means?'

He shrugged. 'Is taboo word, same as cunt.' His fingers slipped back up her thigh, the tips ferreting amongst her pubic hairs. 'Enough foorish chatter. A *doogu* I have which in need of this is.'

'Cock?'

'Tool.' As she watched, utterly fascinated, he stripped off his fine silk shirt to reveal the splendidly tattooed folk tale on his chest and stomach. He unbuckled his belt, unzipped his jeans, then swung around to her with his noble lion family which curved and rippled in their jungle glade as he bent to take off his Reeboks. Standing, he climbed out of his jeans and pants and turned to face her, displaying a fine, proud erection.

Tanaka crawled back on the bed and knelt near Coco's face. 'My *doogu* you may suck some, should you wish,' he muttered as he cupped a hand behind her neck and pulled her head up towards him, rather negating the words of choice.

'I wish, honey, I wish.' Her eyes ran sexily from his genitals over his folk-tale and melted into his black eyes, which were smoky with lust. 'What is the word for sucking *doogu*?'

'*Shakuhachi*,' he told her, his voice gratingly thick. Swaying towards her he pulled her lips to his lowering glans. 'Do it.'

Gladly, she took his penis deep into the warmth of her mouth. Out of the corner of her eyes, she noticed a movement. She saw that the wall at one side of the bed was mirrored and that the movement was her head bobbing on Tanaka's stiff cock. Raunchily, she watched herself performing the colourfully named *shakuhachi* while sounds from the lilting samisan music in the next room rang prettily in the air.

To her surprise, after less than a minute of being fellated, Tanaka withdrew his penis from her mouth and climbed off the bed. 'Is enough. Is good, but for now is enough,' he said.

'You just love to tease,' remarked Coco. 'Don't you, Tanaka?'

'Us I tease, sure. Much of sex, games must be. Now, one of the best we pray.' From a drawer in a wardrobe he produced a bulging plastic bag with handles and with the name of a boutique printed colourfully on it. He pulled out a large armful of soft, white rope which he dropped at Coco's feet.

Coco's eyes went very wide. 'Ah – bondage?' she asked, hesitantly. 'You planning to tie me up?'

Tanaka grinned. 'Not. But that other interesting thing.'

'Oh, yeah? Good old Rape Man, huh?'

'No. For now, no.' He began to spread the ropes out on the bed and Coco saw that they were joined in a mesh like a fishing net. The holes in it were rather smaller than playing cards. When he was done, the mesh covered the bottom of the bed, an area the size of four big cushions. 'Now, prease,' he said, his erection unaffected by this strange change in activity, 'on the ropes you sit. In middle.'

'I, I sit on them, do I?' repeated Coco, mildly worried but not altogether alarmed about just where this was going to lead. 'On the ropes I sit? But you won't tell me precisely why?'

He produced a twisted smile. 'Is surprise.'

'No doubt. No doubt.' Taking her courage in both hands, she sat straight up, bumped herself across the bed and parked her behind on the ropes, which she found as soft as pyjama cord. 'Now what?'

'Your knees tuck up, tight under chin.'

'You're going to tie me in this thing?' But she did as she was asked, wrapping her arms around her shins.

'Tie? No. Encrose. Rike this.'

'Enclose, huh?' muttered Coco, as the mesh was, indeed, pulled up on all sides of her body and Tanaka closed it over her head with a drawstring made of the same rope.

'Enclose,' she weakly repeated. She saw that the drawstring rope was in a largish coil; there must have been three or four yards of it. As Tanaka took this coil in his hands and stood over her on the bed, her eyes shot to the pulley in the ceiling, which she had noticed earlier. Her heart skipped a beat. Of course, it had to do with Tanaka's plan. He was going to hang her from it!

'Heh, heh, heh!' Coco protested, struggling in the mesh. 'Now just a minute, honey – I am no meat carcass.'

With the rope still coiled, he crouched down and kissed her on the cheek through the mesh, a gentle kiss of reassurance. 'Is a Japanese expression meaning *nekko*, pussy in basket, what I to you do. Is preasure magnificent, no pain. This on my honour as a *yakusa*, you I promise.' He kissed her again, this time on her ear, wriggling the tip of his tongue inside, bringing her a little thrill. 'Is okay?'

'Okay,' agreed Coco, but wondering about his honour as a gangster.

Standing, he let the rope fall out of its coils. Its end in his hand he reached above his head and threaded it through the pulley system and began to tug it through, taking up the slack. Coco looked on apprehensively as the rope went tight above her head.

Tanaka wrapped one end around his wrist and gripped firmly while his other hand took up the slack on the other side of the 'basket'. Sitting beside the trapped Coco he treated her to a broad affectionate grin. He then laid flat on his back with his hard-on pointed straight up at the pulleys. He coiled the rest of the slack around his wrist and forearm – and gently heaved.

Coco felt the mesh tightening around her naked body, crushing her arms in to her sides, flattening her hair, but causing only the slightest initial discomfort. Then she was off the bed and in the air. Tanaka supported her bottom with his free hand until she was above his body, and then he let her go and she swung all the way across him and back again, jogging his cock on the way.

Catching her, he steadied her. He crawled his hand under her to her pussy, which was perfectly exposed, framed in a square of mesh, and worked two fingers inside. 'So,' he breathed, 'then not too much I scare you.' He jiggled the fingers. 'Wet and ready. Is good.'

To her delight it now became perfectly clear to Coco why she was suspended in this mesh basket, hovering directly over Tanaka's waiting penis. Her guts performed a rapturous lurch. All traces of apprehension drained away, and Coco waited with seething sexual impatience for penile penetration. Tanaka poked his fingers inside her once more, twisted them, withdrew and poised her open pussy directly over his glans. Inch by delectable inch he lowered Coco onto his cock until he was hotly buried all the way in her.

Coco hangs in the air looking down on her young Japanese lover. His cock is tight up in her belly. Her buttocks resting on his heavy balls. His eyes catch hers, hold them in lecherous amusement. He murmurs, 'Now you understand.'

Only one hand is needed to hang onto the rope as the pulley system absorbs most of Coco's weight. With his free hand Tanaka holds Coco steady as he begins to slowly, tantalisingly, pull her up and down on his cock. It is an extraordinarily horny, wonderful feeling, this deep, deep penetration whilst suspended in mid-air above a man she has contact with with only her pussy and, occasionally her buttocks as they gently bump against his balls. Coco is in sexual heaven.

One of the pulleys has a slight creak. As Tanaka steadily lifts Coco up and down his cock in a fuck almost as slow as it had been at his father's house, this noise, akin to the sound of bedsprings under copulating bodies, somehow adds to the amazing carnality of the situation.

Tanaka screws her like this without the slightest change in tempo, on and on. Five, ten, fifteen minutes pass and Coco hovers once more on the brink of climax. 'I'm coming. God, I'm coming,' she moans.

Tanaka urges her, 'Wait! One second.'

He stills her, holding her with a little over half his

cock buried inside her. The hand that has been steadying her now begins to spin her around. 'Now, you come,' he tells her. Her eyes have been closed but she opens them to catch her spinning reflection in the mirror. The room appears to be turning around her; the sensation in her vagina as it goes through a series of little contractions on the cock on which it gyrates is of overpowering ecstasy. As she spins for the fifth time, her orgasm rushes over her and she screams it at her passing reflection then collapses into sobs.

But this is not yet the end. Tanaka, specialist in protracted coitus, is himself gripped with orgasmic fever. Letting go of his famous control, he begins to yank furiously on the rope, jumping Coco up and down on his cock, his jerking hand moving as fast as in climactical masturbation. Sweat beads his forehead; he arches his back off the bed, grits his teeth, grunts noisily through them, and his sperm gushes upwards into Coco in three great spurts. His hand stills. He holds her fully impaled on him. Miraculously, yet another climax takes hold of Coco as she feels the hot outpouring within her, her wrapped body shudders in exquisite pleasure and she sobs again, this time holding back her scream.

Tanaka's rope arm travels slowly towards the ceiling and Coco rolls at matching speed off his cock. As he lets go the rope, she is dumped heavily onto her side on the bed where, trapped in her wondrous cage, she feels utterly sated and content. She closes her eyes as Tanaka's hands flop to his sides and his hard-working cock begins to wilt.

'I'm beginning to feel just a bit like a netted dolphin,' Coco lazily grumbled minutes later.

Tanaka turned his head to her with a smile. 'And even prettier you are,' he said. Stretching out a hand, he partially opened the drawstring. 'In there, trapped you are not. See?'

She bent her elbows away from her sides and the

mesh gave way, then she worked her hands up through the slackened hole at her head, opened it wide and pulled it down over her shoulders. With a giggle, Coco struggled to her knees and the whole basket fell around her like an empty sack. The rope spun the pulley wheels around, unravelled itself and dropped over her shoulders. For once she had nothing to say as she lifted it off her. Gazing down at the pile of white mesh, then up at the ceiling, she shook off her head in wonder and disbelief.

Climbing off the bed, Tanaka suggested, 'Some more sake, maybe?'

'You have whisky?' asked Coco, feeling a definite need at this point for something a little stronger than rice wine.

'Yankee whisky. Bourbon. On the rocks, you rike it?' Tanaka's lions rippled as he walked to the door.

'I rike it,' said Coco.

He came back in, carrying two, dimpled, highball glasses filled with dark bourbon and ice. A Jack Daniels bottle was tucked under his arm. He handed Coco her glass and put the bottle on the floor by the low bed. Sipped his bourbon, he stared intently at her as she tipped her glass to her lips. He had changed the music and sounds of Joe Cocker drifted into the room. Coco's needful slug of the strong liquid slipped easily down her throat to invade her belly with fire.

'Rike a man, you drink,' he observed.

Coco contradicted this with a splutter. 'Not quite honey,' she said. 'What happened to the samisan?'

'Too much Japanese music no good.'

'It's okay. I dig Cocker, he's kind of earthy.' Coco was wondering how to broach the subject of Akiko and Kiki. Now seemed as good a moment as ever. With studied care she leant over the bed and put her glass on a low table next to a pile of comics. She shifted herself off the mesh and, as she pushed it together into a heap, watching her hands she said, 'I wanted to ask a special favour of you, Tanaka.'

'Sure,' he said. 'Shoot.'

Falteringly at first, but with mounting confidence, she told him the story. Sitting there naked on the edge of the bed, steadily sipping his Jack Daniels, he appeared to be listening with a certain amount of sympathy. At least he was making the right noises. When she finished by saying '. . . so I thought perhaps you would ask your father if he could persuade Okiwa to let poor Kiki go free?' he looked at her for long seconds, saying nothing, unblinking. He was slightly unnerving her and she downed a hefty, burning dose of bourbon.

Finally he said, 'The position I have with my father you must be understanding. In his business I now am, very good to me he is. But for some years yet, exactly as I am ordered I must do. Question him I may not about such a thing you ask.' He laid his hand gently on her knee. 'This is not possible. I really wish otherwise. To help I want, but,' he shook his head in genuine regret, 'no. Very, very angry he would be.'

'Oh,' murmured Coco, deflated. At least his reaction had not been like Noguchi's, which she had feared, but it offered no encouragement either. She had put her case, he had stated his; there seemed to be no possible meeting point. The Irishman had been quite right. 'I am not going to plead with you,' she said. 'I, I think I understand.' She moved into his side, snuggling up to him, finishing her bourbon. The combination of the Jack Daniels and the previous sakes began to make her head a little light, which was something she was grateful for. 'Then I guess it'll have to be plan C,' she sighed.

'Pran C? What this is, prease?'

'I'll tell you perhaps a bit later. Maybe there you can help.' Right now she felt she ought to get off the subject for a while. Too much of it would possibly irritate him and prove counter-productive to what she now had in mind; she would keep him happy with sex.

Putting her empty glass on the floor next to the bottle, she kissed his shoulder, got up and went into the other room where she uncased her camera. Before going back

154

into the bedroom she attached a flash unit to the Nikon and adjusted the focus to eight feet. Then she poked her head, viewfinder to her eye, around the half open, paper screen and took a quick shot of Tanaka, who was admiring himself in the mirror whilst running a hand through his hair.

He objected, but only mildly. 'A picture of me with no crothes on you take?'he said. 'This is bad girl, no?'

'You won't be the first. Bad girl, yeah.' She readjusted the focus. 'But your whatsit . . . Your *doogu* wasn't on display.'

He grinned. 'Ashamed of itself it is not.'

'I should think not,' Coco retorted. 'Now, please stand up.'

Stooping, he reached towards his small heap of clothes. 'Then my underpants I put on.'

'It is not ashamed of itself,' Coco reminded him. 'What other way would I shoot your wonderful tattoos but with you starkers?'

'Starkers?'

'Naked.'

'Oh.' He faked alarm. 'My rions you are going to shoot?'

'Only with a camera, honey. Now, come on, stand up.'

Coco took a dozen pictures of nude Tanaka, discovering, unsurprised, that he was a natural poser who had no qualms in the least about having his *doogu* photographed. How she would love to get him like this on set with a couple of naked cuties at *Sophisticats*. When, satisfied, she put the camera carefully on the pile of comics, he said, 'Now other special thing for you I have.'

From the same drawer that the rope mesh had come out of, he produced a small, black-velvet covered box which he opened with theatrical show. Inside, cushioned in more black velvet, lay two little silver balls. '*Rin-no-tama*,' he said. 'Bell balls.'

She smiled at them. 'For the *nekko*, no? I've heard of such things but I've never seen them.'

'Then is coming for you now such a thrill. Take them, Coco.'

Picking them up with her right hand, Coco put them on the open palm of her left hand. They were light, with a weight inside them which made them unsteady, as if infused with a life of their own.

'Your hand make wobble, and risten,' Tanaka instructed.

As she did this, both balls vibrated. She seemed to detect the faintest of noises and put them close to her ear. A tiny, high-pitched sound, just within the range of human hearing was coming from them. 'Why do they do that?' she asked.

'Inside one some mercury, and other a piece of copper.' He shook his head. 'Why they do it I not know, but a thing most exciting inside the woman it is.' He held out his hand. 'You will now see.'

She gave them back to him and he sat on the bed in front of her. Putting a palm on the inside of her thigh, he coaxed her legs apart. Making her wriggle and bringing two sharp intakes of breath to her lips, he popped the balls into her vagina. They were pleasurably cold at first, but as they warmed she quickly discovered their true function. Tanaka told her to sway her hips in time with Joe Cocker and when she did so they constantly knocked together and vibrated within her. The sensations made her gasp; it was as if tiny fingers, fingers more arousing than any she had encountered, were playing a sexual tune inside her pussy.

'Oh, wow!' she exclaimed, closing her legs tight and running a hand over her breasts, 'I can hardly stand it.'

'Many woman there are who much use them,' he told her. 'Woman without men, nymphomaniac woman. But for the man and woman together also they are. This you are finding out in a moment.'

'They are incredible,' gasped Coco, snaking her hips some more, the vibrations within her sending tingles of pleasure through her belly. She noticed that his cock was raising its swelling head towards her. Reaching down she took it in her hand. 'But it's me that's wearing them, not you.'

'Just this to know, most exciting to me it is, you understand?' His cock went very quickly hard as she tightened her fist on it and rubbed.

'With the *rin-no-tama* in place we fuck, and what they do to me I exprain. Come.' Shifting his buttocks to the very edge of the bed, he put his hands on her hips. She let go of his hard-on as she was turned around, her back to him. Then he took hold of her knees, parted them and pulled her towards him, so that her thighs were spread over his. He urged her down. 'Sit.'

Coco fumbles between her legs for Tanaka's cock, grabs it and directs it into her as she bends at the knees and sinks down on it. His hands, back at her hips, push her all the way down. The little balls vibrate in her at the same time, the tingling excitement reaching beyond her belly all the way up to the back of her throat. Her eyes fix on the close-up reflection in front of her. Tanaka is deep inside her; all she can see of his genitals is his heavy, hairy scrotum hanging below her pussy.

The soft, gentle, experienced young Japanese hands steal up from Coco's waist and around her to enclose her breasts as Tanaka puts his mouth to her ear and mutters. 'Now – you the fucking do. Bounce!'

Further encouragement is unnecessary. Coco shifts her palms from where they have been resting on her thighs to the bed on either side of Tanaka's backside and uses them to help her do exactly what he told her – to bounce. This is fucking with quite a difference. The added sensations which the vibrating balls induce within her is exquisite bordering on ecstatic. Her hair is in one long, thick bunch hanging forward over one shoulder, the ends swaying back and forth over her knees. Her tits are warmly, comfortably grasped in Tanaka's hands, nipples pinched between his first and second fingers, and she rides the boy's cock as if post-trotting a horse. She nips her bottom lip with her teeth as her eyes lasciviously feast on her actions in the mirror – on Tanaka's vanishing and reappearing, solid length of penis, on his trembling balls – the sight yet more food for her turbulent emotions. Tanaka is grunting, a sure sign that something special is happening to him, too, as she has only heard this just prior to his orgasm.

The pressing of his hands on her tits suddenly increases. He growls, 'Enough,' and she stops, fully impaled on him. 'Now,' he mutters, voice somewhat weak, 'what this does for me, I exprain. As up and down you go, the *rin-no-tama* up and down my *doogu* also go. As you know, all the time they vibrating, and I, as you, great excitement from them get. You see, onry within *nekko* can I use *rin-no-tama*. Woman lucky – any time can use.'

Coco swayed her body to one side so that she could catch his eyes in the mirror. 'And why not all the time, Tanaka?' she muttered. 'I never felt anything *like* this. Christ!'

'No. Such preasure to be taken in small doses, this I have been taught. Too much, it sours. No good.'

'Is that so? How a kid of your age knows so much beats me.' She wiggled on him and the vibrations cursed through her. He stilled her again.

'Okay, just so long as you won't let me move . . .' She stretched a hand to the bedside table and picked up her camera. Holding it in both hands to one side of her body she pointed the lens at the mirror, angling the flash to lose any bounce.

'Pictures of this you take?' He protested. 'Not!'

'Why not?' She glanced towards the wall of highly explicit, erotic prints. 'You dig porn, obviously.'

'Yes, but . . .'

She interrupted him with a half truth. 'These will be strictly for you, to add to your collection. I'll give you the negs.' After I've taken a set of prints for myself, she

158

thought, as she fired off a shot, the flash hitting the top of the mirror and bouncing over the ceiling. 'They'll be a bit off balance, but that's cool, they'll be good and horny.' Moving her arms to her other side, she took another picture.

'Is okay,' he said. 'Some more take, no?' He lifted her by the waist until only his glans impaled her. 'Like that, yes?'

'You bet.' The flash went off again.

'So.' He ran his hands over her breasts and kissed her shoulder. 'In many positions we fuck, the *rin-no-tama* enjoying, and each time so not to come we rest, you more pictures shoot?'

'Let's go, baby.' Coco laid her camera down on the bed near them, well away from the edge. 'My turn to give the orders, huh?' she suggested. Lust sweeping through her, she climbed off him, had him lay on his back, took him briefly in her mouth then straddled him. She sat straight up, facing him, legs doubled on either side of him and heaved her buttocks up and down until, in a very short session, she was close to climax. Then she stopped, fighting to control herself – and took a picture.

In this way their copulation seethed on: change position, ball to the threshold of orgasm, stop, capture the scene on film, rearrange their interlocked bodies, fuck once more, take more pictures.

Actually, it was Tanaka only who managed to control himself throughout in this manner. Coco was unable, naturally, to endure all this without occasionally going over the edge. The combination of Tanaka's prolific cock and the *rin-no-tama* was doing the most wild things to her. By the time, a full hour after this photographic fuck had commenced, they exploded in massive, mutual orgasm. She had enjoyed three lesser climaxes along the way – and the camera was out of film.

Tanaka was the first to recover. Flat on his back next to Coco, he murmured, 'The *rin-no-tama* you keep. A present.'

She turned on her side to face him, and even that little movement made her aware of the teasers inside her. 'Thank you,' she said. 'I don't think I'll ever take them out!'

'But you must,' he told her. 'Too much excitement on itself feeds until nothing there is left.'

'Then you must give me the box, too, otherwise I'll lose them.' Poking two fingers inside herself Coco fished the balls out one at a time. Tanaka took a Kleenex tissue from a silver container next to the pile of comics and handed it to her. She thoroughly cleaned their mingled juices from the balls. He gave her the box.

Popping the balls in the box, she snapped closed the lid with a smile. 'For whenever I need a man and can't find one,' she said.

'Such a thing is possible?'

'It happens. I do tend to be choosy, you know.' She put the box by her camera.

'Yet to sex parties you go.'

'That's different.' She took his hand. 'Anyhow, I chose you, didn't I?'

'No. I chose you.'

'Have it your own way, macho kid.' Her eyes lingering on him, she took a deep breath, deciding that now was the time to brief him on Plan C. 'Listen, Tanaka,' she began 'about that poor kid Kiki . . .'

When she finished he was staring at her in consternation. He was sitting cross-legged next to her on the bed, his hands loosely draped over his thighs. 'But, to help you do this I cannot,' he protested. 'You get caught, dead you are!'

'You say cannot. But you probably could help me, if you wanted to.' She looked at him with grave, pleading eyes.

'Yes,' he said, carefully. 'Perhaps, but . . .'

'No. No buts, Tanaka, please, huh?' she interrupted him and laid a hand on his upper arm. 'You see, I made a promise, which means it's a matter of honour – something very important in this country, no? I desper-

160

ately need you to help me, no one else can. I'm not asking you to involve yourself personally at all, just to tell me what I need to know. Besides,' she added, 'I can take care of myself, I'm an aikido expert.'

'Hah!' he scoffed. 'Tokyo this is, Coco. A city full of martial arts experts.' But from the tone of his voice she got the impression he was relenting.

'We'll be on the ball, I promise you.'

His eyes darted over her, brooding, worried. 'I not rike. But . . . okay. A name I give you. A place. Then, up to you it is. But most dangerous this thing is.'

'Yeah,' said Coco, heavily, 'And don't I know it baby.' She grinned fleetingly. 'Anyhow, living's dangerous, didn't anyone tell you?'

Chapter Nine

Tender Trap

The following evening was the night of the Asakusa pageant. This took place in the old, north-eastern quarter of Tokyo, one-time red light district gone respectable and full of splendid fine art and traditional craft shops. The area of the famous Asakusa temple was thronged with people, the atmosphere was boisterous, the crowds there to cheer on the yearly courtesans' procession, a custom dating back more than three centuries.

While Magee sipped Old Bushmills from a hip flask, Queenie and Coco hung on to his upper arms. He pulled a face at one of the two beautifully carved and crafted *enma*, ferocious guardians against evil, which flanked the temple's entrance. As yet unaware that he was shortly going to be inveigled into the girl's scheme to free Kiki, he said cheerfully, 'Ugly beasts they are, make no mistake.'

'I rather like them,' said Queenie. 'By the way, how's your book research coming along?'

'The book is still a gleam in its creator's eye, but sure it's almost a foetus. Ideas are pressing on me from all sides.' He took another sip of his whisky. 'And how's the article?'

'We've more or less enough to cobble it together.' Queenie told him. 'We, um, we may be able to give you some first-hand experience for your thriller.'

'Just what do you mean by that?'

Coco chuckled. 'We thought we might add to your ideas.'

'Sure, and haven't you given me enough ideas already?' Magee asked. His eyes travelled quickly up and down her body. 'And aren't I getting more right this moment?'

The conversation was interrupted by a surge in excitement in the crowd. There was the sound of approaching music and the regular beating of a gong. A minute or two later, an extraordinary procession approached them. It was led by this year's *oiran*, the woman selected to represent the courtesan. For some odd reason a large, fat lady in her forties had been chosen, her appearance bordering on grotesque. Tottering on nine-inch high, black lacquered sandals, beneath a multi-coloured paper umbrella held by a male servant, she walked with a most peculiar, awkward looking figure-of-eight gait. She was wrapped from head to foot in heavy brocade, her face was painted chalk white, with vermilion lips, and her hair was styled in an enormous pile decorated with a tracery of large wooden combs.

As the *oiran* drew almost level with Magee and the girls, the gong sounded twice. She stopped. There was a pause in the music and her brocades were carefully straightened while a young boy fanned her face. It was a cool, early evening, but all that clothing and the pancake make-up clearly made her uncomfortably hot.

The gong sounded once more, the pageant continued. Behind the *oiran* trailed a long procession of brightly attired, heavily painted geisha, many of them well past the prime of life. Behind them, in front of the musicians, a crowd of old ladies beat their breasts and howled as if in pain.

It was all very strange. The procession took close to half an hour to pass because of the frequent stops to adjust the *oiran*'s brocades and to cool her down. As the penitent old ladies went by, the crowds dispersed.

'Weirdsville,' commented Coco.

'Amusing, I thought,' said Magee.

'Absolutely.' Queenie studied him. 'Didn't you say you're staying somewhere around here?'

'Just around the corner. Why?'

'I fancy a change from sitting down to a Japanese dinner. Why don't we seek out some good old hamburgers and take them back to your place? What say you Coco?'

Coco shrugged. 'That suits me fine.'

'Is it evil designs on my person you two have, then?' asked Magee, a twinkle in his eye.

Shaking her head at him Queenie in mock reproval, 'Now, Sean you should know better. I have designs on a hamburger.'

'Right,' Magee responded. 'Mackodonaldo's it is, then.'

He took them to a nearby McDonalds which was the same in most respects as any such an establishment in the world except that it was, indeed, called Mackodonaldo's. They loaded up with a selection of the welcome junk food, bought three bottles of sake from a shop next door and in cheery mood made their way to Magee's loaned accommodation.

It was over an art shop and most unremarkable, a tiny studio affair with four worn *tatami* mats, and a futon on the floor against one wall. But it was neat and clean with a smattering of pleasing prints. There were a number of large, puffy cushions around a foot high, square, red lacquered table, a small bookcase and that was it.

'To hell with tradition and bird-sized cups,' said Magee. Producing three glass tumblers from the bookcase he put them on the table, where Queenie was unboxing the hamburgers, opened a bottle and almost filled the glasses, emptying the entire contents.

Grinning happily, Coco announced, 'Am I going to enjoy this.'

'Nothing here but bloody chopsticks, of course,' said Magee.

'That's great.' Queenie vigorously shook a small ket-chup bottle. 'I love eating this stuff with my fingers.'

As they tucked in, Magee saved them the trouble of bringing up the subject which was foremost in their minds by asking Coco, 'You saw Tanaka last night?'

'Sure did,' she told him, popping a heavily salted chip in her mouth.

'And?'

She washed the chip down with sake. 'You were right, and you were wrong. No way would he talk to his father about Kiki, but he has helped.'

'The devil he has, has he?' Magee looked surprised. 'By doing what exactly, may I ask?'

'He gave me a key name, and a time and a place where we will be most likely to run into this, er, person.'

'What the hell is this? You're going to get yourselves mixed up in this rotten business? Did I not tell you to drop it? If you don't you're surely going to walk slap into a whole pile of trouble.'

'Absolutely right, Sean. We plan to walk slap in.' Briefly, Queenie explained plan C.

Magee looked as if he had been smacked hard in the face. He stared for long seconds at Queenie as he drained his glass, opened a second bottle and filled the glass to the rim and drained a third of that before he said, measuring his words, 'I know you both well enough to realise that any attempt at dissuasion will be a waste of my breath, so I won't try. But I'm telling you now, before you utter another word, that I'll have no part in this.'

Coco, hamburger, gerkin and chips polished off, wiped her lips on a paper serviette then sipped her sake, eyes taunting Magee over the edge of her glass. 'Well, yours is only a bit-part, really,' she casually informed him.

'Oh no. Oh no it's not.' he told them emphatically.

Shifting herself around the edge of the table towards him, Queenie laid a hand lightly, high on his cordu-

165

royed thigh. 'We already decided you were liable to object, so we worked out a contingency plan, Mr Magee,' she said, squeezing his thigh.

'Did you now. Well it has as much chance of success as a dog swimming the Irish Sea.' He shook his head firmly, swallowed more sake and added, 'No way, girlie.'

Coco's hand found his and her eyes, suddenly heavily seductive, hooked his eyes. 'You wouldn't happen to have sex in your plans for this evening, would you?' she purred, tongue tip wetting her lips.

Defences on red alert, Magee growled, 'And what if I have?'

Queenie's hand wandered higher up his thigh, almost to his crotch, and Coco's steamy looked turned into a wicked grin.

'Well, just in case you have, we will discover how persuasive we can be,' said Queenie. 'In the meanwhile, let me tell you what it is you will do to assist our little enterprise.'

'I don't want to hear it!'

'Well, you're going to.' And she explained, as his eyes grew wider.

When she was done, he told her. 'No part in it, thanks for your kind offer. I will not be dragged into a mad affair such as this. You two want to get yourselves bumped off, or worse, sure it's up to you.'

'Right, Sean. If that's how you're gong to be.' Queenie unhanded him after another suggestive squeeze and got to her feet. She began to pick up the cushions one by one from the floor around the table and to throw them onto the futon. Coco chucked hers over and sat back on the *tatami*. When all the cushions but one were heaped over the futon, she yanked the one out from under Magee.

'Just what in the name of God is going on here?' asked the Irishman.

Queenie slipped off her sweater and began to undo

her blouse. 'Pressure group,' she said, nodding at the futon. 'Over there.'

'Little sales talk, Magee,' Coco told him. Standing, she unzipped the side of her black, pencil skirt.

Magee's jaw dropped and he ran a disconcerted hand through his mass of springy grey hair as the two most enigmatic, most gorgeous young women of his entire lifetime's experience, took off their clothes with an air of calm determination.

Stripped to their undies – Queenie braless and in tiny white mesh knickers, Coco in a matching, celadon-coloured, three piece set from New York's Sonia Rykiel with sheer, white stockings – the girls arranged themselves in provocative poses amongst the cushions on the futon as Magee watched in astonishment.

'What are you standing there staring for?' asked Queenie. 'Don't you want to sample a little action?'

Coco crooked a finger at him. 'Come here, Sean.'

'Oh, oh, oh,' muttered Magee. He might have been a hooked marlin the way he was drawn to them. He sat down between them. The futon was too small for the three of them, but the cushions spilling off it onto a *tatami* mat made up for it. As he dumbly sat there, his amazement gradually gave way to lust, Queenie removed his tie and undid his shirt buttons while Coco busied herself with his shoes and trousers. Within a minute he was naked except for white slips, a hard-on rising beneath them under Coco's administering hand.

They pushed him onto his back and moved their bodies in on him, cuddling and caressing him. Queenie licked his nipples as Coco folded his pants down to free his erection and began spiritedly to masturbate him. Moving her face slowly, tantalisingly down over his muscular belly, Queenie dipped her tongue in his navel before trailing it into his pubic hairs and on up his cock from its root as Coco let it go. She took it in her mouth and sucked on it while Coco squeezed his balls. Letting loose a long groan of pleasure, Magee put a cushion behind his head. Female tongues, mouths and hands brought him to an exquisite pitch of excitement as he closed his eyes.

But, moments later, the attentions ceased. he raised his head to see the two of them briskly climbing to their feet and reaching for their clothes.

'What's this?' he complained. 'What in the name of . . . ?'

'We'll be off now,' said Queenie casually as she pulled on her blouse. 'Thanks for dinner.'

'This, I don't believe!'

'You'd better, honey,' breathed Coco with a wicked little smile as she climbed into her skirt. She nodded at his hard-on. 'No doubt you can do something about that on your own.'

'Since you've turned out to be a bit of a wanker,' added Queenie, buttoning up her blouse.

'Well, thanks,' he said. Then he protested, 'You can't do this to me. Jesus Christ!'

'Oh, but we can,' said Coco, pulling her skirt over wriggling hips and zipping it up. 'And are.'

'What you're doing is downright criminal.' Magee propped himself on his elbows. 'Leaving a man in this condition, so help me!'

Queenie planted her hands on her hips, her eyes roving over him. The situation didn't exactly feel great to her, either – Magee's penis fresh from her mouth pointed towards her from the floor and she was very firmly switched on herself. 'Your attitude is criminal, too,' she told him, 'refusing to help us to rescue those poor girls.'

'So that's it,' he said, his gaze lingering on coppery whisps of pubic hair which strayed around the edges of Queenie's panties. 'Sexual extortion!'

'One way of putting it,' Coco agreed. She stopped dressing. 'Either you pay our price or we leave you like that.'

'You're wicked, wicked hussies, the pair of you. The devil is in you, so he is.' But the gleam in Magee's eye belied his anger. Unfaded lust was added to by the

168

faintest glimmer of amusement. 'And the devil take you!' he went on. 'Now, be getting your clothes off and come back down here.'

'You pay?' asked Coco.

Queenie started undoing her blouse again, knowing full well that they had won this too-easy battle. 'You'll do exactly what we want?'

'Aye, vixen, which you both are. And Jezebel and Messalina rolled into one!'

'Messalina, is it? Strong language, Sean Magee,' exclaimed Queenie. Her breasts fell free and she taunted him with them, thrusting them forward. 'Well? do we have your solemn promise?'

'I said yes.' He glanced with fast flickering eyes from one to the other. 'You have the word of an Irishman.'

'Hah! Not good enough, baby,' said Coco, but she was stepping out of her skirt. 'We want a solemn promise – your personal word.'

Craving close contact with the silken thighs between Coco's stocking tops and her knickers, Magee growled, 'You have it, girlie. May Heaven preserve me.'

'Say, "I promise",' insisted Queenie.

'I promise, dammit. Now, get your mouth right back where it was, if you please.'

Chapter Ten

Whore-dition

On leaving the Imperial Hotel two afternoons later, Queenie and Coco were subjected to inscrutable, searching looks from the reception staff. Usually immaculately turned out, they were wearing old jeans and crumpled sweaters, and they both carried a full, cheap hold-all. Their make-up was rather carelessly applied, and their hair brushed short of perfection.

Tanaka was waiting for them outside in a taxi. All the way to their destination, which was close to Ueno Station in the north of the city, he tried to talk them out of their intended course of action. When they were almost there, realising the uselessness of this, he lapsed into moody silence.

The taxi crawled through some busy, sleazy back alleys, passing several unappetising cabaret clubs. As they went by a particularly dingy looking café, Tanaka, half covering his face with his hand, pointed to it. 'There,' he said. Fifty yards further down the street he had the taxi stop.

'This madness not to do?' he tried for the last time as Coco swung her feet from the cab.

'The only way we change our minds is if you persuade your father to have the girl freed,' said Coco.

He looked extremely unhappy. 'You know that possible this is not.'

'I know.' She planted a kiss on his cheek and stood

up on the dusty pavement. 'Come on Queenie, into the jaws of the tiger.' she said.

The café was as dismal inside as it was dingy out. Three oldish, scruffy men sat around the only occupied table, two of them playing I-go, the third watching. In fading, peeling shades of green, the establishment looked as if its last lick of paint had been half a century before. Queenie dumped her bag on the floor and sat down at a formica-topped table, and Coco went to the counter where a runt of a man in a greasy apron with a cigarette drooping from the corner of his mouth was washing some cups and glasses.

'Hi,' Coco exclaimed, as cheerfully as she could muster. 'We'd like some sake, please. And we're looking for a man called Shintaru?'

The man carried on with his washing up, jaded, browless eyes blinking twice, otherwise expressionless. He said nothing.

'Do you understand English?' Coco asked him.

This time there was a response. 'Some,' he said, ash falling into the washing-up water as the cigarette jiggled.

'We look for Shintaru?'

'Ah, Shintaru.' It was as if he had not understood her at all the first time, yet he dried his hands on his mucky apron, produced a bottle of sake and two cups and deposited them in front of Coco. Then he turned to a phone on the wall surrounded by faded, curling photos. 'I try,' he muttered, punching some numbers.

Coco carried the bottle and cups to the table, where she and Queenie sat in silence for fifteen minutes, sipping the wine, depressed at their surroundings and more than a little nervous at the prospect of what they were letting themselves in for.

They knew this must be Shintaru the moment he set a gleaming, black and white brogue shoe through the door. Every inch the cartoon Chicago gangster from his broad lapelled, double-breasted, black and white chalk-striped suit to his cream fedora hat, he came directly to their table and sat down, shouting a couple of words to the man behind the counter who brought him a sake cup. Filling it, without asking, from their bottle, his exceptionally hooded eyes wandering over Queenie and Coco with, it seemed, the sole purpose of undressing them. He asked, 'Who sent you to me?'

Coco tried to disguise her increasing nervousness. 'I never knew his name,' she lied. 'It was more than two weeks ago. A man in Manila, a *yakusa*, he drew us this map.' She produced a crumpled piece of paper which Tanaka had prepared for them. It showed the area of Ueno, the station, and pin-pointed the café. Shintaru's name was ringed around at the bottom of it.

The man downed his sake in one and refilled his cup, neglecting the time-honoured courtesy of topping theirs up after his own. He seemed to be a champion of bad manners, and Coco briefly wondered if he thought it enhanced his image. 'You of course have experience in this work?' he asked. There was no question of what the 'work' comprised.

'In Manila,' said Coco. 'But we heard from the *yakusa* that in Tokyo we can earn much more money.'

'Perhaps.' He took a cigarette from an elaborate silver case and lit it with a gold Dunhill lighter, a heavy gold chain dangling from one wrist and a flash gold watch with tiny diamonds on the other. He was missing the top joints of both his little and third fingers of his right hand. 'What is your name?' he asked her.

'Coco.'

He glanced at Queenie. 'And yours?'

'Queenie,' said Coco.

'I ask her – why she does not tell me?'

'She's dumb, she can't talk. Sad.'

Slightly raising an eyebrow, the gangster shrugged indifference. 'It is not necessary for her to speak. Sometimes it is better that way.' He waggled a finger with arrogant authority. 'Stand, let me look at you. And you, Queenie, you understand?'

Queenie nodded. Feeling most unreal, as if she were

acting a part in a play, she got to her feet. Shintaru
moved his imperious finger in tight little circles. 'Turn
around.' Uncomfortably, they did so, and at the same
time they were forced to enjoy the amused stares of the
other men in the café. They hated being treated like
this, like hunks of meat inspected for defects. 'Yes,'
breathed Shintaru in evident satisfaction. 'Yes. Sit
down.'

Coco tipped a cupful of sake down her throat, wish-
ing it were something stronger. As she replenished the
glass she said, 'We were told that you have a house
where the girls have rooms of their own, that it's clean
and comfortable and that the clients are all rich men?'

'Our house is the most renowned in all Tokyo,' said
Shintaru. 'The whores are all young pretty, very
special.'

That was something of a gut blow, his casual use of
the word whore in reference to themselves. 'We are
special, man,' Coco managed.

'I think maybe yes. But first I must see you
undressed. Come.' He put out his cigarette on the table
top and went to the counter, dropping some change on
it. 'We go to the house now,' he said.

Forty-five minutes of traffic jams and thick smog later,
they were back in the Ginza, alighting from a taxi with
Shintaru in front of the same wooden doors which Sean
Magee had tried unsuccessfully to enter four days previously. They were let in immediately and crossed a
neatly laid out, well-tended garden to the ivied walls of
the house. The front door opened on a spacious hallway
in pastel yellow; a huge, circular staircase with elegantly
carved wooden bannisters curved grandly up through
four floors, and a glass dome at the top of the house
let daylight down onto it. A hefty man in jeans and a
bulging T-shirt, evidently some sort of a guard, sat in
a chair near the door cleaning his nails with a thin knife.
He nodded to Shintaru and payed only fleeting, bored
attention to Queenie and Coco.

There was not a great deal to indicate that this house

was a brothel. As Shintaru led the way up to the third floor, they passed only two girls, both extravagantly sexy; they exchanged a few words with Shintaru who gave them hardened, searching looks. The house was quiet. The only other sign of activity was an elegantly dressed man pulling on an expensive topcoat as he emerged from a room on the third floor. Soft music came out with him but silenced with the closing door.

Shintaru took them into a pleasant, simply furnished room whose main features were a large, low bed and a mirrored ceiling. As he closed the door on the three of them, Queenie and Coco found themselves more nervous than ever as hordes of butterflies fluttered in their bellies.

An oval, padded chair faced a wooden dressing table. Shintaru sat on the chair, crossed his legs and made a small production out of lighting a cigarette while Queenie and Coco hovered uncertainly by their bags.

'Remove all your clothing,' said the gangster, with a twisted, cynical smile.

They did not dare show the slightest offence at this peremptory instruction. To do so would surely arouse suspicion in the man. They were playing emotion-toughened whores, and whores they had to be. Queenie watched the floor as she fumbled to remove her clothes, and Coco managed the feat of staring blatantly at Shintaru as she quickly undressed, catching a glimpse of her reflection behind him.

His face betrayed little sexual interest. When they were naked Shintaru had them parade around the room. Both women, who frequently got great enjoyment from being nude in front of men and who would gleefully strip for a sex party, felt uncomfortable in their nakedness, even rather embarrassed.

'Let me see what clothes you have brought,' he ordered them. They unzipped their bags to hold up each item against themselves as he told them to do; it was the sort of sexy gear they imagined might be appropriate for the life of a prostitute.

When they had half of the clothes unpacked and draped over the bed, he said, 'Excellent. Now I must be sure that you are practised in a certain art very much in demand here.' Without preamble or even the most fleeting show of emotion he unzipped his chalk-striped trousers and dragged his penis into view from under yellow satin slips.

They had, of course, expected something of the sort, but so apparently clinical and disinterested had his inspection of their naked bodies been that neither was prepared for the fact that he had a big, knotty erection. 'You first,' he said, crooking a finger at Coco. 'Some head for Shintaru, no?'

Approached in such a cold, sudden way, Coco found the prospect of fellating this unlovely creature, an act which under normal circumstances she revelled in, bordering on the disgusting. She swallowed hard and glanced around the room. 'The custom is to bathe it first . . .' she said flatly, '. . . but I don't see a bowel or towel.'

'Is okay, I wash,' he agreed. He stood and, erection poking through his buckled trousers, he crossed the room to a small doorway.

With a certain amount of relief, Coco heard the sound of running water. 'Oh boy,' she said to Queenie, taking a long, deep breath. 'Oh, boy!'

The gangster returned, hard-on undiminished. Sitting on the dressing table chair, holding his cock, he muttered with an utterly immobile face, 'Come.'

Coco takes a cushion from the bed and drops to her knees on it between Shintaru's opened thighs. Trying to muster some relish for this familiar act, she finds none. He lets go of himself, and Coco takes him in hand, slides the edge of her palm down to the thick base of his penis and ducks her head to it. Flickering her tongue over its bulbous end, she is at least gratified to taste soap. She takes it deep into her mouth, sheathing its underside with her tongue and begins to duck her head up and down on it whilst masturbating the root with finger and thumb.

Standing nearby observing this reluctant blow job, Queenie gets none of her usual pleasure from this sort of voyeurism. There is a hollowness within her, her thoughts are jumbled, incoherent. Coco's head bobs with feigned enthusiasm as her hand drags his yellow underpants down to free the man's balls which she treats to a warm squeeze.

He watches her intently, but Shintaru makes no sound, nor does his expression change in the slightest. There is no indication whatsoever that he is deriving any enjoyment from this. After a few minutes he takes Coco by a handful of her hair and pulls her head away from him. He nods at Queenie. 'Now you, dumb one,' he growls.

Queenie takes Coco's place on the cushion. It is Coco's turn, feeling curiously flat, to stand by and watch.

It mercifully lasts but a very short while. Queenie, with as much faked enthusiasm as Coco, gives Shintaru head for less than a minute before he moves her mouth off his cock and pushes her face down to his balls. As she takes one of them in her mouth, he wraps her fingers around his penis, jerks them up and down on it then lets go. 'Hard. Fast,' he commands. He fishes a silk handkerchief from his top pocket, holds it over his glans and, with a single, quiet grunt as Queenie's hand pumps away, he ejaculates into it.

Coco blinks surprise at this. She had assumed that one of them would be obliged to take his semen in her mouth and is relieved at Queenie's reprieve. Shintaru rudely pushes Queenie's head away from him, wipes the top of his rapidly wilting penis, rolls the sperm-filled handkerchief over itself and tucks it back in his top pocket. He stands, puts his cock away, and zips himself up. 'Is okay,' he says, nodding. 'Is very okay.'

Having been fellated expertly by two beautiful naked women, this curious, unlikeable, Japanese gangster still shows no emotion and acts as if more or less nothing has taken place. 'Then you both have work,' he tells them. 'The money is good, as you will discover. You,' he nods at Queenie, 'take room next door. Both are free to enter and leave the house at certain times. You must do so by door at back.' He glances at his Rolex Oyster. 'Downstairs is a bar. You should be there at seven o'clock, dressed very sexy.' And he leaves.

As the door banged behind him, Queenie and Coco looked at one another with troubled eyes. Queenie sighed. 'Well, we passed the audition,' she said quietly, her first words in more than an hour.

'That man is . . . ugh!' Coco exclaimed. For once not happy in her nudity and feeling somehow soiled by her experience, she got into her knickers and sweater while Queenie found a cotton dressing gown in her bag and slipped it on.

'Not talking was harder than I imagined,' said Queenie, digging to the bottom of the bag and producing a radio phone.

Coco managed a weak grin. 'Can't be so difficult with your mouth full!'

'Shut up, love, huh?' Punching the buttons on the phone, Queenie got through to Magee who was at that moment pacing the streets in the area of his flat, a habit he got into whenever turning over novelistic plots in his mind. 'We're in, Sean,' she told him. 'We have a job and a room each and we'll be checking out the place later.'

'Holy mother of Jesus!' was Magee's helpful comment.

'I'll be talking to you when we know what the next move is.'

'The next move is you're both going to get laid, so you are!' Magee held a hand over his ear and winced as a loud motorbike roared by.

'If we have to get laid, then we get laid.' Queenie

paused. 'There's always a chance that the punters might be nice.'

Magee decided not to reply to this, knowing that she was taunting him in her typical way. 'Did Tanaka fix you up with some self-defence?' he asked.

'A useful little gun.'

'You're in it up to your ears now, aren't you? May God preserve you.'

'I am a crack shot,' said Queenie. 'Now, don't you dare go anywhere without that phone. You hired a car?'

'I did.'

'Don't be too far from that, either, there's a love?'

'I read you girlie,' Magee responded. If he was not so scared for them, he might have even been able to enjoy his role, a role which would normally be confined to the pages of his thrillers. 'Take care.'

The call over, Queenie said, 'We have a couple of hours. Let's do as the man said and get dressed very sexy and nose our way around the place.' She put the phone back into the bottom of the hold-all, brushing her fingers over the reasuring coldness of the gun next to it; on top she piled her clothes back in. She took the bag next door into a room, which was a replica of Coco's. Just as neat and functional, its purpose was evident from the big mirror on the ceiling over the bed.

Looking around, she tried to come to terms with the fact that many thousand of Tokyo's wealthy had probably taken their pleasure here with prostitutes over the years, and that, unless they achieved their mission remarkably quickly, she was going to have to play the complete role of a whore that very evening. She might even, if things went very wrong, she reflected with a little surge of fear, meet her end here.

Thinking it over, Queenie found she was not seriously worried about the eventuality of being obliged to service one of the brothel's clients; there was always the chance of the experience proving okay, and if not it could hardly be any worse than had been their ordeal with Shintaru. The only sane course of action if the worst came to the worst, she decided, was to take the advice offered by cynics in case of rape – lie back and enjoy it.

She hid the radio phone at the back of a drawer, pleased that she had thought of the possibility of there being no phone in the house they could conveniently use under the circumstances; there wasn't a phone in the room.

The only other item she unpacked, apart from her outfit for the evening, was the pistol, a thirty-eight calibre Browning automatic which she stared at for thoughtful, scary moments before patting it and tucking it under the mattress.

Chapter Eleven

Cats with Claws

The house, they discovered whilst exploring it a little later, was remarkably tranquil, considering it was Tokyo's most exclusive bordello. They wandered from floor to floor, meeting almost nobody. There was music, never loud, behind many of the closed doors, and here and there noises suggested sexual activity, but nowhere was there the boisterous flaunting of sex they had somehow expected.

They found that the back door was guarded by a man of similar impressive proportions to the goon on the front door. When they came across it he was leaning against it reading a *manga*; Rape Man again, Coco noticed. He looked them over nonchalantly and refused to let them out. Six o'clock in the afternoon was apparently not one of those 'certain times' that Shintaru had told them they would be free to come and go. Through a lace curtain and slightly parted shutters, they could see a bustling traffic-free alleyway.

The bar, when they first stuck their noses in, was devoid of any drinkers or staff. Like the rest of the house, it was reasonably tasteful. Coloured wood-block prints were scattered around the walls, reminding Coco of the ones at Tanaka's room at Lake Chuzenji. The furniture was low and comfortable looking: upholstered chairs in light velvet; small round, walnut tables. The bar with its varnished wooden top and mirrored wall behind the rows of bottles might have been anywhere in the world.

This 'bawdy' house appeared to deny the adjective. It seemed no more racy than some small hotel. Yet somewhere here was Akiko's sister. Perhaps she was not the only girl who was being held and used against her will, behind a closed and locked door.

Coco – wearing a red satin cheong-sam, split to the top of her thigh, and Queenie in a black mini-skirt with very high heels and a low-cut blouse which clearly revealed her lack of bra – returned to the bar at seven. Except for a taciturn, or non-English speaking, barman, they were the first. The man had no trouble however understanding that they wanted whisky and poured them the generous measures they were both very much in need of.

Their idea to have Queenie act dumb was to protect against anyone recognising her very upper-class English accent and smelling a rat. Even with this uncommunicative barman she could not risk talking and the two women sat together at a corner table in silence, warming their bellies and soothing their nerves with the whisky.

Up until eight-thirty, young women, all of them attractive and blatant with their sexuality, drifted in, either alone or in twos and threes. The atmosphere livened up. but there was still not what might be considered a brothel feeling; it was more of a night club with hostesses waiting for the first of the evening's customers.

Men, most of whom seemed to be familiar with many of the girls, started making their appearance, mingling and chatting with many of the whores. Several eyes fell on Queenie and Coco at their little corner table. Oddly, no one approached them.

Shortly after eight-thirty a young girl with hair as long and as black as Coco's came in with Shintaru at her heels. Coco's foot jabbed Queenie's shin under the table, she nodded towards the girl who, looked subdued, leaning back against the bar. Opening her evening bag, Coco slipped out a snapshot, glanced from it to the girl and showed it to Queenie. There was no doubt about it, the girl was Kiki.

There was a stirring of interest amongst the males. Shintaru, still at Kiki's side, rang a bell and there was a sudden silence as everyone stared expectantly towards him. Shintaru said something loudly in Japanese, and a hand was raised. He said something else and the hand went down as another went up. The procedure, clearly some sort of an auction, went on for several minutes until an ageing, paunchy man waved a handful of yen in the air and there was a smattering of applause.

Queenie and Coco communicated the fact that both realised what was going on with meaningful glances; these men were aware the Kiki was a prisoner, a sex slave, no mere whore. She was being used at great profit to feed the national male fantasy of rape, each act of cohabitation with her was rape and they were willing to pay well over the odds for the kinky pleasure.

Impatiently pushing the unprotesting Kiki in front of him, the old man left the bar with a vigilant Shintaru behind them.

Coco decided to make an ostensible trip to the toilet and went out after them, horribly aware of the many eyes on her and her exposed length of thigh. She was also nervous that she might be caught spying.

The toilet was tucked under the foot of the circular staircase, but she had no intention of using it. The goon was in his place, sprawled in his chair reading a newspaper. With a confidence she far from felt, she started up the stairs. If Shintaru saw her and asked her what she was doing, she would say she had left her lipstick in her room.

The three ahead of her had reached the first floor landing and were continuing up; if Coco stayed close to the wall it was unlikely she would be spotted. She needn't have worried about the goon's reaction; he merely watched her legs over his paper as she ascended.

Jittery, heart thumping, she carried on, getting to the first landing as the group ahead of her arrived at the second where they went out of sight down a corridor. Hurrying, she reached the landing in time to see, as she cautiously peered around the end of the corridor, the old man roughly shove Kiki into a room five doors down, living his fantasy to the full. Shintaru closed the door and locked it. Not waiting to see him slip the key in his pocket, Coco fled down the first flight of stairs and then went as fast as she dared down to the ground floor; the goon this time ignoring her altogether.

Coco was back in the bar before Shintaru got to the first-floor landing. She was telling Queenie, under cover of a cupped hand, voice drowned in the babble of conversation, what she had found out by the time Shintaru returned to his place at the bar.

The gangster rang his bell again. There was another restless silence. He hooked a finger at one of the girls who went resignedly to him. This one was not oriental; she was blonde and petite, dressed more or less as a schoolgirl with little make-up and her hair in two plaits. Another auction was held. The girl, who looked no more than eighteen, was sullen throughout. This time, two young men were spirited in the bidding against one another. When everyone else dropped out, they came to a noisy, laughing agreement between each other and carted their victim off for a forced threesome, Shintaru again following.

Coco fetched their third large whisky from the bar. Unable to get a reply from the barman when she asked him if it was free, she assumed rightly that the bar was a complimentary part of the brothel's services.

When Shintaru got back, his unreadable eyes fell on them. Then he lifted an arm, gold chain dangling over the cuff of his jacket sleeve and crooked that maddening finger at them while with his other hand he hit the bell.

Were they to be auctioned, too? wondered Coco, as, standing, she drained her whisky too fast and spluttered. Surely not – where was the rape fantasy in laying two supposed hardened whores from Manila?

Resigned to their fate, they approached Shintaru who, jabbering loudly to his audience, had them each do a couple of pirouettes. 'What were you saying?' dared Coco, when he had done.

Surprisingly, he obliged her. 'It is a custom that ladies new to the house are offered to the most important men present on their first evening. This man who is about to speak has first refusal.' He glanced at Queenie. 'I tell him is most interesting you cannot talk.'

A man, taller than the others, about forty, came across to them. He was slender, not unpleasant looking and dressed in an immaculately tailored black silk suit whose elegance was only slightly marred by a rather flashy, handpainted silk tie. And he smiled! This man who was possibly about to buy one of them flashed even, white teeth in a most genial manner.

The two men exchanged several words. Then Shintaru said to Coco, 'This honourable gentleman wants to know if you two do chick-chick?'

'Chick-chick?' exclaimed Coco, smiling inwardly. 'Lesbian stuff. I guess you mean?'

'Right,' said Shintaru.

Coco's eyes fixed on the man's. She was most relieved to discover she was getting good vibes from him. 'Absolutely,' she said, not breaking the eye contact.

There followed a lengthier conversation between the two men, all of it seemingly polite, but including one or two of the universal gestures of bartering. Then they shook hands. 'He take you both for the entire evening, perhaps the night. You must be very, very good to him. The honourable gentleman is most important customer.'

A great deal of money changed hands, then the three of them, followed by the barman bearing a tray of whisky, sake, a bucket of ice, cups and glasses, went up to Coco's room.

As soon as the waiter had departed, the man laughed

loudly. 'What a bullshitter that Shintaru is!' he said. Mimicking the gangster's accent he went on, 'The honourable gentleman is most important customer.' He laughed again. 'Of course he doesn't know that English is my second language.

Delighted at this revelation, Coco giggled. She was warming considerably to the man.

'Whisky for both of you?' he asked, pleasantly, pouring Chivas Regal over crackling ice. 'I noticed you drinking it earlier.'

'Great,' said Coco.

He handed them a glass each and fixed himself a cup of sake. 'Cheers,' he said, drinking it straight down. He put the cup back on the tray and went to the wardrobe, opened it, took off his jacket and hung it up. 'Where is your dumb friend from?' he asked Coco, as they watched him casually undo his belt and the top of his trousers and unzip himself.

'Manila,' Coco told him. 'Same as me.'

'With such a complexion? And red hair? I never saw a girl from the Philippines remotely like her.'

'Yeah, well, we've both got kind of mixed blood. Her mother's English, my dad was a Yankee GI.' Sipping her whisky, Coco gazed at the man with a certain amount of fascination as he continued to strip himself without the slightest inhibition; he might have been in a men's changing room. He draped his shirt and tie over a hanger, then slipped off his shoes and socks and put the socks in the shoes. In briefs which were in startlingly white contrast to his lean, tanned body, he poured himself another sake and knocked it back in one. Then he took off his underpants and stuffed them in a jacket pocket. His mid-section was as brown as the rest of him. He had an impressive flaccid penis.

'I enjoy getting naked early in these sort of proceedings,' he remarked with another of his friendly smiles. 'I somehow feel more comfortable that way.'

'Er . . . right,' said Coco, sitting on the edge of the bed, glad that the whisky was beginning to act agree-

185

ably on her. She took hold of Queenie's hand. 'How did Shintaru say it? The honourable gentleman wants us to do chick-chick?'

He chuckled. 'The honourable gentleman has a name. You can call me Kafu.' He lowered himself into the same chair in which Shintaru had been served with his lightning blow job just a few hours earlier. Contrary to the reaction the gangster had had on them, they found the sight of this pleasant, attractive naked man rather arousing. 'Yes,' he said, 'I would. For me to watch two lovely females such as yourselves making love to one another I find particularly exciting.' A first gleam of sexual enthusiasm crept into his eyes. 'Whenever you're both ready please undress each other. But take your time, we have all night.'

'Some music, perhaps?' asked Coco.

'No. No music. I very much enjoy the sounds of zips being undone and the rustle of clothes coming off, followed by the noises of love making. Such a pity to drown that with music.'

'You're the boss,' responded Coco. 'Here's your first zip.'

She reached for Queenie's mini-skirt, unhooked it and slicked the zipper down fast, producing the sort of sound she imagined might bring him satisfaction. She pulled the skirt over Queenie's hips and let it drop to the floor. Queenie stepped out of it and Coco turned her so that she was facing Kafu. 'Shoes,' she instructed. Queenie kicked them off and, slowly, Coco peeled her tights down, pausing when they were at her knees to kiss the back of a thigh. Peering around it at the man as she did so, she observed a narrowing of his eyes. Queenie's knickers were of fine, white lace, her heavy red bush showing through and creeping around the edges.

The tights went the way of the skirt and, beginning to get into the swing of this, a familiar, welcome horniness stole over her. Coco slipped a hand from behind between Queenie's thighs and up and over her pubis to hook her fingers in the waistband of the knickers. Remembering the word Tanaka had taught her, she muttered, 'You are about to behold the sweetest of *nekkos*, Kafu.' She pulled the top of Queenie's panties down to the fork of her thighs, and curled her middle finger came off the waistband into Queenie's bush. 'My favourite plaything,' she added, as Kafu's eyes narrowed further and there was a stirring in his loins.

Teasingly slowly, Coco slid Queenie's panties all the way down her superb legs. 'Please throw them over here?' asked the man in a pleasant, thickening voice. 'We Japanese have a fetish for knickers.'

Coco bunched them up and tossed them to him and he deftly caught them. 'Knickers and rape, huh?' she remarked, then risked adding, feeling that this man would not take offence, 'Good old, cultured Japan!'

With a twisted smile, saying nothing, he scrunched the knickers in one hand, held them for a second close to his nose, then put them in his lap, where they draped across his pubic hairs behind a fast rising erection.

Reaching up and around Queenie's body, Coco made a production of undoing the buttons of her blouse, from the bottom upwards, pausing after each one. Then she pulled the blouse back over her shoulders and off and Queenie was facing Kafu naked except for two long, thin gold chains around her neck and an ivory, gold-threaded band on one wrist. Coco cupped her hands over Queenie's breasts and rolled them together, making her girlfriend squirm and causing Kafu's erection to attain its full, eight inches.

'You are such a beautiful young lady,' he murmured, eyes clinging to her. 'Too lovely for even a high-class brothel such as this.'

Queenie smiled at him, catching herself just in time from thanking him. Aroused, delighted that this evening was apparently not going to be the dreadful experience she had feared, she sunk to her knees, turned around and began to undress Coco, starting with her elegant, patent-strapped shoes. When Coco was nude,

Queenie climbed on the bed and pulled her into her arms.

Both are very ready for mutual pleasure. The fact that a good-looking stranger is watching them, aroused by their actions, even the fact that he is paying them, adds a certain spice and they make love with a fire which has little to do with the acting of a lesbian 'show'.

By the time, after a lengthy session of kissing and caressing, they position themselves mouth to crotch in the classic sixty-nine – each of them hungrily eating a pussy which runs close second favourite to their own – Kafu is standing over them at the side of the bed. With Queenie's knickers wrapped around his cock, he slowly masturbates through them. Queenie fails to notice this, as she is on top, her head busily buried between Coco's thighs, but Coco, who has been watching their reflection in the ceiling mirror through the cleft of Queenie's buttocks, does. She finds that the sight of the distinguished Japanese wanking with Queenie's knickers as his eyes lech with mounting greed on the two of them adds yet more fuel to the fire of her seething libido and her tongue goes deeper, stabs faster, a furious little cock which is bringing Queenie rapidly towards climax.

Queenie's legs jerk, they double at the knees, her heels drum on her buttocks and she comes down with a drawn-out moan muffled in Coco's pussy and enclosing thighs. But she is aware that Coco has not quite made it. Seconds later, she raises her head, affording Kafu a momentarily clear view as she slides two fingers deep into Coco, then blocking his view with the back of her head, she brings Coco off with her fingers, while her teeth nibble her clitoris.

Coco's stubby little toes with their red-painted nails go rigid, her thighs clamp tightly over Queenie's ears and she gasps her orgasm – 'Oh yeeaaaahh, oh shiiiit!' – into Queenie's crotch.

Kafu has sagged. His knees indent the bed near

Coco's head, his teeth are bared, his hand works fast. He takes Coco's hand and replaces his with it over the knickers, allowing her no time to recover from her climax. But the feel of what she has grasped is welcome; she opens her eyes to the reflection of this, gripping the panties and their throbbing enclosure with enthusiasm. She treats Kafu to a short, energetic, climatical wank and he explodes in a series of grunts, his sperm arching and falling in three long spurts over Queenie's lower back and buttocks. He collapses on the bed, his wilting cock still in Coco's hand, in the now wet knickers. He closes his eyes, breathing heavily.

Minutes later, with Queenie and Coco unentwined and lying head to feet, Kafu, on his back, looked up at them in the mirror and drawled, 'I've no idea what you two are up to in this place, but of course it's perfectly obvious that you're not the whores you pretend to be.'

Coco's eyes went wide, a stab of fear attacked her belly. 'What makes you say that?' she asked him.

'Over the years I've visited some of the finest brothels in the world. I know whores and neither of you has exhibited even one of their universal character traits up to now.'

'Oh,' muttered Coco, head in a turmoil. Was this trouble?

Kafu rolled off the bed and poured himself some sake. He seemed, at least, unconcerned about his opinion and friendly enough. 'Have some,' he suggested. 'After sex it's more refreshing than whisky.'

'All right. Coco sat up. 'Want some, Queenie?'

Queenie nodded, troubled.

He poured the dregs of the whisky into the ice bucket, rinsed their glasses around with ice cubes, filled them and handed them to the girls who both drank thirstily.

'You're just not hard enough, you're not hardened enough – what's more you're altogether too gorgeous,' said Kafu, with a smile. 'Young ladies such as your-selves generally marry money – which I suppose often is a form of prostitution – but they don't sell their bodies on a daily basis.' He swallowed a cupful of sake, eyeing them thoughtfully. 'Tell you something else. I've had dozens of lesbian shows put on for me by whores and there's always been a bit of an act about it. Not you two – that was for real, and how!'

'We happen to . . .' began Queenie and, too late, stopped herself, a hand over her mouth.

He grinned astonishment at her. 'That rather settles it, doesn't it? Everything – except the way you make love – is a charade about you two. Dumb, eh?' His eyes travelled admiringly over Queenie's nakedness. 'You happen to what?'

Queenie bit her lip. 'I was going to say we happen to be in love.'

'I believe it. But whores? No.' He sat on the bottom of the bed. 'What's the angle in pretending you can't speak? And that's an upper-class English accent isn't it?'

'Which is exactly why,' Queenie admitted. 'Nobody's going to believe I'm a whore from Manila with this bloody twang, are they?'

'No. So what the hell are you up to?'

Coco remembered their friend Frannie, Lady Ballington, and her libidinous life. She seized on an idea. 'We're on a sort of a sexual adventure trip,' she said. 'We're always looking for new thrills, we figured we'd dig seeing what it's like to work in a brothel, get our rocks off in one, if you get my meaning?'

He studied her, amused, shaking his head as, feeling the lie written all over her, she nervously gulped down some wine. 'Somehow I don't think that's quite the truth either,' he said. He shrugged, laying a hand on Coco's thigh. 'I reckon you've conned your way in here for some very special reason. You're certainly up to something – but then it's none of my business. I must try to act the honourable Japanese gentleman as described by the villanous Shintaru.'

Both girls experienced a surge of relief. 'Then you won't tell him?' Queenie anxiously asked.

'Certainly not. Why should I do such a thing? I might enjoy the sort of house he keeps but I have no love for the man or obligation to him.'

Coco, relaxed again, letting spill what might have been an inadvisable question. 'You go for this rape fantasy business? Auctioning off sex slaves?'

'Sure, just occasionally,' he confessed. 'It seems to be a part of the male Japanese soul. Besides, those kids would only be living a life of misery in some slum or other.' His hand travelled up over her hip to her breast. 'So that's it, then? A foolish rescue mission?'

'I didn't say that.'

'We told you why we're here, insisted Queenie without much conviction. 'It's a sex adventure.'

'Sure it is,' he replied. 'And I count myself a very lucky man to be part of it. So, you're not whores, yet here we are the three of us, naked together, and I've bought you for as much of the night as I wish. So, what's next?' He squeezed her breast firmly – just short of hurting her.

Reaching for his flaccid penis, Coco took it in her hand. 'On with the sex adventure, that's what,' she murmured. 'We ball, honey. You've paid for it and, believe me, you're going to get as much as you can take!'

Which, as it turned out, was a considerable amount. Especially fired up by the excitingly peculiar situation in which he found himself and incredibly horny as men inevitably were in the sexual company of Queenie and Coco, Kafu proved to be a great stayer after his initial ejaculation through Queenie's knickers and copulated with them vigorously for the ensuing three hours, taking them in every conceivable position and orifice. When, after his fourth orgasm, and their string of them, he had had his fill, he quickly recovered and showered and dressed himself, appearing under the circumstances remarkably fresh.

Queenie and Coco were comatose on the wrecked bed, totally satiated and deliciously lethargic when Kafu, before leaving, honoured them with a short head bow. 'I thank you both,' he said. 'That was a night to remember and cherish for the rest of my life.' He grinned, 'I would ordinarily leave a massive tip, but then you're not whores, are you?'

'We'd be kind of offended, Kafu. We had a great time, too,' Coco told him.

'I get a feeling you'll be out of here by tomorrow,' he said. 'But if not I'll be back for an encore.'

'Leave your address?' suggested Queenie.

'I never leave an address. Give me yours?'

She thought about it. 'I guess it's better not to.'

'Prudent of you. But I won't let on, should you get away with whatever you are doubtless now going to attempt. *Sayonara!*' Halfway through the door he stopped, turning his head. 'Take the greatest care,' he warned. 'These people are killers.'

'We know it, buddy,' said Coco, to the closing door.

Queenie lay still for a moment, thinking. Then she got up, crossed the room, and cautiously stuck her head out into the passage. The house was alive with stirrings and soft music. she slipped into a bathrobe, went next door and fetched her bag and the gun and phone. Shut back in with Coco, she took a small alarm clock from the bag. It was twelve-thirty, she set the alarm for a quarter to five. 'A quick shower, no?' she suggested to Coco. 'then we should grab some shut-eye. Let's hope the damned house is asleep when we wake up.'

They showered together. Before going to bed, Coco made a close inspection of the lock on the door. As in the interiors of most Japanese houses, when not a sliding paper screen, the door was hardly any thicker than double cardboard, its lock slotting into a metal box with barely a centimetre of wood between it and the air.

Coco explained carefully how the deed was to be done. They rehearsed it as best as they were able. Then they went to bed where they fell asleep almost immediately in one another's arms like very young girls after an innocent, late-night party.

The low buzz of the alarm droned rudely through Queenie's dream which she instantly forgot as she fumbled for the stop button and shut it off. She listened for long moments, holding her breath. The house seemed very quiet and still.

She roused Coco with a shake of her shoulder, drawing incoherent complaint followed by nervous awakening. 'Time to get dressed, sweetheart,' she said, quietly.

When they were dressed in the jeans, sweaters and trainers in which they had made their entrance to the brothel, Queenie found the radio phone and put in a call to Sean Magee as Coco carefully printed a short note.

Magee was drowsily grumpy. 'Don't you know it's bloody five o'clock in the morning?' he grumbled.

'Shake a leg, Sean,' Queenie briskly told him. 'Out of bed and have the car around here in twenty minutes. We're going into action.'

'The devil we are,' said Magee, to an already dead line.

Coco had printed, 'Kiki, we're friends of Akiko. We're going to get you out of here in fifteen minutes. Be ready. Tap twice on the door if you understand.' She read it through herself, scrambled her nerves together and said, 'Okay honey, wish me luck.'

'Luck,' muttered Queenie, eyes wide.

Carefully, Coco inched open the door. The passage was in darkness, she heard only far away snatches of soft music. Fast, on tiptoes, she made her way to the stairs which were eerily lit by light from the three-quarter moon filtering through the glass dome above her. The music was slightly louder, drifting up the stairwell from a crackly radio. She met no one and heard nothing but the music as she approached Kiki's door where she stopped and listened, her ear close to it, holding her breath. There was no noise from behind it, the girl was evidently asleep.

Coco began the first of a series of gentle raps on the door, apprehensive as she did so that she would wake someone else up. After a minute or so she was rewarded by a mumbled 'What is it?'

'Sssshhh,' warned Coco. 'Look under your door.' She slipped the note through and moments later there were two confirming raps. Turning around, she hurried back the way she had come.

'That was the easy part, she'll be waiting,' Coco told Queenie as she let herself in.

'I'll make sure Sean's on his way.' Queenie dialled his number.

Magee was still grumpy. But he was behind the wheel of his car, and he said he should be there within ten minutes. Queenie rang off and the two girls began to cram those clothes that they were reluctant to leave behind into one bag. That done, Queenie checked the gun, clicked off the safety catch and slipped the Browning into her belt. They were ready.

'Let's do it,' muttered Coco, nerves taut as piano wire.

When they were outside Kiki's door Coco tapped lightly on it.

'Ready,' Kiki whispered.

'Stay clear of the door.' Coco turned her back on Queenie. 'Support me the way I showed you.'

Queenie hooked her arms through Coco's under her shoulders, spreading her hands on her own shoulders. 'Lean well back and stand firm. Here goes,' whispered Coco. Sweeping both legs off the floor, she brought her knees into her breasts and slammed her feet forward in a karate-style kick, hitting the door in the area of the keyhole with the balls of her feet and all her force but ending the kick precisely there. Inertia, as Queenie staggered back, completed the job.

With an alarmingly loud cracking and splintering the door crashed open, smashing into the wall. As Kiki hovered uncertainly into view, Queenie grabbed the hold-all in one hand and slipped the gun from her belt with the other. Coco snatched at the girl's hand. 'Run!' she urged, and the three of them hared along the passage and down the stairs.

Halfway down the first flight they saw that the goon on the door was on his feet by his crackling radio, looking up at them. The knife he used to clean his nails was held up menacingly. As they were just about down the stairs, Shintaru appeared in a dressing gown, holding a gun.

The girls were seething with adrenelin. That and surprise were their advantages. Queenie clouted Shintaru's gun-hand with her bag, a bullet buried itself in the floor, and Coco followed up with one of her aikido armlock throws, hurling him into the sharp corner where the hall wall met the passage. His head connected with an audible crack and he crumpled into an unconscious heap.

The goon was almost on them with his knife. Queenie, deadly calm now, took quick aim and shot him in the kneecap. The man healed over with an agonised roar, dropping the knife and clutching his shattered knee.

Mayhem, the entire house started to wake up. As they tore through the garden, lights went on everywhere. The lumbering guard from the back-alley door came shouting after them with another man right behind them.

Coco fought for dangerous moments with the garden doors; Queenie prepared to fire at their pursuers. Then the door creaked open, and they spilled through it and Coco pulled it shut in the men's faces with the metal grill.

To their dismay, there was no sign of Sean Magee.

'Shit!' exclaimed Queenie. They all three looked up and down the deserted road before dashing off in the direction of the Nichikegi theatre as the door behind them crashed open and the men came running after them.

They had covered about a hundred yards with the men closing in, when a car squealed to a stop beside them and the side doors were flung open. They piled in and Magee accelerated away from the defeated *yakusa*. 'Going somewhere in a hurry, were you, then?' he asked, with a grin.

Chapter Twelve

Dear Randy Reader . . .

My fearless, darling friends got away with it! They
departed from Tokyo with great speed, I can tell you
– the *yakusa* are far from partial to such disrespectful
treatment. Fortunately they had gathered together all
the interviews and photos they needed to put together
their article; it has appeared while I have been writing
this book. I read it with interest, it was most informative, and skilfully organised – however, I hope that my
readers will find the other side of their Tokyo exploits
more interesting!

As well as a whole series of Queenie's amusing little
notes about their sexual entanglements, I had a copy of
the video of the two of them cavorting with Sean Magee
in the love hotel and the photos Coco took of herself
and Tanaka in his mirror to guide my pen.

Sean Magee is not the thriller writer's real name. They
are still enjoying the occasional tumble in the hay with
him and when he heard I was working on this book he
insisted I change his name – Catholic Ireland is light
years from being ready for such a revelation! All the
other names are, however, real, and I can assure you
that Tanaka is as young, attractive and as accomplished
a lover as described.

I have had a tremendously exciting time putting all
this together. My regular readers will know by now that
when I sit at my old typewriter and describe sexual

adventures I get as turned on as I hope they do when they read them.

I have not myself gone off on the sexual trail for almost two years – that last trip where I got rather over-involved in devil-worship and so forth – *Frannie Rides Out* – almost cost me my life and rather put me off. But I must say that writing up Queenie and Coco's Tokyo frolics has put me very much in the mood to taste forbidden sexual joys once more. Perhaps when my two darlings go off on another of their Far East journalistic missions I'll catch up with them somewhere along the way . . . ?

In the meanwhile, *au revoir*. Keep doing it!

F.

Letter from Esme

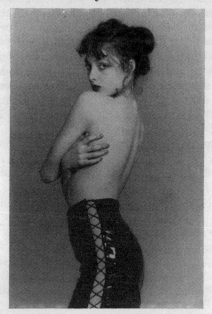

Dear Readers

At last! Spring is in the air, my favourite season of all.
Even in the high heels I like to wear, I certainly have
a bounce in my step. It must be the sight of nature
bursting forth in all its glory. And it's not just the
daffodils that are popping up everywhere. I'm sure you
naughty readers must know what I mean!

But spring will be turning into summer by the time
you read this. And let's hope the weather will be every
bit as sizzling hot as the stories coming up in this
month's Nexus books! So what has that lascivious-
minded publisher cooked up for you this time?

Choosing Lovers for Justine is by one of the most

popular of all Nexus authors — Aran Ashe — who wrote the successful *Lidir* books. This time we are not in the mythical principality of Lidir, but London of the Edwardian era, where some of the less than genteel ladies and gentlemen of the time exact their perverse satisfaction from the submissive flesh of the young Justine. Chosen to live a life according to discipline and subservience, Justine experiences every imaginable shame as she tries to please her strict guardians.

Things *were* hard in those days by the sound of things. All those repressed desires and hidden lusts — I'm sure people were even kinkier then.

Then we move on a couple of decades to *Blue Angel Secrets*, set amidst the lights and glitz of Tinseltown. Hollywood in the 1930s was full of wild women, hellbent on getting as much wicked fun out of life as possible. Now, doesn't that sound like someone you know?

Anyway, we follow the fortunes of German heart-throb Hugo Klosterman, as he strives for the fame and fortune a life in the movies can provide. But it seems he has to prove his talents in the bedrooms of his amorous admirers before he's allowed to perform for the cameras. Poor thing!

Also up for grabs this month is *Queenie and Co in Japan* — the second story in the series. This time that sexy, red-haired reporter and her exotically beautiful Oriental assistant are posted to the fleshpots of Tokyo, where the world's most bizarre erotic tastes are catered for. However, investigating the lifestyles of rich Japanese businessmen involves more than a couple of interviews. Queenie and Coco are expected to participate in kinky orgies where anything goes. Needless to say, they don't get much copy writing done, but their investigative work is so rewarding, they simply don't get the time. I know just how they feel.

I have found time though, to look at the books being prepared for next month. There are two Nexus books for you in July, plus the special new imprint I told you about in last month's letter. More about that later.

First up is *Helen – A Modern Odalisque*. And what a naughty girl she's been! Although the book is set in modern-day Britain, poor Helen is subjected to all manner of old-fashioned chastisements. Not only is she punished soundly with a variety of instruments of correction, she is forced to keep a diary recounting her filthiest misdemeanours with her husband's 'gentleman' friends.

Imagine if someone got hold of my diary – it wouldn't be for the faint-hearted, I can tell you. There are things in there that even the Nexus publisher doesn't know about. Although he's begged me to divulge my rudest secrets on more than one occasion (and it was hard not to give in, as I'm such an exhibitionist) it's a girl's prerogative to keep men guessing *some* of the time, isn't it?

Hot on the trail of *Queenie and Co in Japan* is *Queenie and Co in Argentina*. This time the girls are posted to the land of the raunchy rancho, where they become embroiled in the very depraved activities of the corrupt Minister of Finance. His taste for using the whip leaves our darling twosome more than a little saddle sore!

And now for the really exciting news! In July, the publishers of Nexus are launching Black Lace, the new series of naughty books for women. But of course, I'm sure they will also appeal to men as they're no less steamy or kinky than good old Nexus books. I've had a sneak preview whilst I've been paying my regular visit to the Nexus offices, and they certainly had the desired effect on me. Where they differ, is that they tend to eroticise the male a lot more – turn him into a sex object – which is what you men have been doing to us for years! The covers are subtly erotic – so subtle that you wouldn't mind being seen reading these books on the train. But don't be misled. The contents are so arousing, there's definitely no mistaking what these books are about.

Well, I'm so busy, I must go now, but let me know what you think about the new Black Lace books, and indeed, about Nexus books in general. I'm always willing to read your letters; even though I can't possibly find the time to reply to them, your comments don't go unnoticed. and it's such fun reading them.

Esme ♡

Nexus

THE BEST IN EROTIC READING

The Nexus Library of Erotica – almost one hundred and fifty volumes – is available from many bookshops and newsagents.

A complete list of titles, with prices and information about ordering by post, is available from the publishers. Please send a large, stamped and addressed envelope to:

Nexus book list
332 Ladbroke Grove
London
W10 5AH